VIKING VILLAGE

A Novel
By Steven Cutts

 en Press

First published in Great Britain by Pen Press

All paper used in the printing of this book has been made from
wood grown in managed, sustainable forests.

ISBN13: 978-1-907172-90-8

Printed and bound in the UK
Pen Press is an imprint of Indepenpress Publishing Limited
25 Eastern Place
Brighton
BN2 1GJ

A catalogue record of this book is available from
the British Library

Cover design by Jacqueline Abromeit

For David
The best of men

"For long duration space flight has no parallel in terrestrial aviation. It is a lifestyle. It is a physical ordeal and the man left standing at the end of it is the winner. It's like choosing to live in a prison where the only luxury is sex."

The Physiology and Psychology of Deep Space Flight
P Reichebner and R Reichebner
May 2034 AD

Acknowledgements

Front cover illustration supplied by NASA.

"Do not go gently into that good night" from *The Complete Works* by Dylan Thomas, reproduced with kind persmission of Dent Publishers.

PART ONE
THE AJAX

CHAPTER ONE

When he dreamt of Taiwan, he dreamt of a man in white. The whites of an officer in the United States Navy, neatly pressed and yet to be tarnished by the madness of war.

Hopping down from a screaming jet copter, David Hewish traversed an empty tennis court and looked to his left. The bomb damage was minor here and buildings were mostly intact. In particular, a vast smoked-glass office block seemed to have been built to show his reflection and it was here and at this point, that this one defining portrait was burnt on his brain.

All around him and across the city, people were running for cover. The streets were tense but not yet frantic. This was Taipei. People panicked with a purpose and a sense of direction. As a flight surgeon from their aircraft carrier the *Lexington*, David had always envisaged treating his wounded on his ship but the situation in Taipei was becoming desperate and there was something about this conflict that had drawn him in.

He ran a little further and found a small reception party. They led him to a MASH outfit just short of the helipad and asked him to change into greens. In the week that followed, he never got clear of the tents. Bent double beneath a dark green canvas, he was soon giddy with the heat and the humidity. Dreams have a habit of changing with time but there were still a few constants that stayed in his mind.

Early on in his first day, he saw the flash of a press photographer, standing to his left. Some healthier than average specimen from the Marine Corps was grinning from his bed, a pristine bandage wrapped tight round one his hand. The saddest thing about that guy was that apart from his hand, he couldn't have looked any better. Now – David realised – he was dead.

And if there was a point of maximum realism in his dreams then it was the things that he heard. The overbearing noise in Taipei was neither cannon nor the scream of the wounded. Like the space ships he had once served in, the soundtrack in Taipei was dominated by an endless, white noise. It started on the third day. He hadn't slept and his legs were starting to fail him. Fifty-six hours in, one of the local orderlies passed him a bottle of beer and asked him a question. He couldn't hear him. David had just de-scrubbed and the feel of cold glass on his fingertips was a rare and unexpected joy. To his immediate left, he saw a pile of amputated limbs. They were beginning to smell. He had little formal training in chest or abdominal surgery and they were sending him the mangled feet.

After the beer came a string of Marines with scalp wounds and he banged in a few burr holes on physical signs. If anything – he realised – he was a better surgeon drunk. The head injuries dried up and he progressed to burns. The unit had acquired the feel of a 19th century production line, the wounded and the dead being their raw material and the bleary eyes souls in post op, their half finished produce.

Some time on the fourth day, the white noise receded and the smell of death took over. Like mulled oil and burning peppers. Like garlic. Something extreme and yet never so severe as to stop him working. They seemed to have slipped to a place where the US Army simply wasn't supposed to go. The tent was acquiring the feel of a crowded subway station, packed to overflowing, in desperate need of a train.

In between cases on day six, David Hewish closed his eyes and tried to will the Chinese to lay down their arms and die. Seconds later came an explosion, about a hundred yards to their rear. There was a fresh artillery duel in the west. His will alone had failed.

And suddenly, there was a *bang,* a deep sustained bang, like the extended boom of a passing freighter. The sound was sufficiently intimidating to make them cower as a group, crouching from the waist as if the sky was about to hit them. It wasn't. Not yet. David tried putting a cannula in a man's vein. His hands were loathe and cold. He couldn't.

One of the orderlies dropped a bag of blood and he watched it spread out around his feet. He tried to get clear and slipped down again. Clambering upright a second time, he felt it on his hands. Blood was a working material to David. He knew it to be a thicker, darker more viscous fluid than urine, though it was the latter that seemed to be streaming down his leg now. In an effort to stop it, he even got a grip on his urinary sphincter. It didn't work. He made a third attempt to stand and skidded, as if on ice, his left thigh cold and un-cooperative in the dark.

And because memories are insecure, he remembered little of what followed, 'til he came round in a jet copter, hearing his ears pop with the rising altitude. Beneath them, Taipei was receding, streaked in white ash and intermittent fire. David blacked out some more, never seeing the coastline or the endless blur of the South China Sea. The next sharp image in his head was coming round near the Lexington and seeing that ship through an open exit at a range of less than one mile. And then he saw a flash, a bright white flash that seemed to linger, like the boom from the howitzers, all seducing and coming from the west. He thought they'd taken his leg. He was wrong.

Beijing had nuked Taiwan.

And that's where it ended. Every time. His dream was on a loop and it was still being played from beginning to end. It ended in consciousness and a return to reality.

David Hewish rolled over. The world of the present was warm and humid. His elegant lover, Christine was waiting for him there, conscious and upright. The line of her mouth was long and flat.

"What was that?" he heard her say.

And for a few seconds David was afraid that she could actually read his dreams. That she had watched and heard his nightmare, as he slept, as if on TV.

"Bad stuff," he murmured. "It'll go soon."

"You'll never go," she told him.

The woman climbed off him and he felt more naked than before. Outside, behind the windows, the Washington freeway was a muffled roar. He crawled after her and found her in her kitchen, in a bathrobe, leaning forward, not looking up.

"The Lexington's a good ship?" she asked him.

His response was a reflex.

"The best."

"Taiwan was five years ago."

"She's been revamped," he retorted, always quick to defend his ship. "When she gets out of dry dock, she'll be good again."

"She *is* out of dry dock."

David fell silent. The combat status of the Lex was classified information. Had he said something in his sleep? Or had she guessed?

4

"Your tour with the Pentagon ends in six weeks."

Unable to deny this one, David declined to reply. The kitchen seemed smaller than it had before, colder.

"Maybe they'll extend it," he lied. "They like me in the planning department. I'm a big hit."

Christine shook her head.

"No," she said, with considerable confidence. "You'll sail with the Lex."

"But I'll come back. There'll be a time, a time when the fighting is over. Another year and I can come home if –"

"She is your home."

"She's a good ship."

"And if that's not enough."

"Then the sea's as good a grave as any."

Christine shook her head, ever so slightly and a voice in his head acknowledged what he had previously sought to ignore. It was over.

David dressed slowly, trying to find his clothes. His body seemed reluctant to bend double. Standing at the door he turned back for one last look.

She was 31. She was beautiful and until this moment she had been his. But they were different people. There were things in Christine's life that she wanted and everything about her that was good was a mechanism by which she planned to get it.

"So …" He began to feel awkward. "I'll call you in the morning."

"No you won't."

The door banged shut and he found himself alone on a freezing sidewalk. A cluster of cleaning droids seemed to sense his anger and he heard them run for cover. They needn't have. David, who had already been thrown out of his first country, was not one to take it out on a robot. Hunched forwards, fists thrust deep into regulation

5

pockets, he marched alone. His father – though an Australian citizen – had been a refugee from the then British Isles and though his memories of that man were indistinct, he'd learnt enough to hold it all in when it mattered.

Freezing on the steps of his own apartment block, David glanced up at another door. Hidden sensors read his iris and he waited, blank-faced whilst the locks snapped open and a holographic receptionist grinned, lasciviously from behind the desk.

"Hi, David! Your friends are waiting for you."

"My *friends*?"

"Your associates …" The software had detected the strain in his voice. "…are awaiting your acquaintance."

Who the hell could that be?

The elevator was out of the question. David made a dash for the staircase and quickly discovered that the door to his apartment was off the latch. Then, as he reached for the handle, there was a moment of hesitation. Who could this be and what was he walking into? Christine didn't have a key, neither did his colleagues. It had to be thieves, the navy or someone from the estate. David wasn't armed and he might have waited longer if an unfortunate burst of conversation hadn't come his way.

"Hey, Virgil," he heard some guy say. "Hey Virgil, do you think this guy has nightmares?"

"What? Like about his past?"

"No way!" cried a third voice. "He'd be too afraid to sleep."

Stepping into the living room of his own apartment, David paused to take it all in. A group grown of men in full combat gear were drinking his tea on his sofa. Having arrived a few hours ago, the Marines had spread themselves across his furniture and made themselves at home.

The military had come for him. This was it.

"Colonel Hewish? Colonel David Hewish?"

Over by the breakfast bar, a gauche young captain was trying to sound proper. This was David's pad and if it hadn't been for the gravity of the situation, he might have said something about the taking of liberties. In the circumstances, his eyes had fixed on the gleaming white envelope in the captain's hand and his mouth had sealed over.

"'Orders from the Pentagon," said the captain, pausing only to glance at David's face. "I am to escort you to the Washington helipad. Immediately!"

A cold wind of apprehension blew over the colonel. From the day he first set foot in this country, he had been training for battle with Beijing but now that the moment had come, he couldn't help but feel unprepared. Conscious of his new entourage, David spoke without inflexion.

"For the Pacific?"

"No," said the captain, dismissively. "For Mars."

CHAPTER TWO

David had been summoned to an undisclosed location in Texas. The details were sketchy but his mission had become a matter of national priority and his departure from Washington would be in style. The air force had provided a state-of-the-art jet copter and he was driven to the helipad in an open-top jeep.

Champagne leather seats, an unnecessarily lithe female hostess and a couple of brutish-looking men in camouflage. All of these observations seemed to be telling David that this was going to be no ordinary trip to Texas. And as the jet copter soared skywards and the city receded, the woman leant over him and asked what he'd like to drink. David was her only quarry and she hung on his every word. Later, when the troopers had chilled out and his tea had gone cold, he started to notice something else. This was more than attention. This was *reverence*.

And he hadn't even done anything yet.

They landed at NASA headquarters just before dawn. The clouds were turning orange and as he stepped off the helipads, David saw the outline of two identical aircraft some 300 yards to his left. Their rotor blades were silent, their engines cold.

His escorts led him down from the helipad and into the building, uncomfortable memories erupting in his mind. A few years ago, the space agency had dragged David into a broad conference room on the 8th floor of this same complex and told him that his career with

NASA was over. He had been de-selected from the astronaut training programme. It would be an exaggeration to say that this was the worst day in his life. The days in David's life got a lot worse than that. But the lights and the style, indeed the very feel of this Spartan complex were reminding him of defeat and he didn't like it.

And them, just yards from their final destination, David glanced up at an imposing doorway and caught his breath. They were standing on the 8th floor.

Well I'll be damned, he realised, *it's the same room.*

In contrast to his erstwhile lover in Washington, David had a talent for self-control. Idle between his guards, he showed no outward sign of surprise. Then, suddenly, the doors of the conference room sprung open and a line of three men strode out.

"Chabod!"

Directly opposite him and flanked by a pair of identikit US Marines, the jilted figure of Doctor Antonio Chabod was clinging to his briefcase like a frightened child.

Christ! thought David, *they've dumped Chabod.*

And for an instant, Chabod actually returned the stare and offered a smile of recognition. The two officers were old friends. At medical school, they had competed endlessly for the number one slot in their class. But for all their martial discipline, neither man had ever made any secret of their true ambition. Like Hewish, Chabod saw the navy as a stepping-stone to another world.

The smiles were short-lived. Glancing back over his shoulder, Chabod offered this warning to an old friend.

"Don't listen to them!" he yelled, "*it's fucking madness!*"

Conscious that his own career might be in jeopardy, David Hewish wanted to hear more. But it was not to be.

9

Chabod's guards were getting frisky, driving their man onwards with a newfound haste.

Several seconds elapsed. Chabod and his guards cleared the corner and David's escorts gestured to the door. They were leading him into that very same conference room that had just ejected Chabod and where his own termination had once occurred.

The panel had changed but the stage hadn't. Powerful lights shone down onto a narrow desk whilst the peripheries of the room remained in darkness. David had the awkward feeling that there was a larger audience hidden in this realm although in the circumstances, he felt forced to focus on the visible. A well-known general was flanked by a couple of civilian administrators. David recognised both of these men from his days with the agency. Their names were Kurt Mason and Tom James.

Like many modern technocrats, Mason had the annoying habit of reading from a head-up display in his spectacles. Science had virtually abolished the need for glasses and optometry was largely a dying art. Spectacles – David knew – were only really worn out of habit or for data. At the opposite end of the table, Tom James seemed to prefer a hard copy.

"Colonel Hewish," the man in uniform was speaking, "glad you could join us. My name is General Greaves and I will be chairing this meeting. You are familiar – I assume – with the other members of this panel."

The colonel nodded.

"Colonel Hewish, I understand that in the course of your career you have, upon occasion, been seconded to the American space agency, NASA."

"Yes sir, that is correct."

"Two missions into low-Earth orbit …" The general's gaze had returned to his notes. "Eighteen months preparing for Mars."

"That is correct, but the Mars flight never happened. 'Funding restrictions, finite crew requirement. I have since returned to the navy. Chief medical officer on the Lexington for the last two years."

Greaves had yet to look up. "Colonel Hewish …" His eyes were on his documents but his mind – David sensed – was somewhere else. "You have an instinct for survival."

A cold silence engulfed the chamber.

All eyes turned to David's face. No response was forthcoming and after a several seconds, Mason felt the need to speak.

"Colonel Hewish, what do you know about the situation in Viking Village?"

"Viking Village on Mars, sir?"

"Clearly."

"There's a manned relief flight on standby. As a matter of fact, I know the crew."

"Who would that be?"

"I'm quite familiar with Jones, sir, and also D'Alonzono."

Sometimes, even the most transient delay contains a message.

"Colonel Hewish, it is my …" Greaves seemed to pause for effect. "… *sad* duty to inform you of the failure of that mission."

"In what sense?"

"Total loss of vehicle crew and payload. Evidently, a foreign terrorist cell was looking for an opportunity to torpedo the US ambition in space."

"They *blew it up*?"

"Yes. Using a missile from the back of a truck. One of the most audacious terrorist attacks of recent years. However, the Mars exploration vessel – known as the *Ajax* – remains docked at the international space station.

11

Despite the loss of the Jones mission, the crew of that station continue to prepare the Ajax for deep space."

Taking the initiative, David decided to get things going.

"So you're looking for a new crew?" he asked. "Six men?"

Entering the foray for the first time, the scrawny figure of James held up the index and middle fingers of one hand.

"Two. Your objective, emergency re-supply of Viking Village and recovery of the ten personnel in that settlement."

If these first few figures were alarming, there was much, much worse to come. Almost immediately, David felt the need to interrupt,

"But there are *11* astronauts on Mars, sir!"

They ignored him.

"Colonel Hewish, you will be briefed on this mission in the course of the next *24 hours*. At the end of that period, this panel will re-convene to discuss the practical implications of your flight. In the meantime, I'd like to take this opportunity to introduce you to your commanding officer for this mission, Nobohito Kazu."

Having hidden in the sidelines for some time, Commander Kazu made his entrance in full dress uniform. Although they had never been formally introduced, his face was recognisable to David from the flight deck of the Lexington. The product of a less than conventional Japanese-Irish upbringing, Nobohito Kazu approached his colleague as if on the parade ground and the flight surgeon, who had never really bought in to this kind of ritual, rose to the occasion and offered a perfect navy salute.

CHAPTER THREE

Twenty-four hours. They meant it.

For an ordinary man, trapped in the ordinary world, a day is a distinct unit of time, punctuated by periods of work and sleep and by the rising and falling of the Sun. But in the life that David Hewish was about to begin, such divisions would lose all meaning as one breathless moment merged into the next.

Perhaps predictably, both members of the flight crew were offered amphetamines. Perhaps predictably, both men refused, choosing instead to stay awake on a heady cocktail of caffeine and raw adrenaline. The mission under discussion was daring but not impossible. Where Antonio Chabod had resisted, David gave way. Where he had panicked, their latest candidate stayed silent and the management was grateful for it. At the opposite side of the lecture theatre, there were engineers with flip charts who seemed too embarrassed to describe the proposed trajectory out loud. "Ya see," blushed some young post doc from MIT, "ya see fellas, nothing like this has ever been done before. People have talked about doing it but never actually done it." He reminded David of his more sensitive colleagues in military medicine, unable to look a relative in the eye whilst he broke bad news and he thought less of him because of this. As was the convention in manned spaceflight, neither astronauts would show self-doubt.

Elsewhere in the organisation, this kind of confidence was thin on the ground. Ever since the death of Jones, staff at the Marshall Space Flight Centre had been trawling through every personnel file in the building, racing to find another pair of would-be volunteers. And in a matter of hours, it had become obvious that there were virtually none. Many on the NASA payroll simply would not countenance an interplanetary mission. Even a Near Earth Asteroid visit wouldn't have been difficult to staff at short notice and the purgatory that was Mars had few realistic candidates. Then, when all hope seemed lost, NASA had turned to the navy and struck gold.

Exhausted by a second day of back-to-back lectures, David Hewish was called back to the briefing room and asked to face the panel. General Greaves began with a reference to an old friend.

"Colonel David Hewish, just to kick off, I'd like to apologise for – the incident – yesterday with Doctor Antonio Chabod." The colonel smiled politely and they invited him to pitch questions. As the only surviving doctor on the mission, he was concerned about the welfare of the crew.

"What about the people on Mars?" David asked. "What sort of shape will they be in? By the spring?"

Mason answered frankly.

"Without a relief flight? All of them dead."

David nodded. Their options were clear-cut. Like many in the navy, he preferred it that way.

"Colonel," said Mason, "I understand that you came to the United States as an Australian citizen? With direct experience of starvation?"

"It took us three weeks to cross the Pacific, sir." Then – interrupting himself sharply – David Hewish added, "But I claimed American citizenship at the dockside, sir."

Right beside Mason, Greaves glanced at his notes.

"Did you know Major Smith?"

"I – we met at NASA, sir."

"And before that?" The colonel buttoned up again and his superior and probably everybody else in the room sensed a dead end. "So in essence," said Greaves, "what we're proposing here is a manned rescue attempt using the only Mars-worthy vessel we have left, that's the Ajax. The Ajax was designed for a six-man crew, or in the emergency situation, a crew of 12. Ordinarily, we'd be looking at 27 weeks for the outbound journey but because of your ..." Through the corner of one eye, David actually saw Mason wince. "Because of your – *unusual flight plan* – we calculate that you ought to be on Mars in 17 weeks. We can't predict the exact date of your landing, but we would expect you to be in Viking Village in time for Thanksgiving. And boy, what a Thanksgiving that will be!"

Chipping in from the sidelines, Mason tried to improvise.

"Best since the first one."

Greaves continued.

"Colonel Hewish, this mission has been deemed unsuitable for civilian personnel. It's the kind of mission that a man has to volunteer for and that he has to be ordered to do. Do you get my drift?"

"Yes – sir! I'm your man!"

The panel erupted in smiles.

"Well spoken, Colonel! You've heard of the Right Stuff? Keep this up and they'll be saying you had more than most."

And they chuckled openly amongst themselves until the moment ended and Greaves added, "Oh, and erm, Colonel, we'd ask you to reconfirm your Will."

CHAPTER FOUR

As a serving officer in the United States Navy, the colonel already had an existing Will on file and felt no real need to change it. The publicist, Christine, got her hands on most of what he had, partly because of his residual feelings for her, but mainly because he didn't have anyone else to give it to. His parents were gone, his siblings long since slaughtered. In the service, David had often encountered deck hands prepared to leave it all to their shipmates. Seeing as anything that saw his own demise was likely to finish Kazu too, this idea hardly appealed and he decided to sign in the appropriate box and maintain the status quo.

With this delicate matter over, the flight crew returned to the briefing rooms and waited patiently for their next speaker. Sensing a delay, Nobohito Kazu took the unusual step of initiating a conversation.

"Do you know who he was?" David must have looked surprised. "*Ajax?*" Kazu explained. "They said you liked to read."

"Yes sir. I do. Off the top of my head, I'd say he was Greek. I'll try to look it up."

Seconds later, the door swung open and a veteran mission planner by the name of Hutchings ambled into view. A greying, crusted figure on the edge of retirement, Hutchings had lost count of the men he had sent into space. Hutchings had once worked as a tutor at the astronaut academy and it was possible that the agency had consciously chosen to show this face.

If it was conscious then they had done well. This was a difficult man not to like. More than anything, Hutchings reminded David of a Frank Sinatra song. Not any particular Frank Sinatra song: *all of them.* He spoke without a break for the best part of an hour and when he had finished, it fell to Colonel Hewish to ask the first question.

"What about the sail?"

Their tutor smiled, relieved perhaps, that his audience hadn't ventured onto more sensitive ground.

"Well, you've obviously heard about our *large* solar sail. It set off for Mars a few months ago and may be making an appearance during the course of your mission. I think you've got to bear in mind that the sail's going out there as a technology demonstrator and doesn't actually carry any cargo. As you know, we've got people looking at alternative application for that sail but frankly, I'm not optimistic."

Since this was their only query, Hutchings returned to his script.

"There's only going to be the two of you, so we envisage quite a gruelling workload for the outbound flight. Maintaining the ship, learning the layout for the base and trying to familiarise yourself with the dynamics of the crew. Because you're going to need that crew on side if you want to get home."

This was a poignant statement and it might have made a lasting impression on David's mind if Kazu hadn't distracted him with this, rather pointed query about suicide.

"Will we be taking cyanide tablets?"

"Suicide tablets do exist on Mars," Hutchings explained, "as do a small number of firearms available to control any outbreaks of … *extreme behaviour* in the crew. As you know, there are people in the Marshall Space Flight Centre who regard suicide as a more … humane exit strategy than some of the other, more abrasive mechanisms available in the village."

"But if the Ajax is successful," countered Hewish, "on a high-thrust trajectory, would you see that as being necessary?"

Hutchings shook his head with all the self-effacement of a second-hand car salesman. "With the double burn on offer? No, of course not. I don't envisage anybody dying of hunger or anything else." And then he fell back on patriotism. "Gentlemen, you know – both of you know – just how many allies this nation has already lost: *dead countries.* Countries that stopped believing in themselves. Whatever happens next, we've gotta stop America falling into that trap. When NASA pulls off a good one, the people of this country start believing they can do stuff again. And gosh, if you can pull this one off, they might just start believing we can do *anything.*"

CHAPTER FIVE

Ever since the end of the Cold War, the NASA management had been learning how to lean on their colleagues in the East. Whilst the overall American attitude to Russia remained one of patronising superiority, the persisting Russian ability to launch men and cargo into space could not be ignored. At this crucial moment for America on Mars, the Kennedy Space Centre was out of bounds and Hewish and Kazu would fly in the Russian-built *Klipper* spacecraft, blasting off from their base in Kazakhstan, accompanied by four men for the rotating station crew.

Their choice of launch vehicle was reassuring. The Klipper was the most tried and tested manned spacecraft in the world. During 28 years of operation, this machine had become the workhorse of the Russian space programme and China's later-day enthusiasm for low Earth orbit had been based on a blatant copy of this hull. To avoid confusion over language, the Ajax crew were helped into their seats by a balding Scottish refugee engineer and briefed in English through the ascent by computer.

An 18-minute, high-thrust flight culminated with the strange and frankly nauseating experience known as *zero g*. Conscious that his people in Houston might be watching, Hewish held back from the vomit bag. Like the Klipper crew up ahead and the four rotating space station astronauts behind him, Hewish and Kazu had been dosed up with ondansetron before blast-off and this ought to save them from the worst. If they started to retch, a tiny surgical pump on the left forearm was on stand-by to provide a second shot. Thus far, on this flight, everyone had kept their composure.

Another 18 hour passed by.

The astronauts were allowed to remove their helmets and drink lemonade from a straw. Some guy up front decided to defecate in his suit and they all had to sit there whilst he grunted. Then, about three hours into the second day, Kazu offered his crewmate yet another vision of the future. Having produced a spring-loaded exercise beam from under his seat, he began pumping the thing in mid-air as a form of "upper body exercise that can be performed in the seated position" actually using that expression on the com.

"Er, that's great, sir," replied Hewish, uncertain what else he should say.

"This session will enable me to spend more time to my abdominal crunches after we break orbit," Kazu explained.

Seconds later, one of the rotating station crew leant towards Hewish and spoke in hushed tones.

"Rather you than me, buddy."

Shortly after docking and with his colour vastly improved, Colonel David Hewish completed the short journey through the universal airlock and into the station itself. After a cursory tour of the construct, the Ajax crew began to make themselves at home by their respective sleep stations, hanging out their kit in the orderly manner of the military. And in the midst of their excitement, one of the space station regulars drifted down to their location and asked, thoughtfully, if they'd heard about the *ghoul*.

"What's that?" asked Hewish, answering for the pair of them.

"The Great Galactic Ghoul, man! Haven't you heard about that?"

They had not.

"It's this great ghoul and it lives out there, between Earth and Mars. The Great Galactic Ghoul's been swallowing all the space shit going out to Mars since the Cold War. You remember the Soviets –"

"That's enough, young man!" snapped Kazu. "I won't have riff-raff like you distracting my crew!"

Since his crew consisted of the good doctor and nobody else, Hewish found this comment faintly amusing.

The kid continued.

"Those Soviets, man! Those Soviets beat NASA into space! Sputnik *and* Gagarin. And you know what? Not one of them Russian rockets ever made it out to Mars! They got to Venus! They got onto the surface of *Venus*, time and time again. But they never got one damned ship out to Mars. 'Cept for the ones that kept crashing –"

Kazu, who was accustomed to the order of a fighting ship, responded in kind. "Kid! What's your name? I'll be speaking to your commanding officer!"

The kid had begun to scarper, whizzing off like Peter Pan and looking back over one shoulder.

"Watch out for that ghoul, man!" he taunted. "All the way to Mars!"

But the ghoul would have to wait until later, as the Ajax crew rather feared that it might. Right now, time was of the essence. A mere six days had elapsed since the colonel's recruitment in Texas and NASA had attempted to cram six months of pre-flight training into that period. What the Ajax crew suspected and what the NASA people already knew was that neither Hewish nor Kazu had anything like the ability as D'Alonzono and

Jones and that the mission would be on a knife edge from the day they broke orbit.

If they could get underway and if they were able to complete routine maintenance tasks, then the rest of the journey would be dominated by what the agency was calling "ongoing professional development". As far as David could make out, this would mean "reading".

Meanwhile, their ship was undergoing final assembly. An unmanned re-supply vessel had delivered additional cargo canisters for the Ajax. These had being hauled towards the main fuselage by a party of space-walking astronauts. Hewish felt the urge to go outside and lend a hand but a safety-conscious NASA management forbid it. Instead, he would have to satisfy himself with a tour of the vessel from the inside, where his enthusiasm for the mission did a nosedive. The spaceship was packed tight with supplies for the village and her crew were destined to linger in the occasional crevice between their cargo. Much of this material had been destined for the Moon and there were some awkward rumours as to the problems this might create for the next lunar explorers. Worse still, there were parallel questions as to the viability of that same hardware on a Red Planet.

Finally, and in defiance of several last-minute setbacks, the Ajax was ready and a joint Russian-American crew assembled in the airlock to bid them farewell. In a poignant gesture to their more usual service, Kazu chose to enter the vessel in US Navy whites. The only thing missing was his hat and in the absence of gravity, this would have been difficult anyway. It was a move that would make little impression on their mentors in Mission Control. For them, it was the aesthetics of the men that would stay in their minds the longest. The contrast between Kazu's dark-brown eyes and jet-black hair and the blue-eyed blonde beside him could not have been starker.

Blast off was unspectacular. The Ajax drifted from her birth at a snail's pace and was scheduled to break orbit within the hour. Ten kilometres out from the space station, she prepared for full throttle. The last few minutes before ignition provided a period of quiet reflection for David Hewish. Strapped into his couch, he turned very slightly towards his commanding officer and tried to read his thoughts. He failed.

As in the Texas briefing room, as in the cargo bay of the Klipper, Mission Commander Kazu retained the impenetrable scowl of a Japanese warlord. Somewhere in the archives, they said that he was Irish, though the evidence to support this view was thin on the ground today. That being said, casual fraternization was never going to be easy on the Ajax. Their ship was littered with tiny cameras and their every move was about to be analysed. Whilst the concept of recall was about to become meaningless, the Ajax crew were career officers and reluctant to bring any slight upon their names.

Finally, with the hour of their departure fast approaching, the great Nobohito Kazu began to speak. "Will this flight help?"

"I'm sorry, sir?"

"With your career? I was planning to make captain on the Lexington, before I hit 40. Didn't you ever want that?"

"No, sir," said the colonel, confessional with the moment. "No medic ever craved the helm of a ship."

"I guess it's a different job. A guy that gets to lead never gets to be close." Then, "You were on the *Serpentine*, weren't you?"

David bit his tongue. His escape from Oz was an open secret but he hadn't realised how much.

"Yes sir."

Suddenly they were interrupted.

"Firing in 40 seconds ..."

This was a real time signal from Mission Control and David Hewish was grateful for it. In the days and weeks that followed, the Ajax crew would come to miss this kind of punctuality.

"Twenty-eight, twenty-seven ..."

Glancing down at his home planet, David let his eyes linger on a distant ocean, felt the soothing waters of the South Pacific break across his flesh and reflected that he could have been there – with a heat shield – in less than an hour. Such was the warmth and beauty of this world. There would be no oceans on the next and in an effort to calm his nerves, he found himself reciting a line from the greatest space pioneer of them all, Konstantin Tsiolkovsky.

"The Earth is the cradle of reason, but man cannot stay in the cradle forever."

Chabod had declined this mission and Chabod was going to have to live with that. The Ajax was an absolute gem of a spacecraft and she was about to fly to Mars.

CHAPTER SIX

Five days out from the home planet and the Ajax was rapidly changing shape. A couple of spent fuel tanks had already been discarded and would be soaring towards Jupiter for the next six years. Near real-time radio communication with Houston was still possible, although the inevitable delay in transmission was becoming clear. Soon, the very idea of a conversation with mission control would be a thing of the past.

In a rare break from the monotony, Kazu produced a gas-powered dart gun and they test-fired the weapon in turns. Their improvised target had been placed at the end of the 8-metre-long tunnel that led up from their couches and through to the aft bulkhead. It was just wide enough to allow a man to crawl through and represented the gap between their bulging stores. Loathe to abandon a good dart, Kazu had the annoying habit of retrieving the things in person, and in time the game became boring. Later, Kazu found a more conventional weapon, designed to use live ammunition, and the atmosphere changed as they slid in a blank cartridge and tested the firing pin. Hewish for one, felt uncomfortable with this exercise. Blowing away his own colleagues wasn't on his agenda.

It was almost midnight. The astronauts had spent their day moving stores around the Ajax. Her original design team had planned to offer distinct quarters to all six passengers, but for this mission, every room had been crammed with cargo. For the first few days, Hewish had slept at the aft end of the ship, his loose cotton sleeping bag tacked up against the hull. But the nights had proven difficult. The constant flood of cosmic rays had ruined his sleep and the naval officer beat a hasty retreat to the storm shelter.

That same shelter was a cylindrical compartment in the very heart of the vessel, little more than a metre wide. It had been designed to function as a refuge during one of the intense solar storms that tend to cause problems for space travellers. For this reason, the walls of the shelter had been lined with a thin layer of lead. It's unusual for an interplanetary mission to actually need a shelter and when a solar storm does occur, it rarely drags on for more than a week.

Stretching out in its cramped interior, Hewish closed his eyes and collected his thoughts. In particular, he continued his deep-seated intellectual quest to comprehend his commanding officer, Nobohito Kazu.

The only thing these two men had in common was that as children, they had been threatened by China and that as adults, they had –

"Christ!"

Hewish bolted upright in his sleeping bag, all but head-butting the opposite wall. A streak of light had shot across his mind.

It was a problem he had been prepared for and it was a problem he was fighting to accept. Invisible cosmic rays were ripping through the spacecraft all the time. One of them had just drawn a line across his retina causing a whole row of light-sensitive cells to discharge. During the day shift, with his night vision bleached out, it would have gone unnoticed.

Conscious that some sad bastard back on Earth might be watching him on television, Hewish resisted the urge to scream.

"Cosmic ray?" Kazu's voice was distant on the flight deck.

"Yes, sir."

"When I was a kid in the desert, it was the coyotes." called Kazu, his voice barely audible through the white noise. "Used to hear them screaming in the night, wherever we pitched the tent ... You'll get used to it."

Hewish inhaled slowly on the noxious odour of space. This place was dour, but he could take it.

CHAPTER SEVEN

Their time was divided between sleep, reading and those mundane janitorial rituals that an astronaut finds difficult to ignore. There were carbon dioxide filters to be changed and repeated acts of sanitation to perform. On-board alarms had an annoying habit of interrupting their dreams and when they were awake, it was considered mandatory to perform five hours of physical exercise a day. Bored senseless by the bulk of it, this was not the first crew to try and squeeze two tasks into one.

Drifting down from the storm shelter, David would often catch sight of the animated figure of Nobohito Kazu, his trademark exercise beam held high above his head. Chatting to Ground Control, Commander Kazu was "maintaining his upper body strength". For his part, Hewish preferred the cardiovascular exercise of the static cycle machine, a device that was ideal for pedalling whilst listening to music.

In lighter moments, Hewish read and re-read the handful of battered paperbacks he had managed to salvage from his bedroom in Washington: the poetry of Dylan Thomas, an abridged collection of Shakespearean plays, *The Waste Land,* Auden, Wilfred Owen, *The Last Days of Socrates.* Shortly before blast-off in Russia, he'd asked permission to bring a copy of the *New Testament* and was told that this would be available on computer.

"That's not the point," he had replied to the "non bookish" technician. "There are a million books on computer."

"Ah! I understand," said the technician, who didn't. "It's a hard copy thing."

It was a hard copy thing. When he wasn't actually reading them, he kept the books taped to the wall of the storm shelter, that they might do their bit to shield his brain. Whether or not Dylan Thomas had ever stopped a cosmic ray was open to question but the guy's presence at either side of his skull made him feel better. In the mornings, they awoke to popular music and did their best to share breakfast. For much of the journey, internal pressure would be held at about half sea level and one of the more unwelcome consequences of this was a marked reduction in the boiling temperature of water. Hot drinks have always been a disappointment in space. Food comes out of a can. Anything that could have been described as fresh had been eaten in the first few days and for the rest of the journey, the astronauts sustained themselves as soldiers do, with the regular cracking of mess tins.

With his duties all over and the demands of his stomach quenched, David returned to his studies. Ever conscious of his terrestrial audience, he glanced down at his commanding officer and noted that the guy was playing with an empty tin can and a roll of sticky tape. Some of their meals had been stored in cans and the flattened metal cylinders were beginning to form a wall around Kazu's brain. Bombarded by the same cosmic rays as his colleague, Kazu had decided to construct his own storm shelter.

Hewish looked away and checked out his inbox. His emails were of relevance to Kazu too, but he was under orders to conceal them.

MESSAGE FOR COLONEL DAVID HEWISH –
USN – FOR YOUR EYES ONLY

Since the significance of the liquid oxygen leak was first discovered, Viking Village has been functioning at subsistence levels. The subsequent failure of their automated supply vessel made economy of action even more important and the crew have been ordered to consume a diet that is inadequate both in terms of calories and content. However, crew survivability is now considered highly probable and mission controllers remain committed to the imminent second burn.

Rolling away from the screen, Hewish reached for a familiar paperback and a bottle of glucose water. The combination of literary pleasure with sugar rush would help to distract him from the biggest un-kept secret on this ship.

The second burn.

CHAPTER EIGHT

By now the Earth was a small blue orb, its only moon a tiny crescent to one side. In more ordinary times, the astronauts might have feared that they might never see their world again. But these were far from ordinary times and the unspoken fear on the Ajax was that by the time they returned, the Earth might not be there for them.

Their next big challenge was the upcoming second burn. Ever since she broke orbit, the Ajax had been flying without power, hurtling to Mars in the manner of a cannon ball. Re-igniting their engines would provide a mid-course correction and welcome boost to their speed. The difference on this mission was the size of the velocity interval required.

Reluctant to face the g-force on a full stomach, the crew decided to skip breakfast. Instead, they shared some water on the flight deck. Squirting the last few drops into thin air, Kazu made a show of gulping them slowly with an open mouth. Then he checked the clock. "Colonel Hewish," he said, "I can't predict what the outcome of this action might be."

"I know that, sir."

Up against David's receptionist in the Washington apartment, Kazu sometimes struggled to appear human. Given the speed of his own heartbeat, David was able to admire him for it.

"Second burn in 30 minutes."

The computers were trying to be helpful.

Kazu added something about time and fate and the privilege of being asked to be the first. And then he said something else.

"In the service, it's not always best to ask why. I guess you already know that. Came down from the sky in Taiwan, came down from the sky and they called me to the bridge." Kazu's brow remained un-furrowed and yet he seemed unduly concerned by this story "And they offered me command of the squadron. And I said, 'Why are you offering me command of this Squadron?' And they said, 'Don't ask us, Nobo. Don't ask us why. Just tell us you'll take it.' And I told them, 'Yes. Yes, I'll take it.'"

It wasn't an easy anecdote to absorb but David Hewish tried his hardest.

"Sometimes," he said, "they ask a lot of you."

Sometimes they ask a lot of you. The Ajax crew broke up and made their separate tours of the spacecraft, checking the hardware along the way. Whatever doubts were in Kazu's mind, he elected not to voice them, as did David, who took this opportunity to thank his estranged girlfriend, Christine, for having disposed of him when she did. Now his only allegiance was to this ship. Now he could do this thing and not ask why.

The checks were done. Non-essential light sources were fading out and well beneath them, the propellant pumps were beginning to stir. Cruising down to the flight deck from 'above', Hewish got a grip on the pilot's seat and strapped himself in beside his colleague.

"How long have you wanted to fly on Mars, Colonel?"

"Pretty much all my life, sir. For the adventure mostly. Maybe a little science along the way."

"Ain't gonna be no science on this mission."

"You never know, sir. We might just be the guys who make some big breakthrough."

What neither man was saying and what both men knew was that the second burn was a done thing. Most spacecraft burn their engines in interplanetary space. The difference here was in the mathematics. How many tonnes of fuel? How much delta V? The answer to these questions might well have been the first reason that Chabod had cited for refusing this assignment although it wasn't hard to think of others.

"Sixty-five seconds."

David looked at Kazu and saw a pool of black sweat, oozing out from his armpit and down across his chest. From every other angle, Commander Kazu was completely at ease.

The colonel tried his hand at humour.

"If we screw this one up, what are they going to do with us?" he asked. "Dock my wages?"

"I don't even know what scale we're on."

"Fifteen seconds."

"Could be joint chiefs out here. What the hell are we going to spend it on?"

"Zero!"

Engine start!

Not a sound in the cockpit.

The Ajax pressed gently into their butts at a steady one third of a 'g'. Pretty much the sort of gravity they could expect to find on Mars. Though the engine note was constant, vehicle vibration was on the up and David took comfort in the tightness of his straps.

"All engines running – 70% thrust."

"Copy that."

This was an unnecessary call. The thrust readings were on the monitors and the telemetry was already –

"Shit!"

They could *smell* something.

"Fire!" shouted David. "Fire in the spacecraft!"

David Hewish extended his neck. Less than 30 feet above their heads he saw an incandescent ball of flame. Five minutes ago, he could have bolted up there like Superman. With gravity back in the picture, it was hopelessly out of reach.

"Masks!"

An ecstasy of fumbling in a smoke-infested hull. Grabbing his oxygen mask in the mounting blackness, David inhaled wildly on a cold and tasteless gas. Now he could actually feel the heat on the back of his neck, now his entire ship was going up in flames. Beneath his feet, he caught sight of a bright orange fire extinguisher, rolling out across the floor.

David was already holding an extinguisher in his left hand. This one had to belong to Kazu. He had dropped it.

"I'll take it!" called David. "Stay with the flight deck!"

Grabbing the hand rails, David pulled himself closer to the flames, felt his closely cropped hair begin to singe and at 15 feet, stable with one foot on the storm shelter and the other on the wall, leant into the hull to free his hands. Far beneath him, Kazu was barking the obvious.

"Get it out! Get it out!"

David's grip tightened and the extinguisher responded with an awesome burst of CO_2. Five, maybe ten seconds passed by. He fired some more and watched the flames recede and then flare up again in his face, just in time for another burst.

Impatient on the flight deck, Kazu decided to climb the opposite rails. Hanging on with one hand, pointing the extinguisher gun with the other, Kazu fired and went down with the recoil, reaching the floor a few seconds later. Still in position, David let off one last burst from his gun.

The flames were gone. They could hear hissing.

"It's the oxygen!" he shouted. An oxygen cylinder was hanging halfway along the spacecraft. It must have broken free during the course of the burn, twisting the tap on its way down. "Ignited on its own spark!"

With the extinguisher secure in his teeth, David freed his hands and reached over to close the tap. Seconds later, gravity deserted them and the astronauts were weightless again.

"BURN OVER! BURN OVER!"

The burning was over, that much was certain. Having put the thing out single-handed, Hewish was exuberant, calling out his pleasure with a wild confederate whoop and a gratuitous blast from the CO_2 canister that saw him soar across the spacecraft and up to the bulkheads.

"Get a grip, sailor!" called his superior, visibly irritated by the irregular use of a fire extinguisher. "This is a government vessel! It's not the fucking fun-fair!"

You're so right, Commander. I only put the fire out!"

But Nobohito Kazu remained troubled, a sorbo rubber strap still tight across his neck. Bouncing back along the blackened utility wall, David Hewish flew back down to free him.

"That's the Great Galactic Ghoul for you, Colonel!" spat the mission commander, as close to gratitude as he would ever come. "The little bastard's out to get us!"

Prior to this moment, the only bond between these men had been the Pentagon. That situation had changed. Kazu and Hewish were trapped in the same tin can with the same cindered cotton. They had nowhere else to go.

The Ajax was the fastest spacecraft ever to fly to Mars and the fastest manned spacecraft of any kind. In a world bedevilled by crisis, it was an achievement that the media would eagerly overlook and in many ways this was probably for the best. Burn-out velocities of this magnitude have never come cheaply. Hewish and Kazu had just exposed themselves to a new kind of risk, risk that few on Earth and none on Mars could yet understand.

CHAPTER NINE

The entire ship was a mess.

The highly celebrated fireproof bulkheads had been blackened as far as the flight deck and the taste of ash and smoke would stay with them to Mars, narrowly surpassing the mild lavatorial smell that had followed them this far. One of the computer screens was down and refused all attempts at resuscitation. Further afield, a bundle of clumsy-looking shovels had come undone, their 19th century image strangely out of place amidst the hi-tech haze of a spaceship. In the end they tossed it all into the same airlock as their spent fire extinguishers and gave them up to the almighty.

Watching it all disperse in the vacuum, the colonel turned to his colleague and offered this warning: "We can't get home without shovels."

Kazu responded sharply. "Do you think I don't know that?" Then, more softly, "There are other shovels in the canisters. We can still make it."

And so it went on, numbing their minds with its dreadful repetition. Fighting to remain sane, David coerced himself into reading one of the bedrock documents of Western civilisation, *The Last Days Of Socrates,* and in the final minutes of their arbitrary days, he even took to reading it out loud from the storm shelter and waited for Kazu's response.

It never came. Kazu never asked him to stop and he never told him to keep going either. As far as philosophy went, Kazu kept his own counsel.

Their journey achieved a routine. Conversation remained sparse. For men who had spent half their adult lives at sea, the Ajax was a familiar institution where white noise took on the hum of the engines and zero g replaced the gentle rolling in the waves.

Then, five weeks after the second burn, Colonel Hewish checked his inbox and found this rather stark warning.

COLONEL DAVID HEWISH
MEDICAL UPDATE – FOR YOUR EYES ONLY

Our perspective on Viking Village has been further compromised by the refusal of the crew to submit themselves to medical examination.

This unfortunate attitude has been paralleled by the deliberate sabotage of a number of cameras in the village, restricting digital surveillance. Psychologists at the Marshall Space Flight Centre now anticipate a significant behavioural problem within this community.

In the meantime, mission planners continue to evaluate the option of landing the Ajax by aero-braking alone. Whilst such an approach would obviate the delay involved in parking orbit, it would also be associated with a significant risk of catastrophic failure during the re-entry process and/or landfall at a logistically difficult site.

At this stage, David Hewish had studied the flight plan in depth. The Ajax crew were caught in a trap. Too fast and the mission could end in disaster. Too slow an approach and the Martian crew might be dead by the time of their arrival. To paraphrase their most memorable tutor in Texas, they needed the village crew to survive.

CHAPTER TEN

The Ajax was ten weeks out from the Earth, a mere six weeks from the planet Mars. Constrained by higher authority, David had not yet attempted to contact the Americans on the planet. Though he lacked the manic discipline of a fighting man like Nobohito Kazu, David had spent his formative years in a naval boarding school and his adult life as a commissioned officer. Such a background had left its mark and he had yet to query his orders from Houston.

His mind numb from another day on the spacecraft, David escaped to the storm shelter and decided to review the medical records on the villagers. Flight crew selection is a demanding process and it was not inconceivable that NASA had sent a bunch of bad eggs to Mars. At medical school, he had once heard his psychology professor go off record just to ridicule the space agency. Astronauts, he declared, should never be the subject of analysis. They were simply too dull. Ever since its inception, NASA had been stamping out every worthwhile character trait it had ever found in a man and your average outbound spacecraft is packed with a bunch of geeks. *"Man,"* his maverick professor concluded, *"has yet to fly in space."*

Well, David Hewish reasoned, it was a free country. Or at least it had been a free country in his Harvard days. Pushing this particular anecdote to one side, he decided to focus on his work.

From the time of his arrival on the planet to the time of his death, Major Smith had issued regular medical reports from the settlement and David decided to run through these quickly. He noted that the astronauts were all on routine prophylaxis for muscle wastage, radiation sickness and bone mineral density. Medication of this kind was standard and they received it once a week. Several had actively sought treatment for sexually transmitted disease. Again, this had been noted in space flight before although not on this scale.

Doctor Tan, the lead scientist on the mission, was complaining of insufficient electrical power for his lab and for some reason this issue had made its way into a medical report. Why? Smith was doubling up as base commander and flight surgeon. Maybe he had lost the ability to distinguish these roles. In a reference to the main laboratory on the planet, Smith had even used a Martian colloquialism: *the forbidden zone.*

But that was *then*, what about *now*? David flipped through some old photographs of the woman believed to be leading the settlement since Smith's death, Kelly O'Reilly.

Fifth-generation Irish, O'Reilly had been seriously Catholic in her youth but had joined the agnostic brigade part way through her doctorate. Earlier on in the mission, she had made a habit of dying her hair red. In contrast, her most up-to-date image showed a mass of grey roots and like many in this rapidly wasting settlement, Kelly O'Reilly had obtained an androgynous physique.

There were three other women on the team. Sarah Connolly was the oldest. Sarah was divorced with two estranged sons back on Earth. Her close friend Charlotte Erkhart was 35 and at 29, the gardener, Rachael Callaghan, was easily the youngest person to have ever flown to Mars. Prior to her academic career, Callaghan had achieved success as a figure-skating champion. Aside from her youth, Rachael's deep red hair was enough to make her stand out. But it would have been foolish to linger on her image for too long and he quickly wiped it out.

Besides, there was work to be done. The interior of the Ajax had been afflicted by some sort of green 'goo'. The mould had a habit of building up around the air vents where the warmth and the condensation seemed to encourage it.

Coming down towards the flight deck, David Hewish soon encountered Kazu.

"How about that sail, sir?"

"The sail's not our business," said Kazu, refusing to look up from his work. "Bottom line is, I ain't relying on no sail. We're gonna start rehearsing the landing sequence this morning. Meet me back here in 20."

And so it went on. Day after gruelling day, the Ajax crew strapped themselves down by the flight deck, rehearsing the landing sequence four or five times before lunch. Within a month, they were better than Jones and D'Alonzono had ever been. The landing on Mars was more than credible and mission planners were already scheming as to how future travellers might be launched, unskilled and taught in transit. Meanwhile, as their arbitrary nights began, the Ajax crew retreated to their cots and did their best to sleep.

But no matter how hard he tried, David could never black out as fast as his boss. He tried exercise before bedtime. He tried exhausting himself to the point of despair but it was no good. His mind remained active for at least the first hour. In contrast, Kazu was the master of his own body. Within seconds of reaching his lonely shelter, the guy was out cold with both arms hanging loosely above his chest. Like some sort of domestic droid, Kazu seemed able to switch on and off from an internal clock. What's more, the commander remained as distant from his subordinate in either state.

Closing his own eyes, and freeing his soul, David Hewish fell back on his past.

He thought of the Serpentine – the ship that had saved him from death – prominent on the dockside in Sydney. Major Smith had been a kid then too and the pair of them had camped on the deck, ready to jump into the Pacific when the enemy missiles struck home, utterly convinced they could cling to the wreckage until David's father arrived. But the missiles never came, which was probably a good thing because his father was already dead. In that sense, things had been easy for him. The dockside hadn't been short on screaming parents that day. Smith and Hewish had been spared all that. Smith's parents had lost sight of him in the railway station in Sydney and David's mother had died in Alice. Whatever other crimes the boys would commit that day, total loss of composure wasn't one of them.

Alone in the storm shelter, 300 million miles from everything he had ever loved, David dreamt of a better life. He listened to the traffic on the Washington freeway and tasted coffee from the comfort of his own lounge. Sipped cocktails with his shipmates on the flight deck of the Lexington. Saw Christine's mother, her uncombed locks wild in an autumn breeze. Bourbon. Morning. The shape of a girl's waist and the colour of her hair.

And then he woke up.

The Ajax was the same but something was different. Overnight, the vehicle had become possessed by an amber haze. Glancing through the forward observation windows, he soon saw why. Their view had been swamped by the blood-red sands of Mars and for several seconds, he found it difficult to look at anything else. In the hours that followed, he would do a deal with God, offering to die in the morning if only he could be allowed to stand upright on this world for the best part of one day.

Reading from his inbox, his heart missed another beat. For most of this mission, his colleagues back on Earth had greeted him with a dozen separate messages. Today there was only one.

SUPPLY SITUATION CRITICAL
AJAX TO LAND BY AEROBRAKING ALONE
BY ORDERS, GENERAL G GREAVES, US ARMY

It was time to bet everything on black. It was time to land on Mars.

CHAPTER ELEVEN

An interplanetary spacecraft possesses fantastic kinetic energy and it takes a lot of rocket fuel to bring a vessel down on the surface of an airless world. But for a planet with an atmosphere, deceleration is a much simpler affair. Here, the energy can be bled off against air resistance, the underbelly of the spacecraft becoming tremendously hot in the process. This was the game plan for the Ajax.

The last few hours before the landing were hectic, with two men trying to complete a workload that might have been better shared between a crew of six. Three hours short of the atmosphere, Kazu did something unexpected. He played music.

"All of me. Why not take all of me ..."

It was the sound of another world, and a voice that seemed to conjure up a value system from another age. It was Frank Sinatra, the Lexington's very own celebrity mascot. Rushing around like a man on fire, the colonel was slow to catch on.

"I see, sir, very appropriate."

Kazu was actually smiling. It was the first time they had shared a joke.

"How about the name?" asked Kazu, absentmindedly.

"The name Ajax? Did you check that out?"

"Not yet, sir. Not so hot on my ancient Greek."

Settling down on the flight deck, they began to study their monitors.

"Well," said Kazu, "there are some great minds in the village. One of them is bound to know."

Ahead of them, the slow and lazy molecules of the Martian atmosphere were about to receive a shock. The Ajax was falling like a bat out of hell and the two were about to collide.

Eight minutes into re-entry and the spacecraft began to shake. It was nothing to the kind of buffeting they could have expected back on Earth, but it was enough to make them flinch.

"Breaking umbilicals!" Kazu's narration had begun.

Behind them, an elaborate array of solar panels was saying goodbye. It would have been unrealistic to bring them inside and they were far too flimsy to take through the atmosphere. As of now, electrical power in the Ajax would come from the batteries.

Communication with Houston was already down. The gases surrounding a spacecraft on re-entry are quickly ionised and radio contact is lost for up to 20 minutes. During this interval, many missions have broken up, with a plethora of machines simply vanishing into this deadly void. If the Ajax disintegrated today, then the dream of an American colony on Mars would die with her, but her loss would be greeted by more than despair. Kazu and Hewish had a duty to the agency that transcended their own lives. They had a duty to report their status.

"Ejecting the first buoy."

A different kind of thud.

"Buoy ejected."

The buoy – no larger than a beach ball – would descend to the surface on its own parachute. In the event of catastrophic failure on the Ajax, the buoy would survive as an independent entity and the engineers back on Earth would receive the data to tell them why. It was one of those sacrifice-for-the-sake-of-the-programme kind of actions.

Nineteen minutes into re-entry.

"Drogue chutes opening …"

External cameras recorded the drogue parachutes on the Ajax, their vast and colourful canopy flapping wildly in an alien wind.

She shook again, this time quite violently and for a few seconds the control panel went blank. What's more, the nature of the buffeting had changed. The bitch was starting to *roll.* Already baffled by the signals from his inner ear, Hewish screwed up his eyes and tried not to retch, and felt his rectum try to tear itself free of his anal sphincter and take refuge in his chest. Somewhere in the storm shelter there was a software package that told you how to land the Ajax. With his teeth clenched and his toes clawed up, David wondered what it said about inversion without power during an atmospheric descent.

Over to his left, Kazu had forgotten the manual and was acting on impulse.

"Dump the heat shield!"

With the heat shield gone, she would lose inertia and respond more eagerly. The electrics recovered, Kazu toyed with the RCS motors and ejected a second buoy. Their trajectory was good, their cargo still attached. The beads on his forehead were beginning to boil off. Picking up on the artificial horizon, he managed to convince himself that the Ajax might yet survive. For an instant, he even saw their heat shield, a giant Frisbee in the South.

"Main chutes opening …"

The Ajax shook again. The chutes were tugging on the fuselage and the last of her kinetic energy was ebbing off. Judging by the view from the flight deck, she might have been falling through the atmosphere of Earth;

breathable, sustainable, ready to greet them as the doors flung open, ready to blow away the appalling stench of space flight and brighten up their day.

No such luck.

"Four hundred metres. Dumping parachutes … ignition."

She shook again. No – it was more than that – she was coming alive.

They saw a barren desert.

"Three hundred metres – and the com is good."

Onboard telemetry was streaming back to Earth. The shroud of re-entry was far behind them and the buoys had become superfluous.

They saw rocks. They saw a New World.

"Engine stop."

And then they felt it! Felt their entire ship kiss goodbye to the agility of flight and stumble on solid ground.

"We're down! We're down!" The pads were in the sand, the engines cooling. There was nowhere left to run. Hewish turned eagerly to his superior. "How did she handle, sir?"

"Like a brick, Colonel!" Three feet to his left, the guy was almost shouting. "Like a 50-billion dollar brick!"

They had done it. They had landed the Ajax! From a standing start and in less than four months they had landed on Mars, the fastest manned transit ever achieved. Without adequate training, undeterred by onboard fires and with neither the comfort nor the safety of a parking orbit, they had reached the surface. The Ajax was intact and upright, standing less than 6 kilometres short of Viking Village, a journey that would have been feasible on foot and that was certainly feasible in the remarkable new vehicle they were about to deploy.

CHAPTER TWELVE

It was 2 a.m. on a Martian clock. There was no time for celebrations. Their first and overriding concern was electrical power. Without recharging, the batteries onboard the Ajax would be dead within a day. They needed to deploy at least one row of solar panels quickly and hoped to hell the sand storms wouldn't cut them out.

Bent double in the crushing one-third gravity, David peered up at the storm shelter, hopelessly out of reach above their heads.

Now my charms are all o'er thrown. And what strength I have's mine own.

Gravity was a nightmare but the training exercise and the rapid transit had saved them the worst. Having secured the ship, they prepared to bed down on the flight deck, waiting for the Sun.

And when it came, that same Sun tore them from their dreams. Disdainful of the virtual, Hewish scrambled up to the highest point on the ship, ready to see the thing in person. Thirty seconds later, Kazu arrived to join him.

"Does the temperature bother you, Colonel?"

"No, sir," David lied.

"I figured the fuselage would have gotten so hot on re-entry it would be OK to tone down the thermo. That way, we save maybe 6% on battery function."

"That's great, sir," said David, hugging himself gently, "what about the sail? Any news on that sail?"

"Fifteen days." Kazu shook his head with undisguised contempt. "Maybe more. I heard the gyros were playing up."

Folding his arms and rubbing his palms across his chest, the commander seemed unperturbed. His assumption that the heat of re-entry would be retained had been largely intuitive and for what felt like the millionth time on this mission, temperatures inside the Ajax were dropping like a stone.

Directly opposite, David Hewish fell silent. It wasn't the cold. In the crazy mixed-up world of his brain, his own performance during the outbound fire had been exemplary. In contrast, Kazu had been the hero during re-entry, dumping the heat shield three minutes ahead of schedule and saving the mission. But Kazu had been in the driving seat and the two astronauts had been tied down beside one another, unable to visualise anything except their instruments. Maybe nobody had noticed.

"Better make contact with the village," said Kazu. "We don't want to waste any time." Facing his only subordinate, he looked for reassurance. "They're keeping you informed?" he asked. "About the state of the crew?"

"Yes," said David.

"That information has been withheld from me."

If this was true then it was surprising although David Hewish offered no outward sign of surprise. The outward journey had been hectic. It was possible that their mentors back on Earth thought it better that Kazu should concentrate on the Ajax. Kazu was a militarist who obeyed orders but he had the intellect to ask questions and he hadn't. Until this instant.

"What have they told you?"

"Sir, it's not good."

Descending to the airlock, they readied themselves for the surface of a hostile world. Neither man relished this task. Donning a pressure suit was one of the few skills they hadn't practised, perhaps because of a shared conviction that they were unlikely to survive the landing. Having gotten this far, suiting up looked set to become the most important skill a man could have.

NASA recommended that 40 minutes should be allocated for suiting by an experienced crew and 70 for first-timers. Even this was a major advance on the early days of space flight. Whilst a modern pressure suit is designed to be used by a single astronaut, in practice the act of suiting benefits greatly from the help of a colleague.

Backpacks were physically bulky but their gas cylinders had been woven from Kevlar and were reassuringly light. Plexi-glass visors filled a full third of the helmets and having never been used before, were as new. The visors would allow safe, direct vision of the dunes and offered an unobtrusive head-up display with written information being projected onto the inner aspect of the glass. Since there was nothing on Mars that was green, standard text would always be projected in green.

"All set?"

Hewish jerked both thumbs in the air.

"I'm going outside," Kazu explained. "I'll orbit once round the base of the ship, then I'll call you out."

"Copy that!"

Whilst Kazu fumbled in the exit, Hewish took the opportunity to review their life support. Muttering into his lip mike, he watched, entranced, as the computers responded to his spoken word.

Internal suit temperature and humidity were within normal limits. There was a tiny straw to the side of his mouth and if he felt the need, he would be free to sup on lemonade. At the opposite end of his body, a latex convene was tugging gently on his penis. In training they had told him he wouldn't notice the thing and he had never had the nerve to answer back. In practice, the discomfort was tolerable and he would be grateful for the opportunity to pass water when it came.

Out on the sands, things were happening. Commander Nobohito Kazu emerged from his space ship, feet first and with the help of a sturdy ladder. For all his reserve during the outward journey, his excitement on the surface was palpable as Kazu revelled audibly in his first few steps on an alien soil – this man's third!

And in time, David Hewish felt his own boots hit the surface. Stable and upright on the deep red sand, he turned to inspect this vast and decidedly *Brave New World*.

As was the norm for a manned expedition, it was a great place to land and a truly dreadful place to visit. The terrain was largely flat, the boulders little bigger than their own boots. Mission planners at NASA have long been forced to compromise between high risks and low-interest landing zones and the dunes in this region were decidedly dull.

"Magnificent!" shouted Kazu.

"Magnificent desolation," came a self-conscious echo.

David looked up and checked a few constants.

Checked!

The sky on Mars was – as they had always told him – pink.

Then, without warning, there was movement. On a planet where nothing really happens, they saw a gust of Martian wind, swirling wildly in the freezing air. It looked, for all the world, like a terrestrial tornado on the cheap.

"Dust devils," called Kazu, still loud on the com.

The term 'Dust Devils' had been coined by NASA scientists some 50 years earlier. The Ajax crew had first read about them during their initial training for Mars. At last, they had seen one for real.

A short while later, the first cargo canister had swung down and a seemingly endless carpet of photo-voltaics rolled out across the sand.

The second canister contained the components of the nuclear-powered buggy. Too big to be hauled as a single unit, the machine had been shipped in segments and would require further assembly on Mars. The astronauts began by inflating a small Kevlar bubble behind the rigid pressurised cabin, quickly doubling the size of the crew compartment. An hour or so later, the tyres were inflating too, lifting her a good 3 metres above the sand.

And by lunchtime, she was alive and kicking, whizzing around the landing zone at a cracking pace. Locked inside the pressurised cockpit, they marvelled at this yet to be soured environment. Fresh sleeping quarters lay behind the main crew compartment along with pre-prepared meals and folded blankets. Still flushed with the thrill of a planetary landing, the Ajax crew set out for the settlement at a good 10 klicks. A few minutes into the journey, Kazu switched to autonomous steering and turned abruptly to face his colleague.

"What's happening on Viking Village?"

The colonel frowned. It was time to come clean.

"There's been a death; their only doctor. Smith."

"Major Smith?"

"Yes, Major Smith. Smith was also the commanding officer on the base."

"They found him dead in the sand," said Kazu.

"Yes, that's right. He'd been missing for weeks. The radio beacon in his helmet had malfunctioned. In the end they had to send up one of those flying wings to find his body. Sounds like suicide."

"This is the guy you were with on the Serpentine?" asked Kazu.

"And the same class at Harvard." Reluctant to be drawn in on this one, Hewish tried to move things along. "Later, Smith and I were on the programme together. For deep space. The agency let me go, Smith clung on." David Hewish decided to reveal something else. "I've seen men kill themselves before, sir. It's not just the man. It's the place he goes to." Though Kazu did not respond, his manner seemed to confer agreement. "Besides, there was conflict in the village before Smith died."

"And since then?"

"One of the relationships broke down. There was a pair of them that came out here as a married couple but it all went wrong."

"Foguet and Erkhart?"

"Yes. Foguet and Erkhart." The commander had been supplied with more detail than he made out. "Then their re-supply ship failed. They were starving."

Kazu, who – to be fair – had been cooped up in a cramped and humourless chamber for more than 16 weeks, spoke with his eyes on the road.

"You know, Colonel, this could work to our advantage. If we get there and find a few of them dead, our logistical problems will be solved overnight!"

The euphoria of the last few hours had run its course. Hewish and Kazu were stranded on a lifeless, alien planet. Worse still, they were about to run into an entirely new problem: *people.*

PART TWO
LIFE ON MARS

CHAPTER THIRTEEN

Alone, emaciated and until very recently absolutely gorgeous, Doctor Rachael Callaghan lay frigid in a makeshift nest. All around her and across the floor lay the scattered remnants of a forgotten Jane Austin novel, the only hard copy document she had been allowed to bring here. Locked in the stinking twilight of a dying world, the gardener had sought solace in the language of a bygone age and when the text had failed to save her, she had progressed to the act of shredding.

Six feet above her, a last-ditch light source was humming on the ceiling. Staring up at the thing, she could see a crown of lichen, bright green around the bulb. No one at Marshall had sent this here. The spores had stowed away in the minutiae of their clothing and spread themselves out on arrival.

Leave the bugs on Mars.

Get me outta here!

But Rachael couldn't get out. She was trapped in this settlement, afraid even of leaving her room, lest the act of leaving forced her to confront her colleagues. For the last 20 days, she had survived in a shroud of blankets and foul underwear, sustained only by the hope of oxygen starvation and ultimate rescue. And now, without warning, what should have been the closing chapter in her life was being rudely interrupted from an open door. It was her friend and fellow astronaut, Sarah Connolly.

"They're here!" screeched Sarah.

Rachael struggled to her feet. Low, dark corridors led down to the epicentre of the village where a vast Kevlar bubble had been crowned with a transparent dome. Having avoided the Sun for the best part of a month, the gardener was practically blinded by the light. Moments later, she picked up on something else. The place was a pigsty. A horseshoe-shaped table was littered with shattered crockery. It was as if an outlandish Viking orgy had been staged some months ago and the cleaners had forgotten to call.

Ahead of her, the skeletal figure of Sarah had already scaled the horseshoe and was attempting to peer out through the plexi-glass dome. Sarah Connolly had seen the buggy. On this – an almost airless planet – its initial approach had been largely silent but she was getting close and the base was in the grip of a heavy tremor.

And then – without warning – a new player emerged beneath the dome. Kelly O'Reilly: one-time career scientist, acting commander of Viking Village and fully paid-up member of the Martian aristocracy. These days, just another starving whacko on the edge of sanity.

"They're here!" called O'Reilly, her voice soured by panic.

Because if there was one unspoken fear on the planet, it was the fear that outsiders might discover what had gone on here. And if there is one word in our language that described this fear it was *shame.* In what could easily have been the bitter end, the villagers had been asked to leave this world with dignity and failed.

CHAPTER FOURTEEN

The planners at the Marshall Space Flight Centre had blessed the village with its very own stable of vehicles and successive waves of Martian explorers had eroded a recognisable path to the settlement. Finding these tracks in the desert, Kazu veered right and decided to follow them. At that moment, the people beneath the dome got their first clear view of their visitor. A long cargo canister had been laid out between the trailers and they actually saw the thing stretched out to full length. Then, as the buggy swung to face them, they glimpsed the warm glow of the cockpit. This was salvation on eight wheels and there were whoops of joy on the table.

Over in the buggy, the Ajax crew were receiving another bleak lesson in the reality of Mars: *Suiting up for the second time in one day is a big deal.*

So big a deal, in fact, that David couldn't imagine leaving the vehicle without a reasonably good cause. Although already half-dressed for the purpose, the addition of helmet, boots and gloves took vastly more effort than they had expected. If Nobohito Kazu were to die on this mission, then David's own fate would become uncertain. How the hell was he even supposed to walk out of this vehicle on his own?

Eighty minutes dragged by. Being excited is a high-energy task and the observers in the village were beginning to flag. Out on the sand, a pair of clumsy figures in pressure suits had approached the southern airlock and were attempting to gain access.

Kicking the airlock door with the toe of his boot, David Hewish waited for a response. The action passed without sound although he would have expected his boot to be audible to the villagers. A full minute elapsed and he hit the door again, this time using an oversized spanner from his tool kit. Neither man wasted energy on commentary. Tiny cameras on their helmets were beaming home pictures every few seconds.

Nothing happened. Seconds later, David became concerned about the feeling in his feet. His lesser toes were going numb.

"Are your feet cold?" The commander's timing was unfortunate.

"Can you tell?"

"My feet are cold."

"I know. I know ..." They kicked the door for a third time, stamping anxiously in the sand.

Houston had prepared for their arrival with a string of carefully worded radio signals directed at the village. It was, however, by no means clear that anybody had read them. Close to the point of despair, David was relieved to see lights appear in the airlock. Through a porthole the size of his palm, he saw an unbelievably scrawny figure, tastefully dressed in two pairs of underpants and a dozen socks. He knew that the villagers had been forced to cut back on their rations and hold out for rescue. Even so −

Kazu raised one hand.

"Look!"

David followed the man's arm.

There was a transverse window at knee height. It overlooked the communal dining room in the village. Through this window, the Ajax crew could see another group of bizarrely clad people scurrying around like mice.

"Ladies and gentlemen, there is life on Mars," muttered Hewish. "It may be crazy, but it is life."

The ubiquitous green gunk had gained a foothold on the inner aspect of the window, remarkable in that quite a large crew had been unable to hold the stuff at bay. The colonel's heart sunk. He had spent the last few months longing for the space and comfort of this base. He was about to be disappointed.

"God, it's going to stink in there!" Kazu was ahead of him. "Why aren't we getting any voice-over? What's going on here, Colonel Hewish?"

"Ahem. Yes. They've been going nuts for some time."

"Nuts?"

"Nuts. That's a technical term I developed on the outward journey. They shut down most of the cameras in the village a few months ago. Covered the lenses with their underwear. Mission Control doesn't actually know what's going on, but seeing as we were outward-bound anyway, they thought they'd bring us down here anyway, just to see what the fuck is going on."

That's *what the fuck is going on* just for the mike."

Kazu offered a blue-collar laugh on the com. Here was another bit of foul language to get the ground staff cringing. Sadly, they wouldn't get to hear it for another 20 minutes. Thanks to the delay in radio transmission, their mentors back in Houston were still watching them tape up their asses in the buggy.

Meanwhile, the door to the airlock had still not opened.

"Let's circle," decided Kazu. "We'll check the place out."

"Roger that."

61

Traversing the perimeter, the Ajax crew came across one of the outrider buggies some 30 yards west of the base. More of an open-top jeep than a buggy, the vehicle carried seats for a sum total of two men. On the starboard side, the tyres were surrounded by sand.

"There's not been a lot of action round here." Seconds later, Kazu bent forward to retrieve an object from the floor. It was a discarded tin can, not dissimilar from the kind of thing he'd used to shield his brain in the Ajax. Watching it rotate in his hands, they both became silent. The can had been damaged by two bullet holes. "Target practice?" Kazu tossed the object back to the ground.

"Look!" Hewish was pointing at the skyline. "Automated re-supply, still upright."

"I see it!"

They could just make out the spire of a second spacecraft, the *Von Braun*. It was the fuel leak on the Von Braun that had caused the current crisis in Viking Village.

The inspection continued. The base itself had been built with a myriad of solar panels, all of them caked in dust. Kazu, a strict disciplinarian and a naval aviator, offered this verdict on the state of the settlement: "I'd say that the photovoltaic maintenance on this planet is about on a par with the green shit situation."

A little further along, a series of structures had been designed to show their colour. The green houses had been surrounded by rows of tin-foil petals, throwing a little extra light onto crops that had long since died.

Other than the greenhouses and the occasional skylight window, anything that could be lived in had been buried. Lacking the dense atmosphere of the Earth, the Martian settlers had defended themselves against cosmic rays using the only shielding available: sand.

By now, the Ajax crew had come full circle and Kazu led the way back to the plexi-glass dome where the woman, Rachael Callaghan, was still visible, this time on top of the dining table. Behind her, a second desperate figure was trying to clear up.

But there was something else here. Something ill-defined and yet unmistakably sexual. Even to the rear of the commander, even through the shield of their respective pressure suits, Hewish could feel it. From the day of their first introduction in Texas, it had been clear to David that Kazu was not married. Kazu had joined the Lexington before David, about a year before women were officially banned from the navy. Ever since then, the ship had been an all-male affair. In the whole of the outward journey, Kazu had never once discussed women and thus far, Hewish had seen his colleague as a man alone.

The girl gestured to the airlock and they went there to discover that the door was in fact open. Turning to face Kazu, David Hewish patted his belt and waited for the man to reciprocate.

It was time to go in.

Sharing the airlock with a whole load of sand, David dropped the tool kit to one side and unzipped the hood.

"What are you thinking?" asked Kazu.

"We're getting some air in here," Hewish replied. He was watching the pressure gauge in his bag – one of the few instruments that wouldn't show a reading on his visor.

"Safe to egress?"

The commander's impatience was plain to see.

"Wait for the hatch." Seconds later – as Hewish had predicted – the hatch clunked open and a gaunt, red-haired woman waved through the gap.

"Come on, come on!" she cried.

"It's like Man-fucking-Friday in there!" This was an aside. Kazu's voice was on a private frequency.

Other people were breathing. It had to be safe.

"OK, I'm gonna try to break my seal," said Hewish, hearing the squeak in his ears as he swivelled his helmet. Kazu did the same and they progressed through the inner hatch.

"O'Reilly!" shouted the woman. "My name's O'Reilly!"

The new arrivals fell silent. From their review of the personnel files they knew that Kelly O'Reilly was female. Up close, her identity was less distinct.

"O'Reilly! How are you, mate?" asked Hewish, a lost Australian twang suddenly prominent with the excitement. "I'm Colonel Hewish. Colonel David Hewish, I'm a flight surgeon and this is – this is Commander Kazu. Captain of the good ship, Ajax! This is the man that flew us out here! All the way to Mars!"

There was a manic shaking of hands. When O'Reilly opened her mouth again, she was shouting.

"Colonel Hewish, I'm the acting commander of this base! I'm in charge of this place. Whatever anyone tells you, I'm in charge." And then she added, "It's mad in here."

A short corridor led into a more capacious living and dining area. This was, by far, the largest pressurised area the Ajax crew had stood in since Kazakhstan and the place was an absolute disgrace.

Discarded cooking utensils littered the floor. The stench of unkempt sanitation was everywhere. Worse still, the dreaded green gunk had managed to encircle every available light source. That said, it was hard to believe that anything could flourish in these conditions. This place was *cold*!

David handed out a few Hershey bars and cracked open a flask of steaming coffee. Following a tip-off from Houston, he was also providing mugs.

By now, some five personnel had ventured into the dining room. Crowding round the goodies like the starving millions, they lapped it up with unseemly haste. It wasn't quite what Hewish had expected but it was a success of sorts and he might have felt more heartened if it hadn't been for what came next.

Up against the wall, Kelly O'Reilly was making her way to the floor. Her hair had thinned steadily these last few months and what little was left had been denied the luxury of colour.

"Tough time? Tough time you've had out here?" David asked, kneeling down beside her. "Mars can be a harsh mistress," he added, unaware of the allusion.

"Mars!" Kelly's face had hit the floor. "Don't talk to me about Mars!"

And then another pathetic figure made an entrance to their left. It was the gardener, Rachael Callaghan. Having being briefly sighted on the dining table, she had hidden in her quarters for a while, returning now with a baggy jacket and a haunting scream.

"Mars!" she cried, *"Mars is a shithole!"*

"Roger that!" acknowledged Kazu, inhaling deeply on the New World.

CHAPTER FIFTEEN

In the course of their hundred-million-mile trek across the solar system, the Ajax crew had sometimes dreamt of a warmer, firmer greeting. But it was not to be. Before their arrival, there had been ten people alive on Mars, the eleventh crew member having expired at the beginning of the current crisis. Assuming nobody else wanted to die and allowing for the addition of the Ajax crew, there were now 12 people on Mars, all of them looking for a return ticket to the Earth.

The Ajax crew had also expected a degree of physical assistance to help them hook up the trailer to an airlock and unload its cargo. One look at the work force on offer said that this wasn't going to happen. Kazu and Hewish would have to do it themselves.

The village was equipped with four airlocks. Each stemmed out from the centre of the base on the points of the compass. All four were functional. If they could link up the cargo canisters to these airlocks, it ought to be possible to unload their supplies without the need for pressure suits.

But this activity would consume time and energy and they needed to convince themselves that the other astronauts were safe before they became distracted. Hewish decided to take a quick tour of the base and check out each person in turn. This was not an easy exercise. In some of the individual crew quarters, he was made to feel unwelcome.

"Colonel Hewish!" he would shout, "US Navy! Rescue mission! C'ming through!"

This mix of stern heralds and formal politeness was ludicrous but he did it anyway. Five or six of the crew had already dispersed to their own sleep quarters and a few others were still not fit to stand. NASA had never really selected people for obesity and by the standards of the astronaut corps, Hewish and Kazu had been fortuitously plump when they boarded the Ajax. In contrast, the incumbent crew in the village had been forced to shed weight they could ill afford to lose.

When the withered figure of Foguet finally appeared, he was hoarse and supine in his cot. Though Hewish had studied the files of every astronaut, he hardly recognised this man. At the tender age of 44, he had been going grey for some time but somehow, his dramatic weight loss seemed to have blurred the clock. Foguet had gained ten years and lost ten years all at the same time.

David Hewish made a misguided attempt to speak in Spanish and quickly realised that the Spaniard was fluent in his adopted tongue. Conversation apart, this once burly figure from Barcelona showed no sign of sitting up. Prior to the landing, Foguet had been discussed as a likely candidate to help with the unloading. Viewed in the flesh, it was hard to see him helping with anything.

Returning to the dining room, the colonel approached his colleague with undisguised concern.

"How are they?" asked Kazu.

"Tired. Hungry." David Hewish came in a little closer. "*Nuts.*"

"I know. How about the unloading?"

"We'll need to get some sugar in them first. Give 'em a couple of days. Three or four or so guys can probably do it."

"If we're lucky! Christ! Get going!"

CHAPTER SIXTEEN

Back in the airlock, the Ajax crew repeated the painstaking task of re-suiting and preparing for depressurisation. Anonymised by silvered visors, the astronauts spoke on a private frequency.

"What do you think?" asked Kazu.

"I don't know. They're nuts alright. They've been cooped up in here for months. It's freezing."

"Why didn't they go outside and wipe down the panels?"

David Hewish tried to shrug although the gesture was lost in these garments.

"Not every post doc can double as a deck hand."

"This is true, Colonel. I have been truly blessed."

Suddenly they were being lectured from behind the door.

"Colonel Hewish!"

Four or so villagers had appeared by the intercom. It looked like a formal deputation.

"We have a list of demands!"

This was Sarah Connolly, speaking – it seemed – on behalf of the group.

"What's that?"

"Firstly ..." Sarah was reading from a piece of cardboard written in a childlike scrawl.

"Firstly, we'd like to request that you and your crew –"

"That would be the two of us?" scowled Kazu.

"Remember that this base belonged to us long before it belonged to you."

"I'll bear that in mind!"

"We would also ask you to turn off your sound and image recorders whilst inside this base and in contact with our people."

"Lady, if we don't in and get on with our work, you and the above-mentioned personnel are going to be *dead* by the end of the month!"

"Cancellation of the onboard imaging is non-negotiable."

Without the mask of a pressure suit, Kazu would have been visibly incensed.

"Then you can die on Mars together!"

"Kazu!" Hewish was butting in. "Kazu!" The Colonel put one hand on Kazu's arm as if in restraint and with his other he reached into the tool kit.

"Take it," he bluffed. "This is my only camera. Hand held." There was a second hatchlike airlock adjacent to the main door. It was intended for the transfer of smaller items to EVA crew who didn't want the hassle of formal decompression. Hewish slid the camera into the chamber and added, "You can put it in a bucket of water if you want to."

"That's if you can find a bucket of water in this dump!" called Kazu, "*I* am ranking officer on this *planet* and it is upon the basis of my decisions that the people in this village will live or die!"

The deputation retreated.

"You've got three hours' oxygen in those suits," said Connolly, rather ominously. "Until we release the hatch, you're stuck in that airlock!"

A new player was on the scene.

"Are you mad?" This was O'Reilly's voice, attempting to intervene on behalf of the Ajax crew.

"Yes," volunteered Hewish, sotto voce, grabbing a bit of 19th century kit from his tool kit. It was a crow bar. Seconds later, he had also found a gun.

"Now you're bringing firearms into the base!" chanted a female voice, a single digit pointing through the window.

It was time to escape from the airlock and get on with the job. The design engineers back on Earth had never really planned for an outbreak of mass hysteria on Mars but it was happening and they were going to have to deal with it. Having struggled at length with the crow bar, Hewish grimaced as Kazu snatched the thing from his hands and had a go himself. Seconds later, their pressure suits were bloating. The gas that had once filled the airlock was on its way to the stars.

"You're breaking it!" shouted Sarah. Totally nonplussed, Kazu issued new orders.

"C'mon," he mumbled, "let's go!"

CHAPTER SEVENTEEN

More than a hundred million miles from Earth and less than two hours since their arrival in Viking Village, the Ajax crew had been evicted by the very same people they had come here to save. Whatever animosity they might feel for the villagers, they had another – as yet unspoken – burden on their minds, one that more or less compelled them to return to the base.

Hewish and Kazu dragged the cargo canister off the back of the buggy and cranked open its rear doors. A concertina-like tunnel stretched out to the universal airlocks and they soon clunked it into place, knowing as they did so that the villagers might yet obstruct it from within. Several gruelling hours later, with everything clamped together, they re-boarded the buggy to rest and de-glove.

Sand had accumulated on their boots and for the first time in his life, Hewish felt the dust from an alien world.

"Gets worse than this on the Moon," said Kazu, as if in passing. You think this is bad? Try rubbing Moon dust down your dick."

In the corridors of astronaut school, it was common knowledge that the dust on the Earth's satellite was more irritative than its Martian equivalent. Activating the voice link to Houston, Hewish found this hard to believe.

"We have an immediate crisis situation here," he declared, brushing down his water-cooled underwear, with real apprehension. "The villagers are agitated. We've had an incident in the airlock –"

"An incident in the airlock?" shouted Kazu. "The bastards tried to kill me! I've a mind to fly home!"

"We can't fly home." This was a literal statement.

"Houston must have heard it all on the com!"

Attempting to provide perspective, David Hewish became blunt.

"Who the hell are we talking to, Commander? There's no one to call but each other. What are they going to do on Earth? There isn't another launch window 'til the end of this year and it would take six months for a second conventional craft to reach us. That's assuming they've got the greenbacks to build another machine and with the kinda shit they're in right now, I'm not convinced they have. In addition, I'd like to take this opportunity to remind you that everything we say and do on this planet is going on the com. There's no such thing as a private conversation on Mars, there's just conversations they can't butt in on whilst you open your mouth."

"*They* meaning the planet Earth?"

Kazu was leaning over the computers, skimming through the architectural plans for the settlement.

"*They* meaning the planet Earth," agreed Hewish. "And that's what's happening every time you go for a piss."

"Not when you take a piss. The latrines are off limits to surveillance."

Kazu was listening to Hewish and doing something else. With his gaze fixed on the screen, he reached for a toothbrush and a tiny bowl to spit in. Like his subordinate, the commander had found his mouth stained by the stench in the village. Time was of the essence but a man can only keep going for as long as his body will let him.

"The only other time they can't film you, Colonel, is when you're straining at stool, 'cause the fixed angle lens won't go that far. That's the agreement. You signed a bit of paper on another world to say they wouldn't film you voiding your bladder and taking a crap! And whenever we raise our voices, they've got it on the flash drive and they're analysing it and there's some geek back on Earth milking some kinda psycho-babble PhD from the thing."

"And that's why they've gone nuts in Viking Village," said Hewish.

"Gotta be more to it than that." Kazu emptied his mouth into the bowl. "Alright! Important safety tip! Remind me to stay sane on another planet. Arm yourself with the dart gun. When we get in there, it's tranquillisers as you feel fit. I'll be holding the live ammunition in reserve. We'll force the airlock if we have to. You can force it from the outside. I just read how to do it. How long can we knock them out for?"

"Two, maybe three hours. Depends on body mass."

"Well, there's not a lot of that!"

"Remember," hissed the doctor, "we *need* these people alive."

Kazu seemed not to hear.

"Piss if you want to, then get suited up! We're going back in there."

Out on the sands, the Ajax crew unwound electrical cables and linked up the settlement to the nuclear reactor beneath the buggy. This ought to be enough to turn on the lights and warm the base. The one thing that would still be in short supply would be water and there was a plan for that too.

But heat energy carried risks of its own. Kazu calculated that a freezing villager would be a pushover for a healthy young man with a gun and he decided to go in quickly. Storming in through the eastern airlock, Hewish threatened a wide-eyed Callaghan with a dart gun and watched her back away. In contrast, Connolly stood her ground and took a tranquilliser dart in her right breast, keeling over long before the sedative could possibly have gotten a grip.

There was screaming everywhere.

"Get back!" shouted the colonel. Most of them did. A couple of other unshaven characters turned up in the dining room and sounded rational. One of them was the acting second-in-command, a Chinese-American by the name of Daniel Tan.

"We're dying here," he whined, the empty sockets of his eyeballs seeming to reinforce this view. Kazu scurried back into the cargo canister and returned with another box. Opening the box, he grabbed a selection of edible goodies and tossed them over the dining table. Just down from the surface, they were all rock solid with the cold. One bearded figure snatched the chocolate whilst another grabbed a drink. They were going to hurt their teeth.

"OK! You're on our reactor. I'm gonna tone down the air conditioning!" called Hewish, practically blinded by the mist from his own mouth. "We're looking for another 15° here …"

There seemed to be order. Ambulant personnel were engorging themselves on the goodies and the temperature was climbing. Hewish ran back to the main canister. When he returned, no fewer than four bodies had littered the dining room floor. Another three rather placid-looking figures were cowering by the doorway.

Nobohito Kazu had been busy.

"Alright!" shouted Kazu. "Alright! I want to see all three of you in that canister, now! C'mon! Get up! Move!"

And it was at this point that a new, rather hapless-looking figure pitched up in the dining room and asked, idiotically, what was going on. The same question was on David's lips though this probably wasn't the moment to voice it. Rummaging through the re-supply box, David grabbed some drinks and slung them in the microwave. A short while later, the base was full of steaming mugs.

If nothing else, the act of holding a hot beverage seemed to keep them still. With his back to the wall and a gun in his hand, David felt himself lean into the Kevlar. How much longer could he function at this level? Unnoticed even by his mentors back on Earth, the colonel had escaped in his mind to another world. It was the world of Washington DC, shortly after his arrival in the Pentagon. Running onto the mass transit system, he heard doors slam shut behind him and felt a soft leather seat press against him. And then, amidst the ordinary, he saw something else.

Some 20 feet away, elegant beside a pair of nondescript office workers and as blonde and as lovely then as she surely was today, he saw Christine.

Several weeks later, their paths would cross elsewhere. Christine had gotten herself invited to a cocktail party in the Pentagon and he saw her again, as if for the first time. She was amusing herself by the band and a guy on the drums proved helpful with an introduction. They conversed at length, rushing through life, work and the more irritating implications of all-out war. But David never told her about that moment on the train. He held that one in reserve, never dreaming that it would return to him, 24 months and a hundred million miles away.

His eyes opened. Temperatures in the village were soaring and with it, bacterial proliferation. The stench was appalling and he became convinced that his eyes would soon water. Looking to one side, he saw that Kazu – who virtually never revealed any kind of physical discomfort – had kinked his neck and was breathing fresh oxygen from his suit.

Hewish set up an infusion of warmed crystalloid on each of the unconscious people and went through the laborious process of sliding a plastic airway between their lips.

Two of the villagers were too weak to have even left their rooms and he found them docile in their cots. There, he proceeded to string up further infusions, hanging the bags of fluid from the roof. One guy peed in his pants whilst he was talking to them but their pants were pretty filthy anyway and they didn't seem to care. In the short term, the intravenous fluid would be enough to keep them hydrated although it wouldn't have much impact on their blood sugars. With regards to sugar, he was going to have to get something into their gastrointestinal tract.

Bose, who had yet to be seen on his feet, was laid out in his own quarters, silent as if in death. Slashing open the man's clothing, Hewish examined his chest and managed to convince himself that the guy was not beyond salvage. Bose was showing respiratory effort and for a second or so, his mouth opened and the doctor watched his eyelids flutter. For a few seconds, there seemed to be a message there but he was quickly distracted by the torso. Bose's skin was coated in a fine, downy hair. This kind of hair had a name but he couldn't think of it.

Over in the dining room, Kazu was bellowing in the obscene. Feeling the need to move on, Hewish leant Bose up against the wall, slid a naso-gastric tube through the left nostril and waited 'til it reached the stomach.

Aspirating with a syringe, he saw what he took to be gastric juices rushing back along the tube. His eyes lit up. He was in! David hooked up a bag of very high-energy supplement to the ceiling and ran off to the next room.

Rachael Callaghan's cot was occupied again. She seemed to have flaked out and then woken up again. David Hewish switched on the overhead lights. This was the first time they had been used in months and it took him a few seconds to appreciate the scene. The woman was weak with ketone breath to boot. He spotted an obvious appendectomy scar just above her waist. He thought she was barely conscious but as he wrapped her up and rose to leave, Rachael made herself heard.

"I know where you're from …" she whispered. *"You're from a dead country."* Their eyes met. Not like with Bose. Searing.

By dusk, things were beginning to happen. Most of the villagers had assembled in the dining room. Everyone with a gag reflex was sucking from this new teat and offering no obstruction. In spite of this, the Ajax crew remained apprehensive.

"Where's the other guy?" asked Kazu, his eyes darting from face to face. "The engineer?"

"Bose? I left him with the feed up," said Hewish. He really should have gone back and checked again. "I'll just go and see."

He saw. Bose was dead, his cold and wiry body propped up against the wall, just as the doctor had left him. The feed from the ceiling had snared in his stomach and quickly overflowed. David's attempts at resuscitation were cursory. He was gone.

Laguna hair.

The word came back to him. A form of soft, downy hair, well recognised in Anorexia Nervosa. Bose was caked in the stuff.

77

"Christ!"

Was this the fate that awaited them all? Or should this man have been better attended? He would never know.

When Kazu walked into the room, David Hewish was still holding the extracted feeding tube.

"That's ten still breathing," said Kazu, without emotion. "Better than I expected." Then, glancing back from the doorway, he added, "We'll bury him on Mars."

CHAPTER EIGHTEEN

Many times in this mission, the Ajax crew had debated how they would cope with death and on more than one occasion, it had occurred to David that by the time they arrived, the entire village might have expired. To have salvaged 10 out of 11 lives might be seen as a triumph but the image of the leaking NG tube would weigh on his mind for months.

With the other astronauts confined to their quarters, David Hewish, and Nobohito Kazu slid the body through to the airlock and left it at the back of their cargo canister, draped in a couple of stinking sheets. Securing a bulky hatch, David felt an awkward wave of déjà vu: *Taiwan*, *Alice*, his own recurring visions of the Serpentine. No matter how hard he tried to deny it, defeat was the only consistent theme to his life.

In the settlement proper, the Ajax Crew performed a brisk clear-out of Bose's quarters. His bedding was a disaster and the worst of it was heading for the sands. Personal effects were thrown in a loose bag and stored in an empty cupboard.

Next, Kazu made a detour to Smith's office and returned with a pair of hand guns. With Hewish on lookout in the corridor, Kazu examined the weapons at length. Only one appeared to have been discharged. The entire indwelling clip was empty. Intended for extreme crowd control, the weapons had been flown out here with limited ammunition. Recalling the can in the sand, Hewish reasoned that this kind of target practice must have been a rare event. Anything else and the ammunition would have been spent.

His inspection over, Kazu secured the hand guns in the commander's safe using a code known only to himself and his first officer. Their own sedating dart guns, they held in reserve, pending the next riot. Together again in Bose's room, the Ajax crew progressed to the issue of on-site recovery. There had been no routine maintenance on Mars for at least 15 weeks and the life support system was on the brink of collapse. It would take a sustained effort to bring it up to speed.

How soon would the villagers be able to help with this work? Previous experience with famine relief had emphasised the danger of rapid ingestion and the authorities on Earth were recommending a staged return to solid food. Kazu was inpatient but able to obey orders. Others had already ignored this advice and the settlement was thick with the smell of vomit.

Forty-eight hours passed by.

The Ajax crew had formulated a plan. On the doctor's orders, the astronauts would eat steadily for the next 12 days, seven days longer than Kazu originally intended although hardly enough for anyone to return to full health. In this same period, Hewish and Kazu would be able to perform a couple of hundred hours of basic maintenance tasks on their own.

Central to this challenge was the security of air and water supply. In an environment of this kind, these two issues were closely intertwined. Quite apart from urine and faecal losses, every astronaut on the planet was losing fluid in the form of perspiration and – at these new temperatures – frank sweat. If the average rate of loss was 2 litres per day then the population as a whole would be losing around 1 kilogram per hour. Since the atmosphere condensers had been unattended for three months, just over 2 metric tonnes of water vapour had been pumped into the settlement and this accounted for much of the frost that the Ajax crew had seen when they first arrived. Kicking the atmosphere condensers into shape returned 30 to 40 litres of water to its liquid form in the first day and they could all breathe more easily. What's more, they now had access to a renewable source of fluids.

On day nine, Hewish took individual astronauts into the shower and scrubbed them down in 2000 mls of water. He had asked for 3000 mls but had been unable to obtain permission from Marshall. Nudity made them seem even more emaciated. Every joint in their limbs was still visible, like knots in a rope and he revised his anatomy as he washed their flesh. Some of them needed help with shaving and he quickly obliged. A lot of toenails were starting to claw and he clipped them back and scrubbed away the stuff that had gotten underneath them.

Pausing briefly by the doorway, Kazu took one look at his junior and disappeared. Like a lot of non-medics, he probably found this kind of thing distasteful. Even with sponsorship from the navy, David Hewish had struggled to survive at Harvard and at weekends he had often worked as an orderly at a local veteran's hospital. Brushing a sponge across another man's balls meant little to him.

Of all the residents in the village, only Charlotte Erkhart made an effort to resist, insisting that he turned away as she escaped her clothes.

Idle in a corner, Hewish glanced over his shoulder and saw Charlotte playing with the soap in slow speed. Eventually, with her hair blackened by the cold fluid, she became more rational.

"Don't listen to them."

"Who?" he asked.

"*Them.* About O'Reilly. O'Reilly did alright. Once Major Smith was dead, it was Kelly O'Reilly that held this place together. She did what she had to do. Don't let anyone tell you otherwise."

Something inside her snapped and she let him through to help with her bathing. Up close, he saw long dark streaks along the small of her back. Toilet paper had been intensely rationed for weeks and this was a common finding in these people. Charlotte curled forward and closed her eyes and pressed her forehead against the edge of the tub, saying nothing as he reached down to wipe her down for a third and then a fourth and then a fifth time. In another week, he reassured her, it would all be gone.

By day 13, all of the surviving astronauts were ambulant and ready to move on. With temperatures well over 18°C, they disposed of their thermal underwear and clad themselves in fresh white cotton. Underwear from the Ajax was a cause for frank jubilation but at this stage, Kazu was uncontainable. There was work to be done and there was nobody else to do it. First and foremost, there was the issue of Bose.

Marnix Gabanna and Fredrick Weissman had flown out to Mars with a better than average body mass and were relatively well preserved. According to the log, they had taken part in the burial service for Major Smith and Hewish put their names forward to Kazu who agreed to their help.

Later that same day, the four of them drove off to a beautiful hillside, some 6 kilometres north of the village where the astronauts had once ferried the much-loved figure of Smith, that he might rest in a location commensurate with his station. As they had done before,

Gabanna and Weissman helped to dig a trench and in time, they carried Bose's body out from the buggy and down towards his grave.

In a short, stifled service in the sand, Kazu offered a reading that might have been better suited to the deck of a fighting ship. The whole affair was being relayed directly to the village but for reasons that were not entirely clear to Hewish, Bose was to be denied a formal eulogy. Aside from the tragedy of his actual death, this refusal to state his impact on life seemed particularly harsh. Even by the standards of the astronaut office, the resume on Bose was staggering. How on earth had one man managed to cram so many achievements into 39 years?

The service wound down. Looking up from the grave, Hewish spied the white cross that marked Smith's final resting place. His colleagues had asked that the two bodies might lie some distance apart.

"God knows why," mumbled Kazu, back in the buggy. Marnix Gabanna and Fredrick Weissman were still egressing in the airlock and out of earshot. "Maybe the two of them didn't get on."

But David's mind was elsewhere.

"Should have stayed with him," he said, recalling the feeding tube and sensing the pain of neglect. "Should have stayed with him, 'til he was good." It was a confession that did not go down well with his superior.

"Don't give me any of this *guilt* shit!" sneered Kazu, snatching up the mantle of David's forgotten drill sergeant. "Bose died because his crewmates hadn't the wherewithal to feed him! And if they hadn't been fucking around with me, you wouldn't have had to double back for crowd control. Blame *them*. 'Cause they fucking deserve it!" Back in the present, Commander Kazu spun round to face the airlock. "What the hell are they doing in there?" he groaned. "Playing with themselves?"

Fredrick Weissman had fainted. Gabanna asked if he could stay with him until he felt better and Kazu became irritated whilst nothing happened. This wasn't a great development. It's true they weren't getting him at his best but in his current state, Weissman was a less than inspiring figure. "I'll be al r-r-right in a minute ..." he whimpered, flat out on the floor of the airlock. Weissman's posture had deteriorated significantly during his forced incarceration in the village and Hewish was beginning to regret his taste in gravediggers.

At the opposite end of the spectrum, Marnix Gabanna was a far more convincing adventurer. With hair as black as anthracite and a mass of five o'clock shadow to boot, Marnix had developed an enviable reputation for womanising in Houston and had hardly lost it in the closed environment of Mars.

Silent beside his commanding officer, David recited his second personnel file of the day: Marnix Gabanna had been born in Quebec and spent time in Europe before the carnage. At the age of 25, he had applied for US citizenship but found this process unnecessary when Ottawa voted for convergence with the Senate. His primary area of expertise was life support and he'd found himself repeatedly reprimanded by Houston for inappropriate behaviour on Mars.

When the hatch finally opened and the villagers poured in, David Hewish felt a pang of guilt that they had asked these men to do anything, let alone dispose of a friend.

"Feeling shit about your choice of gravediggers?" asked Kazu.

"No," said Hewish, much too quickly.

And so it goes. Bose had been laid to rest and the last 11 people on Mars met beneath a plexi-glass dome to share a very sombre evening meal. Nobody bothered to say grace and when David Hewish said it in his head, the voice was mocking. Few, if any of the villagers seemed grateful for anything they had received. To his immediate left, Tan and Eliot seemed to regard this whole near-death experience as another obstacle to their master work. More tangibly, Eliot's beard had the annoying habit of collecting debris from his plate. Nobody else seemed to notice. If this was the norm for Mars then Hewish was going to have to choose his place at the dinner table more carefully.

Next, he looked to the women. Connolly and Erkhart were too frail to actually carry anything and Kelly O'Reilly had become infantile about losing command. Rachael Callaghan was the face that had caught his eye in their first briefing in Texas though her wasted physique would take time to become human. Scooping up the last of his canned apple pie, Hewish wondered if it was realistic for the only physician in the base to form any kind of relationship with these women and concluded – not unreasonably – that it was not.

The meal ended and the villagers dispersed. Alone in his quarters, Hewish checked his only e-mail and felt justified in his contempt: *"Funeral service projected by the sapling as planned. Very poor attendance."* Several of the surveillance cameras in the village were working again and Houston had been able to monitor this activity in detail.

Cursing his new crew, the colonel succumbed to false nostalgia, recalling the Lexington at her most heroic best. He thought of the desperate battle in the skies above Taiwan.

Kazu's squadron had lost aircraft on a daily basis and by the time Hewish acquired his own flesh wound, more than half of the pilots were dead. But that had been another age. Back then, the navy had still been sending women into combat and lives were being lost on a massive scale. Thus far, in this settlement, two men had died and two more had taken their place. If they wanted to get home alive they were going to need a big change in attitude.

Come daybreak, the Ajax crew concentrated on the inventory. Every box on the planet had been electronically tagged and it ought to have been easy to assess the residual stores in the village. It wasn't. Several hours of intense work ended in frustration. Many of these containers had been raided by people who were starving and in some cases, the contents had already dried up. The initial delivery from the Ajax had helped but they would soon need another and Kazu announced that he would return to the Ajax to retrieve more supplies.

This matter was further discussed over supper. For the first time since the relief flight had arrived, several of the villagers began to think out loud, turning over their plans for reconstruction whilst they ate. That being said, some of them saw this as a challenge for other people.

Alone amongst the villagers, Rachael Callaghan asked for permission to accompany the Ajax crew to their ship. David couldn't imagine that she would be of much help but Nobohito Kazu agreed with a nod over coffee.

The following morning, the buggy picked up speed on an open plain.

"How about you guys?" the woman asked them. "How was your trip out here?"

"Colonel Hewish and I remained calm and collected at all times."

"That's how you came down at 6 klicks!" she laughed.

The accuracy of most manned landings was less than 500 metres.

"Would have been easier with an active homing beacon in the village," Hewish told her.

"That's a Foguet thing," said Rachael. "You need to talk to Foguet about that! I just do the grass!"

Pulling up beside the Ajax, the astronauts progressed through the rituals of suiting, egressed out onto the sands and re-boarded their ship. Happy to be rid of his suit, Hewish climbed up to the higher echelons of the Ajax, ignoring the charred remains.

Halfway up the ladder he stopped abruptly and looked down towards the flight deck. There was nobody there but there were tell-tale noises.

"God almighty!"

Kazu was screwing Rachael in the latrine, less than 6 feet from the flight deck. It was the least convincing seduction scene in the known universe although probably the only source of privacy on the ship.

How the hell had he moved so fast? More to the point, why the hell had she –

Hewish stalled. There were tiny cameras all over this ship and his fleeting scowl was already heading back to Earth. The US Navy had banned women from the sea nearly ten years ago. At the time, casualties in the Pacific were so appalling that nobody asked why. He had never experienced anything like this before onboard ship.

But hey? he smirked, *this is Mars!* Maybe the old rules didn't apply.

Their return journey to the village was conducted in silence. At home in the settlement, the gardener's adventure in the latrine remained secret as the new supplies were unloaded. Carefully sealed boxes were soon open and there were edible goodies galore. Charlotte Erkhart threw up. Alone, against a distant wall, Commander Nobohito Kazu watched in silence.

Still shaken by events in the latrine, Hewish returned to his quarters and tore open a sachet of flavoured glucose powder. On the Lexington, he'd drunk this stuff by the gallon and the rush that comes with sugar helped to stay sane. His scalp hit the wall and he sighed audibly.

Their landing, the burial service, this feast beneath the dome, all of this was only the beginning and David Hewish knew – better than the rest of them – that there was worse to come. Seconds later, Fredrick Weissman did his best to prove this very point by bursting into Bose's room and demanding a packet of pills. After a brief discussion, the doctor accessed his patient's medical records and saw that Smith had prescribed a standard issue antidepressant some three months prior to his disappearance. At that time, there had been no reference to a speech impediment.

Hewish hadn't worked with Smith for some years but it was hard to imagine that he would have neglected to mention the stutter.

"Look," said Weissman. "L-lo-look. I need those pills. I can keep going without them. I can keep going, but I *need* those pills."

Having got what he wanted, Weissman left without prompting. Several minutes later, Hewish walked out through the same door, ready to catch a new speech by Commander Kazu. Kazu had dragged everyone he could find into the dining room and had taken up position on the table. "Now, I'm going to review this whole base," he exclaimed, "and I want my second-in-command here to accompany me on that review."

Seeing that his arrival had been timely, Hewish raised one hand as they all looked behind them. The Ajax crew walked along a narrow corridor, pursued by an eager entourage. In his style and his manner, Kazu was the visiting colonial governor in some distant province and his journey began where it would end, in front of a sealed office by the dining room. The office had been built to serve just one man: the base commander.

Many months after his demise, the villagers were still calling this place "Major Smith's quarters".

"We – we haven't disturbed his personal effects," said Rachael. "After he died, we left everything as it was."

"Who took over the base?" asked Hewish, who already knew the answer. After a brief hiatus, Sarah Connolly replied, "Kelly."

Kelly was standing right next to them but had declined to state her own name. Staying with the office, Hewish saw that the doorway had been sealed with adhesive tape.

"As of now …" said Kazu, "… as of now, myself and Colonel Hewish will be making use of these quarters." This was a bombshell. Kazu was striding onto sacred ground. "I want everything the guy ever owned, stripped and locked away. If you don't have to, don't even mention his name."

This was how they had dealt with death on the Lexington and as the commander described his plans, his new roommate surveyed the place with a fresh eye. He saw a washbasin and a few cabinets. He saw a tiny desk with a convincing wooden veneer. As if to cap this trend to domesticity, a broad fountain pen had been left unsheathed on the desk. Incredibly, in a world where any kind of baggage was at a real premium, there were even books!

Major, you were even crazier than me ...

"All things must pass," Kazu went on. "Major Smith was a good man but he's a dead man too. Get over it. We'll have no sentimentality in this settlement and no regrets."

There was a lock on the back of Smith's door. Hewish had already seen this on the blueprints for the base on his outbound flight. The door could be locked from the inside. All the other doors simply swung on their hinges. On Mars, Hewish realised, it really was important to knock.

Rising up onto tiptoe, he stole a glance at some of the higher shelves and saw a pile of plastic Viking helmets, complete with replica horns. Sensing the full weight of their predicament, Hewish became nostalgic for a time when Viking helmets might be regarded as acceptable headgear in the village. That was the kind of welcoming party he had dreamt of, not a bunch of fruitcakes with their fingers on his air supply.

An inch below the ceiling, Smith had tacked his own idea of a motto for the settlement. It was one of the better-known lines from the American rocket scientist, Robert Goddard and he had written it out by hand.

"Who is to say what is impossible, for the dream of yesterday is the hope of today ... "

That was Smith for you and David had to jump to block a new flurry of memories: Smith's puckered face, Smith smiling at Harvard. Overcoming Chabod in a competitive quiz. Drinking the pair of them under the table in the aftermath of the wildest ball. And then he swept the others away. Major Smith was dead. Like Kazu had already stated, Smith was best forgotten.

It was time to move on. A system of flexible tunnels connected each of the habitation modules. To a newcomer, the complex had the air of a rabbit warren although as Hewish correctly guessed, it would soon become too small. Additional crew space had been established in converted fuel tanks. Here and there, a distant skylight window managed to keep the place airy.

The village was also a work in progress and to save on the heating bill, some of the facilities had yet to be occupied. One of the more recent flights had delivered a large room with a distinct ledge just short of a pit. The room had potential to be used as a water reservoir although a quick glance through the entrance confirmed that this pool was decidedly dry. Feigning disinterest, the naval officers passed it by. Later, with their guides out of earshot, Kazu spoke softly to his shipmate.

"If we can find it," he whispered, "that's the place."

Their tour continued. In an annexe that had been built for rest and UV therapy, Connolly and Erkhart had established their own laboratory in miniature with a huge double X chromosome symbol nailed to the door and a row of seismometers stashed against the wall. Identical machines had already been positioned across the planet and if Hewish had been more switched on, he might have asked himself questions as to why these women felt the need to isolate themselves in this way.

Five minutes later, the answer revealed itself. The entrance to Dr Tan's research lab was at the end of a gentle slope and when the Ajax crew descended, it gradually dawned on them that they were not being followed. The others were all staying behind.

The lab had begun its life a spacious affair but a mass of equipment had made it cramped. As Hewish had read on the outward journey, the background music was Mozart. Besides listening to classical music, the senior citizens on Mars were here to do science and a string of delays to their mission had hit them hard. What's more,

Daniel Tan – who was already down here – had some sort of axe to grind about the thermostat.

"They promised me a temperature fixed between 19 and 22°C!" he moaned. "Back on Earth, they promised me all kinds of shit. This heavenly lab where anything was possible and any breakthrough could be made! Well, let me tell you, it was bullshit! Even before the Von Braun croaked out, temperatures were way outside those limits."

"We can see bits of the lab from the surface," said Kazu, trying to sound helpful. "Maybe it needs more insulation."

"Look, Commander, don't ask me to shovel sand! You see, there are two types of people on Mars. There's guys like *us*, doing serious science in this place and there's guys like *them* who like to go outside. A clown like Kelly wants to mess around on the dunes. She likes it. It makes her feel more like a man." Over to the right, his world-class colleague was beginning to smirk. "Don't forget that back on Earth, *we'd* be on the edge of recognition. And by recognition I mean global recognition – the Montreal impersonation of the Noble Prize. That's what this is all about." He gestured to the instrumentation around him. "That's what we gave up to come here."

Recalling his own disappointment at being rejected by the programme, David Hewish stated the obvious.

"There are a hundred other guys who would have taken your place if they could have."

Tom Eliot took it upon himself to respond.

"And why do ya think they didn't?"

Hewish gave no answer and Tan continued.

"Doctor Eliot and I have been sending home an original research paper from this place, *every two weeks*. We won't be going home to pick up some symbolic statuette at the Oscars. Our names will be on the papers we write and in the world of science, it's our names that will be remembered forever."

"By other geeks," said Kazu.

"Well who else are we gonna talk to?" demanded the younger scientist, his voice just about audible above the latest Aria. "Some kind of regular Joe in the street? This whole goddamned thing is an adventure to them!"

Adventure figured pretty highly on David's list of priorities although he omitted to mention that at this stage.

"Look at Charlotte!" said Tan. "Charlotte Erkhart. The girl's still married to Foguet – legally that is ..." Hearing the joke, his colleague started to chuckle. "But she never changed her name. And does that matter? You're damned right it matters! 'Cause when you look under her name, Erkhart's work will appear on the system and for a research worker, that's all you get to show for your life."

Suddenly, Eliot came in on the same point.

"What we've got going here is a coherent plan for the exploration of this planet," he said. "And by coherent, I'm not talking about the kinda balls they churn outta Marshall! I'm talking about our *own* plan, mapped out here in the centre of things by people who know what the village can do and what it can't!"

Ill at ease with these personalities, Kazu interrupted sharply.

"Yeah, OK. Once things settle down, Doctor Eliot, you can get on with your hobbies. In the meantime, I would ask you to concentrate on the issue of mission salvage. Life support, thermostat, logistics. Leave the science for later! And when I say *leave it*, I say that as an order."

Kazu was accustomed to working in a hierarchical organisation and these people were starting to bother him. But David Hewish had a different hang-up. Glancing back at the bespectacled figure of Tan, he tried hard to suppress a deeper distaste. David had not been brought up to hate the Chinese. It was an acquired skill. His last school teacher in Alice had spent most of her time teaching her kids not to hate the Chinese and David Hewish hated the Chinese, in part because they had murdered her. In the last few years, he had given up trying not to although by the strict letter of the law, Doctor Tan could not reasonably be described as Chinese. His family hadn't spoken Mandarin for three generations, but there are some beliefs that a man can never leave behind.

Ascending the ramp, the Ajax crew found the rest of their colleagues where they had left them, slouched against the Kevlar. Regrouping in the corridor, they soon discovered a new kind of smell. It was the greenhouse. Only the woman, Rachael Callaghan, seemed to have any real interest in this section and her prime function on the planet was to keep the greenhouse going. Fresh food had been a reality on Mars for many years but since the fuel crisis kicked in, the farm had sunk into disrepair and they were all eating out of cans.

Standing by the doorway, Kazu's woman nodded in the direction of the farm.

"Needs a little irrigant!"

"Well we're going to get some irrigant!" the commander told her.

"How you gonna do that?" asked Kelly. "You got an atmosphere condenser on your ship?"

The village erupted in an unexpected wave of smiles. NASA had been trying to milk water out of the Martian atmosphere for decades. Nothing had ever come of it.

In the end, it was Callaghan who guessed their plan, her wild and theatrical smile bringing colour to this bleak planet. "I know what you want!" she jibbed. "You guys wanna build a canal? You brought Percy with you too?"

"Yep," said David, "we've got him on stand-by in the Ajax. Still sketching the place out."

"Well it's a long way to the ice cap, Colonel," Rachael told him. "Never forget that."

CHAPTER NINETEEN

Just as General Greaves had predicted, the Ajax crew had arrived on the planet in time for Thanksgiving. It was, however, far from obvious how the crew would respond to this event. The majority of the astronauts on Mars were unable to trace their ancestry to a common Puritanical past.

Foguet, had been born in a country formerly known as Spain whilst Weissman spent most of his childhood on a strip of land that had once been known as Israel. The latest base commander had been born in the States to Japanese and Irish parents. Most of Kazu's paternal relatives remained captive in Japan. As the founding fathers had predicted, such an eclectic mishmash carried the potential for conflict. But on this occasion, the crew were hungry and the food was free. Why would they refuse?

The seating arrangements for the meal were predictable. Since the table was shaped like a horseshoe, Commander Nobohito Kazu would sit in the middle. His trusted sidekick, Colonel Hewish, would sit on his immediate right. As guests on the planet and as the uninvited heroes of the settlement, neither man was expecting to serve.

Keen to make a contribution, Kelly O'Reilly was arranging the beakers beside their plates just as Sarah Connolly raised this query.

"Hey, Commander!" she quipped, "you got a wife to do this for you back home?"

The colonel stiffened. In all the time they had worked together on the Ajax, he had never once raised this issue.

"Got my people on the Lex," said Kazu, completely unperturbed.

"Good shipmates make for a better family," added David, who had no family. "Always have done."

The villagers seemed to buy this one and David felt better for it because in a sense, this reference to crew as family might make the rest of their evening easier.

Foguet's estranged wife, Charlotte Erkhart, had positioned herself on the opposite flank of the table. Quite apart from the issue of marital friction, there seemed to be a generational gap too with Marnix Gabanna and Rachael Callaghan clustering around Charlotte.

In turn, Tan and Eliot were seated to the far left with Pablo Foguet silent beside them. Knowing that he could annoy Kelly at will, Tan went into a rant about women's rights.

"I must say, Commander, I must say, one good thing about you guys getting kicked out of Taiwan was all the things it did to women in our society ..." Neither naval officer responded. "I guess women had it coming to them, though ... You know, when you look back, I can't quite believe how far they'd already come ..." The chief scientist was beginning to enjoy himself. "First they gave them the vote, then they let them drive cars ..." When Kelly was running the show, she might have been able to put him down on this one. Maybe Tan was looking to see how far he could go with his new boss. Glancing up at Kazu, David saw that he was about to speak.

"Well, guys, the American calendar wouldn't be complete without Thanksgiving and it's good that we sit down together, here today, to enjoy this meal with our friends ..."

Without checking on anybody's spiritual affiliations, Kazu broke off to say grace. As with the death rites over Bose, the base commander might have felt more comfortable addressing a military crew but this was the only crew on offer and he went about it in his own way. The villagers waited for him to finish and tucked in. The food was good. The noise level was rising and in view of the bombshell that was about to hit them, this was probably a good thing. Over to David's right, Doctor Daniel Tan had moved on to the history of science.

"The *Miracle Year*. Have you heard of that, Colonel?" David had. "In 1905, Albert Einstein published three papers in one year, any one of which in themselves would have been enough to make him immortal. There is nothing in the history of science to compare with it, 'cept for that year when that guy they call Isaac had a go."

Foguet cracked up and Rachael Callaghan lashed out from one side.

"And you're gonna beat Newton? From your little lab in the sand?"

"There's got to be a few more weeks before we board the Ajax!" called Kelly, flippant at her own end of the table. "You can do it, Daniel! Have a go!"

"And why not?" asked Tan, far too serious. "Do you think Galileo and Einstein were the last of their ilk? Let me tell you, Colonel, some day soon there'll be another miracle year, another moment of explosive discovery. Maybe even here!"

The party had lapsed into a collage of soaring egos and formal disbelief. David would have liked to have heard more but Kazu sensed that his time had come.

"Well, ladies and gentlemen, one of the reasons you're here today, indeed one of the reasons why, some day, you're all going to make it back to Earth, is sitting right beside me now and his name is David Hewish." Over to their right, someone offered a slow hand clap. "Serving officer in the United States Navy, flight surgeon on the Lexington, a man who played a pivotal role in our outbound voyage."

Colonel Hewish addressed his audience from a seated position. Since he had to start somewhere, he decided to start with humility.

"I cannot trace my ancestry back to the Pilgrim Fathers. I cannot trace my ancestry back to the American continent at all, because I came here ..." David hesitated, conscious of where he was. "I went *there* as an immigrant."

The villagers remained expectant. To one side, he received an unfortunate heckle from Tan, *"With Smith!"*

David continued.

"My crimes had little to do with God. My crime was merely to exist in my own country. And in the context of where we are today, I think that what you have to understand about the Pilgrim Fathers – what you have to understand about a group of people that we may at times have been guilty of romanticising – is that these people *suffered* to achieve an objective.

"And after they had been in the New World for over a year, those of them that had survived that year gathered together and tried to celebrate being alive. That's all it was. It's a tragedy.

"The birth of a nation. A story where more than half of the leading characters – many of them children – dropped dead in the first act. Because sometimes, if you want to live in a New World, that's the price you have to pay."

David Hewish stopped and Kazu picked up on the tale. "Following the dual fuel leaks on the Von Braun, the agency reviewed their options. Given the limited resources available it became imperative that myself and Colonel Hewish –"

"What about Colonel Jones?" This was Tom Eliot, making a credible bid for the Martian bad timing awards.

"We got that info," said Kelly, lightening up at the sound of this name.

"We got word that Jones was on your mission. Whilst we were still talking to each other."

David Hewish now spoke on Kazu's behalf.

"That crew was killed … shortly after blast-off."

Too dumbstruck to even stutter, Weissman was working on his squint. Meanwhile, Kazu moved on to his next bombshell.

"Due to the supply crisis in Viking Village, we were obliged to burn all of our fuel on the outward journey."

"Wait a minute, wait a minute!" This was O'Reilly again. "How do you mean, *all* the fuel?"

"We burnt all the fuel for the outward journey. Then – in order to get here in good time – we used the fuel for the return journey to make a second burn. Hence the record transit."

O'Reilly's face was turning black.

"And there's no fuel on the Von Braun," she said, her air of informality all but gone.

"No. Because you had a technical fault – you had some kinda leak in that thing here – and it's all gone."

"So, we're still trapped!" Foguet was getting on his feet. "We could have died with Bose. Now, thanks to these goons, we get to fade out in what? Another nine months?"

"No!" snapped Kazu. "There is a *plan*."

Inexplicably, David's thoughts returned to Bose. That moment of eye contact. What the hell was going on there? He would never know. In any case, it was time to rescue his boss.

"We're gonna drive to the ice lake," he explained. "Back-up plan is the ice lake."

For the scientific community, this was already enough. Driving to the ice lake had been discussed in the literature and their faces were screwing up. Others remained in the dark.

"What about the ice lake?"

But before David could respond, Daniel Tan delivered this furious interjection: "No one has ever been that far North!"

David produced a sheet of printed photograph. Unfolded on the table, it showed a gigantic drop of water trapped within the walls of a huge crater. In an era where the very idea of a hard copy had become a thing of the past, the improvised nature of this illustration seemed only to weaken their case.

"We'll use the buggy," David Hewish told them, "We'll use the nuclear-powered buggy to drive north, grab some water ice by the lake. Bring the ice back down here, melt the stuff, do electrolysis, convert it to liquid oxygen and hydrogen and then use that same combination to refuel one or both of our spacecraft in anticipation of a return flight to the Earth in five to six months' time. Now –"

But he had already said too much. The chorus of disapproval was heading to a new crescendo and Hewish decided to give it a few seconds for them to settle.

"We'll need at least 800 tonnes of ice," he said. "Possibly twice that figure. It won't be easy. Some of the stuff is going to be dust and some of it CO_2. Commander Kazu and I will drive the buggy to the ice lake. With the

101

headlights full on, we should be able to keep moving round the clock."

"It c-c-could blow out!" stuttered Weissman, who might have listed a few other risk factors if he hadn't been sidelined by Kelly.

"Nobody's ever made it to the ice lake!" the woman shouted. "Even if you get there, you won't be able to get through the crater wall. We've been exploring this planet for months! Believe me! Right up until the fuel leak, I was out there on the sands. Every day!"

"There's a break in the rocks." Kazu pointed to what looked like an entirely normal section of the crater wall. "An inlet, probably part of the overspill from the last big thaw. We'll drive through that. Now, it's going to be cold up there."

"Yeah? No shit, Sherlock!"

"So cold, over such a long journey that only the nuclear-powered vehicle can make it."

Over to one side, Tan was more objective. "How long do you plan to take getting there?" he asked.

Kazu shrugged. "I can't predict our speed."

"You can't *predict your speed*!" The repetition was searing but there was worse to come. Lathered up by the prospects of a new disaster, Rachael Callaghan, their resident gardener with a PhD was suddenly more than conversant with the technical issues involved.

"Your suits will seize up!" she warned. "Anything that moves will go solid. It's a nightmare trying to keep stuff warm in the village. You've got the fucking tropics here!"

"Not if we keep it warm!" protested David, defying his own disbelief as well as hers. "There's power in the reactor."

"And when you blow a tyre? When you blow a tyre halfway between here and Boerdis? What happens then?" O'Reilly had acquired the air of a master attorney, preparing to sum up. "Everything on Mars breaks down in the end! Even the people!"

"An officer in the United States Navy does not break down!" said Kazu, making a promise that he might later regret.

"Believe me!" his predecessor jeered. "You *will* break down! And when it happens, I just hope I'm there to see it! And then what? Who's gonna drive out there and throw you a rope?"

"No one!" Many years ago, this particular naval officer had offered his life to his country. To Kazu, this is just another day in that life "These are my orders," he said, "I intend to carry them out."

"And if you can't?"

"Then we all die on Mars together. Like the colonel said, this is *Thanksgiving*. It was meant to be a sober affair. But by New Year – I can promise you – by New Year things will be better. By New Year we will have *food* and *power* and *water* in this base. Believe me! Believe me and it will happen."

PART THREE
THE ICE LAKE

CHAPTER TWENTY

Morning came as the morning always will and the villagers awoke with the Sun. The realisation that their return journey had been put on hold was only one of their problems. Many more immediate concerns hung over them. First and foremost, there was a palpable fear of the cold. As soon as the Ajax buggy was in motion, its nuclear power plant would be gone with it and the settlement would be back to square one with only a solid food supply and the hope of ultimate rescue to comfort them.

Preparing to face another day, David stretched his limbs in his gritty cot. He was lying in the very same room where Doctor Bose had either starved or choked to death depending on how you wanted to look at it and some of the Martian dust had made it into his sheets. He could have been sleeping in the cot next to Kazu but the guy was shacked up with Callaghan and the idea of them cavorting right beside him hardly appealed.

Suddenly, something else passed through his mind, a half-forgotten memory from a troubled sleep. In the early hours of the morning, he had heard sobbing in the settlement.

Who the hell could that have been?

Lifting his pillow, David checked the location of his dart gun. It was still there and it was still loaded. Taking comfort from its existence, he called up his e-mails and watched them flash across the ceiling. As well as the usual nonsense, Marshall had raised a new query.

FOR YOUR EYES ONLY

Academics at the University of Arizona continue to complain of a poor down-link from the lab. Whilst general engineering parameters have remained on stream throughout the crisis, laboratory based instruments remain decidedly off line with routine data retrieval occurring as much as seven to eight days post acquisition. This delay is unacceptable ...

Brushing the message away, David Hewish continued to stare at a now blank ceiling. What the hell was that one about?

The base was beginning to stir and by the time David made it to the breakfast bar, Sarah Connolly had already found a seat. Over to one side, Tom Eliot was feasting on some kind of reconstituted rabbit food. Fragments of the stuff were collecting on his beard and David was trying hard not to look. Instead he asked him about the can in the sand.

"That was Smith," said Eliot, toying absentmindedly with the dregs of his breakfast. "He used to use a can for target practice."

"What? Like, every day?"

"No, I think it was just the once." His breakfast over, Eliot slid his bowl across the table. "But he liked it! If we'd had enough bullets he'd have blasted away at that thing every day of the week."

The great man stood to leave, heaving himself away from the horseshoe upright with the air of a real martyr. Eliot said something about the strength of his quads like he understood something about anatomy and his doctor said something sympathetic. Having cleared the issue of the can, David was reluctant to mention the data.

Instead, he checked out the dining room. On the wall behind the sapling, he saw a dozen pictures from around the base. The digital wallpaper was back in action and it was reassuring to be able to survey the complex with a single glance: the airlocks, the gym, the putrefied mess that had once been called a greenhouse. Marching back to the lab, down the central corridor, Doctor Eliot was making better progress than his exit might have suggested.

David looked to his left. Sarah was a few years older than him but a period of enforced fasting had restored her youth.

"Don't worry," she sighed, "this is not heaven. He only thinks he's God."

"Kazu?" Catching on, he added, "Oh right! Tom!"

Over by the sapling, the surveillance images had faded out and a panoramic shot of Manhattan was taking their place. David turned back to the woman and watched her frown. Her thoughts had progressed to Tan.

"Him and his pious pal with the his-and-his spectacles. Spending all day with Isaac Newton and the like, telling us how their own work is destined to supersede his. There's no sex in their marriage, three people and one of them has been dead for 300 years. And that's all they do. Those guys haven't been out on the sands in months. Did you know that?"

The colonel did know this.

"Ask them to find a pressure suit and they're busy elsewhere. Those egg heads in Marshall, they never think. The bastards just fly another six people out here and bring six back. Can we stand them? Do you know how many times they bothered to ask us about it? Like none!" Sarah brushed away her flowing blonde locks, changing the subject in the process. "You're an Aussie, right?"

"In my previous life." David smiled, recalling his nation in better days. "How about you?"

"Nth generation USA. My ancestors sailed in through Ellis Island. Didn't you come in on a boat too?" His smile faded and the woman changed too. "Oh, I'm so sorry!"

She was sorry. David Hewish was already regretting this particular exchange and went into conference with Kazu just as soon as the guy crawled out from his bed. Soundproofing the door with a rolled-up shirt, they debated the mission in a cautious hush.

The room itself had changed. The fountain pen was gone. Over Kazu's shoulder, David caught sight of the man's bed sheets. Though Rachael had already left, a strand of her hair remained prominent on the pillow.

Looking back to his boss, he tried to concentrate on their work. Any delays to their departure would give the village crew more time to dream up reasons to obstruct them. Storing the buggy for the journey north had become their top priority although they also had to contend with ongoing maintenance work, software updates and an impending miracle. Unknown to the other villagers, the Ajax crew were expecting a visitor and by sheer luck, it was due to arrive in the morning.

Concerned that their fuel status had been slow to go public, David questioned whether they should use the same approach twice. "Don't you think we should warn them?" he asked, "I mean before this thing actually gets here?"

"No," said Kazu, without hesitation. "You gotta be coy when it suits you. Besides ..." he glanced up at a carefully sealed door, "... they're keeping a few secrets from us."

Just before daybreak, the settlement was disturbed by the sound of screaming. There was a new star in the sky.

Brighter than anything that the Martian night had ever seen before, exceeding the combined brilliance of Phobos and Deimos and easily casting shadows around the base. A short while later, when the real dawn followed and when people saw just how feebly it shone beside the Sun, their jaws began to close. But there was more to this new star than spectacle. Beneath the skylights and with your face pushed up against the glass, you could actually feel the warmth on your face.

Several weeks ago, the engineers in Marshall had manoeuvred a large solar sail into orbit around Mars. Following fine adjustments, they had managed to achieve a geo-stationary orbit, so that from the point of view of the settlement, the sail would remain motionless in the sky. Rotating the device so that it functioned as a mirror, Marshall had been able to direct a lot of sunlight onto the base. Initially taken aback, the villagers were quick to recognise its potential.

But for Kazu and Hewish, this was all happening to other people. Houston had warned them that the whole thing might turn out to be a damp squid and in an effort to avoid disappointment, they had continued with their duties and played it cool. Out on the sands, the nuclear-powered buggy awaited them and it was time to change into pressure suits.

Against all expectation, Daniel Tan offered to accompany them as far as the airlock where a fresh pile of their padded undergarments was waiting for them. Losing the ability to speak, David slipped off his clothes and picked up the soft diaper-like flannel. The diapers were reusable but the adhesive tape that held them on had to be applied manually before each EVA.

Pulling the thing around his crotch, David found himself recalling an unfortunate incident with an injured fighter pilot on the Lexington. The guy had just managed to land his damaged jet on the deck of the aircraft carrier and ended up in David's ward, the upper half of his chest having been filleted by the Chinese Triple A. Undressing the guy for theatre, David discovered that the lower half of his flight suit was full of it and the resident chest surgeon had ordered him to scrape it all off whilst he scrubbed up. It took 40 minutes. Those were the days. The days when one man gave an order and the other obeyed and all this guilt and inquisition shit never entered their minds. Whatever happened on Mars, David wasn't going to fill his diaper like that.

A few feet to his left, Nobohito Kazu disappeared into the toilet.

"I mean like, I mean ..." Tan was trying to say something to his rear. "I'm sorry this has happened to you."

David's mind was elsewhere.

"It's no one's fault," he replied, in part to avoid conversation.

"These people," said Tan, "the people here, they're a great crowd, but – you know – they're not a crowd." Bored beside his half-assembled suit, David listened in silence. "When NASA was young, when the agency was young, that's the folk memory. You know, all these guys with short hair and steel jaws, TV crews trailing them day and night. *This* is a different era! Older guys, younger guys. All this skirt in your face. It's 18 months, maybe two years since anyone last saw home and there's no one really watching. No matter what you do, they can't dock your wages 'til you're back on solid ground and practically nobody wants to come here twice."

Doing his best to ignore him, David was starting to appreciate the role of the latrine. It wasn't just for men giving into panic on a threshold. It was about trying to save yourself the pain of using a spoon. A few seconds later, Kazu emerged and the rituals began all over again. Finally, after a full 90 minutes in the airlock, Daniel Tan clamped the commander's helmet and turned to face David.

"Hey, Colonel?" If Tan was trying to be subtle, he wasn't trying very hard. "Colonel Hewish, I just wanted to say we were all really grateful. Grateful for you flying out here and everything. And – and I'm *sorry* about Bose."

God! He's guessed.

This wasn't idle banter. Tan, a tenured professor at Stamford, had waited for Kazu to be cut off from the world before asking his next question. "What – like was he dead? As you walked into the room? I mean –"

Flicking his helmet link onto broadcast, Kazu moved to speed them up.

"Will you stop talking and get on with it!"

The scientist made a show of raising David's helmet and threw in one last question.

"Did he tell you anything at all?"

His helmet sealed. The sounds of the airlock were vanquished and David was glad of it. What the hell was that one about? Did Tan suspect something? Had he discussed it with the others? If the only doctor on the mission had stayed with the patient, he might have seen the overflow on the naso-gastric tube and saved Bose from aspiration. But this wasn't a states-side intensive care unit. There was only one of him and the care he could offer was at best sporadic.

Sealing the inner hatch behind him they waited for the freezing vacuum of Mars and the adventure that awaited him there.

CHAPTER TWENTY-ONE

Their fine new star would prove a useful if inconstant companion and the photovoltaic panels around the base were soon reporting a dramatic surge in power. The anxiety of life without the buggy was over and by noon, the ambient temperature around the village would have risen from -20 to -5°C.

Safe inside their own vehicle, the Ajax crew had discarded their clumsy pressure suits and were preparing to make tracks in shorts and T-shirts. The energy source for their journey was a nuclear reactor and in contrast to the solar panels round the village, it would not be troubled by the night.

"I don't believe it!" The gardener's surprise was genuine. "This is awesome."

"You see, young Rachael," said Kazu, "miracles really do happen. Even on Mars."

The buggy was hauling a pair of empty trailers and heading north as part of a slow, articulated procession. Ten minutes from the village, the additional sunlight had faded out. The sail was sensational, but its footprint was finite. Checking the baggage beneath his feet, Hewish found the dart guns again and also the more conventional firearms they had retrieved from the base. In accordance with orders from Houston they were bringing them all along.

Morale amongst the Ajax crew was high and the privacy of the vehicle enabled them to speak freely. They talked about their mission and they talked about the difficulties they faced on this planet. What concerned them most was their lack of confidence in the baseline crew. Earlier on in the mission, Kazu had planned to recruit a couple of able-bodied people from the village and bring them out to the ice lake. In the light of recent events, he had decided to drive alone.

Then, an hour or so into the journey, a new signal arrived from the Earth. A retired astronaut by the name of Roger was attempting to make contact from Houston. Roger was a veteran of two previous missions. He had driven several thousand miles in a similar machine and his helpful words of wisdom went like this ...

"Now, driving on Mars works out at about halfway between driving on the Moon and driving on the Earth. Until you get used to it, the horizon will be deceptively close. We're talking 4 kilometres for the horizon on Mars versus 6 kilometres back on Earth.

"What you will notice – and what I guess you've already noticed – is that if you build up speed in a pressure suit, you don't weigh much but you've got a lot more inertia than you imagine. All that suit and all that body mass makes you just want to keep going and if you try to stop real sudden, you'll be on the deck.

"If you're not in a hurry and you go outside together, I'd recommend trying to stand up from the horizontal without assistance, just to see how hard it can be and to see if you can figure out how to actually do it 'cause it's a useful skill to have."

Bent forwards in the cockpit, Hewish and Kazu exchanged an awkward frown.

"The same lesson applies to the buggy. If you're trying to make progress and the buggy's going on fine, don't go charging into some impact crater 'cause if you do and she starts to roll, you'll be dead and if you're not dead, you'll just die later 'cause there's going to be no one out there to drag you home.

"So for this mission – and I've familiarised myself with this mission – whatever happens, stay on target. Stay on the path! Don't go searching for some glamorous bit of gravel. You catch wind of that extra-terrestrial daffodil that no one's ever seen before – just remember, they've burnt Sweden. There is no Nobel Prize!

"Don't waste hours suiting up for no reason! Only go out if you have to. Never stray off the path *and never ever* go outside alone!"

Useful safety tips. Except that nobody had ever gone this way before so there wasn't really a clear path to stray from. Roger was talking about a route that had been mapped out for them whilst they flew through deep space and that had since been successfully downloaded to the computers on the buggy.

Night fell and Kazu ordered his colleague to bed. Succumbing to his fatigue, Hewish faded out between their supplies and dreamt of a woman who did not want him. Seconds later, his superior was shaking his shoulder, giving the order to get up. The buggy was driving on automatic.

And it was *cold*! The colonel could feel it on his lips.

"Temperatures down in the night," Kazu told him. "We were expecting that."

"It'll come up with the Sun," said David, optimistic, creaking to an upright position.

"Not much. We've just shifted latitude by about two dead countries. We're talking very cold becoming fucking freezing." Kazu had clad himself in a balaclava. He looked like an urban guerrilla. "Here, put this on!" he added, throwing a similar item to his colleague. "And get the thermo up."

That was the handover. It was almost dawn. Kazu was already supine, drawing the collar of a sleeping bag taut around his neck. Freed from any sense of subservience, David made himself comfortable in the driver's seat, and embraced this new view. They had already driven to a latitude that no human being had ever seen before and the feel of a virgin soil was all around him. A soft orange sky foreshadowed the solar disc and in a few minutes, he would be able to shut down the headlights. The terrain around them was always changing although the actual pace of change was slow. Many times in this journey, this former refugee from Alice would gaze out through these windows and recall the surreal red landscape of his childhood. But that was the past. Australia was dead and there was nothing he could do to change it.

And if there was a future for humans on Mars then Hewish believed that it should be an American future. Like the slumbering aviator to his rear, David Hewish sensed that that same society could survive, even if America itself were destroyed. It might take a while, it might take a century or more but Mars and its endless gardens of sand would wait until man was ready.

The light faded and he waited for the moons to greet him. In the case of Phobos – David knew – this would be but a brief, supporting role. Phobos orbits with a fabulously low perigee and if the driver had ever slammed the brakes, he would have been able to track its movements with the naked eye. In contrast, Deimos would follow them 'til the dawn.

Halfway through the night, his thoughts returned to their mission and the micro-environment of the vehicle. By now, the smell was sufficiently severe to rival the one he thought they'd left behind in the Ajax and in an effort to make things worse, Kazu crawled out from his sleeping bag and made abundant use of the latrine. Human waste was only part of their problem. Most of the stench in this situation comes from the bacterial breakdown of sweat and they had agreed to keep the temperatures low and perform daily sponge baths.

Out on the sands, the Sun was up again. The landscape had become boring and would remain so for most of the rest of the day. Switching the controls to automatic, David retreated to the washroom and decided to freshen up his mouth. Just to the right of the sink, there was a tiny mirror and he took the opportunity to survey his own body.

It was hardly a gripping sight!

He needed a shave but that was a minor problem. His own weight loss was a much greater concern. The grub on Mars was hardly enthralling but in this environment, body fat could be crucial and at this rate he was going to have to start force-feeding himself.

Returning to the controls, he drove until nightfall. Then, at long last, the Ajax crew changed places and the doctor lay down to sleep.

CHAPTER TWENTY-TWO

Idle in the back, David developed a passing enthusiasm for the poetry of Dylan Thomas. Half way there, he found an old favourite and started to read it out loud.

"Do not go gentle into this good night."

At first reluctant to engage, Kazu eventually confessed to the power of the piece. He tried some more but Kazu stopped responding and David Hewish returned to his technical manuals.

In particular, he needed to read everything there was to read about how to find water ice on Mars and turn it into rocket fuel. Since no one had ever done this before, he wasn't expecting this to take long.

The ice lake had been discovered by photo reconnaissance at the beginning of the century. Its presence had surprised many observers at the time who believed that water ice – if it existed at all – would be trapped in the ice cap. But the ice cap was considerably further north and it would have taken another six days to get there. Far-sighted mission planers back on Earth had been eyeing up the ice lake for years although it had taken the recent fuel leak on the Von Braun to get the project moving.

His mind too exhausted to deal in words, David decided to check out some pictures. Doubtless the water in the lake had frozen over after the last big thaw. Since then, the extreme latitude and the crater walls had managed to keep the stuff in the shade. But high crater walls were a mixed blessing. From the point of view of access, the crater walls were higher than he would have liked them to be. This wasn't going to be easy.

Three more days passed by. The mileage on the Ajax buggy continued to mount and the buffeting and jolting that was their journey was beginning to take its toll. His entire body had sustained a low-grade bruising and it was reasonable to assume that Kazu was feeling the same. Bleary-eyed and reluctant to eat, he studied the map and recognised a crucial milestone on this road. It was the point of maximum range for the village buggy and they had passed it two days ago.

They could not go back because they were under orders to go on. They could not beg for help because they were beyond all hope of rescue. Soon, it was the sense of the isolation itself that seemed to be causing them pain. As Daniel Tan had tried to tell him, the era of media excitement in space travel was gone. No one came out here for the attention anymore. And in a way, this pained him deeper still because the thought that other men were watching might have given this journey more purpose.

Then, 12 hours short of their destination, Kazu took the unusual step of bringing the vehicle to a halt and shaving, very slowly, in front of the wash basin. Conscious of his own facial hair, David did the same and when they had finished, Kazu said something about standards.

Why the hell did he say that?

The buggy regained its momentum and they pushed on through a jet-black night. Tracking their progress on GPS, Kazu anticipated a visual sighting on the target shortly after sunrise. If it didn't happen, if it wasn't there, if the ice turned out to be nothing but dust and frozen CO_2, then they would all die on Mars together.

That death, when it came, would be a slow and horrific affair and what David feared the most was being forced to contact the civilians in the village and deliver them the news. Rehearsing the call in his mind, he envisaged reading out some kind of pre-prepared message and then hanging up. It was a conversation that went on in his head a hundred times before the sunrise and by the time their world had brightened, he was certain he could do it right.

For all its glory, the actual sunrise was stunted. Every day that passed by, the sky darkened as their latitude rose and their exact location on the maps all around them was revised in real time. Suddenly, their final destination appeared on one corner. Soon, David knew, they would be able to reach out and touch it and his heart and his breathing began to rise. Since the day of their first briefing in Texas, he had dreamt of the ice lake. As with so much of his internal psyche, he had been able to hold that dream on the tightest of reigns. A fleeting image – a magnesium flare in his heart – almost sexual in its intensity. Chabod was a lunatic. Saying no was out of the question. He had to say yes.

Now they were there. Now they could see the sheer walls of this massive crater and now they could sense the knowing glow of an ancient lake. The Ajax crew had been compelled to make their approach from the south, arriving 5 kilometres short of the fabled northern entrance. Orbiting the crater took time and when they got there, the ground turned out to be more irregular than expected. Driving on manual, David Hewish improvised a path between the boulders. To his immediate left, the mission commander oversaw this manoeuvre in silence. In time, Kazu told him, "If you can't find a way through this thing, we're all gonna die."

Thanks for the safety tip, Commander.

Fifty minutes elapsed and they began debating with themselves whether or not to go outside and blow a hole in the crater wall. There was enough dynamite in this thing to create their own gorge and the idea was not completely ridiculous. The buggy was also equipped with small reconnaissance probes that could be launched from the ground, like Fourth of July rockets. These had been designed to fly over the cliffs and send back imagery on the landscape beyond. It would be useful information to collect and the astronauts would have felt a lot happier to have had it in on-line. Then, just as this idea was starting to sound attractive too, the buggy traversed a dark corner in the rocks and the ice lake revealed itself.

CHAPTER TWENTY-THREE

It was everything they had ever hoped for. It was ephemeral and it was even blue.

And it was vast! Leaping out of a cold Martian soil, that same ice lake provided David with yet another unwelcome reminder of Ayres Rock. Although well inside the crater walls, the buggy was 2 klicks from the actual ice. The ground around them was littered with small boulders and they noted fragments of white material that seemed to hide behind every boulder. At these latitudes, the Sun had always been low in the sky and the snowballs had been preserved in a perpetual shadow.

"How realistic do you think it would be to try and round up some of those snowballs?" David was thinking out loud. "Without actually going to the ice lake?"

"There'll be smart asses all over Marshall trying to tell us that soon. Give 'em 50 minutes."

Kazu's first and only crewmate lapsed into an unscheduled grin. The Earth was 20 minutes away by radio signal and the geeks in mission control would have to wait at least that long to see this view. But with the vehicle advancing and the ice lake looming ever larger in their sights, the snowballs were soon forgotten. Sixty metres short of the base, the buggy ground to a halt. In truth, this was closer than either man had hoped to get.

"What's the temperature out there?"

Kazu glanced down at the monitors and spoke without emotion. "Fucking freezing."

"Do you think it would be better to start the EVA in our boots?"

"We'll take them out there and leave them by the ladder," said Kazu, searching for his specially padded socks. "Boots'll slow us down. Bottom line – if it's too cold to operate, then we can't get the ice. And if we can't get the ice then we can't fly home. Do you want to freeze to death? Right here? Right now? Or do you want to go back to the village and starve slowly like some bearded hippy?"

If David had a view on this one, he decided not to voice it. Instead, he opened the inner hatch to the airlock and unhooked his suit from the wall. It would be more than an hour before they were ready for the sand and in his mind, David had already returned to the training tanks in Houston. *"Here,"* his instructor had taught him, *"here – in my suit – is where I belong. This is my home. This is where I wanna be."*

Nod your head and you'll feel your forehead butt against the glass. *Don't do that.* Speak and you may hear your voice echo in this desperate chamber. *Don't listen.* The world outside your helmet is a bleak and cold and hostile place. Here in your suit, you will survive.

I will survive.

The outer hatch opened on manual. He felt the clunk but heard no sound. As with the Ajax landing, David Hewish waited patiently in the airlock whilst Kazu slid down the ladder and on to the surface.

Seconds later, David was hitting the deck in person, checking out the scenery and noting distinct clumps of material that clung, annoyingly, to the soles of their feet.

"Weird sand!" he whispered, just loud enough to make it on the com.

"I concur," came the overly formal reply. Elsewhere on Mars, sand was a fine powder. Here, presumably the temperature and possibly also the permafrost was clutching it all together.

Some 30 metres from their machine, they erected a rocket probe and prepared to send it skyward.

"It's Fourth of July time!" called Hewish, bounding away from his missile.

"Erm, yeah, David ... I can feel it in my feet."

This was their greatest fear. During a weightless EVA in space, heat could only be lost by radiation. Here, on the surface of a solid planet, the ground pressed up against their feet and heat energy bled directly into the soil. In a few more minutes the cold would be through to the mechanical joints.

Launching the rocket from a safe distance, they watched it rush above the lake. Seconds later, the missile vanished and the data stream ended.

Without any further discussion the two men retreated to the buggy and shuffled into their snow boots. It would have been pointless to delay any longer. The snow boots lifted them another 10 centimetres above the sand and with direct contact removed, they ought to be able to hold out on the sand for longer.

Up against the ice itself, David Hewish raised a geologist's mallet and started to hit the thing, quite enthusiastically. Nothing happened. Resting his arm, he turned to Kazu. At such low sunlight intensities, their silvered visors had proved unnecessary and the commander's face was more than visible, clean shaven and tiny in a capacious sphere. The astronauts exchanged frowns.

He struck again, this time much harder and a large chunk of the stuff slid down beside his feet. Then, for the first time on this mission, Colonel David Hewish fell over.

"I'm coming!" said Kazu, discarding his snow boots like wooden clogs.

"No, I can get up," said Hewish, who was about to discover that he couldn't. Kazu reached down with one hand and helped him onto his feet. Yet the crisis wasn't over. Hewish had been out on the permafrost for nearly a minute, and his skin was noticeably cold. It would be more than an hour before the Earth could report on the imagery from the Fourth of July rocket and for the men at the coalface, this was too long to wait. Kazu decided to act on his own initiative.

"We're gonna go straight for detonation," he announced. "Get the drill. Get moving! We're gonna blow this bitch! Right here! Right now!"

They set up a tripod and a drill by the side of the cliff and began to assemble a modular drill bit, adding one spiralled tube after another. The Ajax crew had rehearsed this task in the village but the venue on offer today was totally different. The overwhelming scale of the lake had already humbled them and the spiderlike drills and power cables only seemed to emphasise their insignificance.

Like Greenland in the winter months, the ice lake was locked in a perpetual twilight. When the reconnaissance rocket had fired, they had seen colours but with those same flames gone, the region had returned to a grey monochrome and in a way, David was beginning to feel cheated.

When they had first told him about the ice lake and the concept of fuel synthesis, his soul had been gripped by a sense of excitement – of real anticipation. The Ajax crew were the first men in history to stand in this place and his residual frustration at having fallen was starting to fade. His own breathing continued to echo in his own head, fast and furious. His own heart rate soared in the secular green of his visor.

Why? What did he feel now? Fear? Reverence? There was a cathedral-like grandeur to this place, that much was certain. And yet his feelings fell short of the spiritual. Not quite. Not yet.

He held out one hand and brushed the surface, hoping – like a child – to gain insight through contact. Through the centuries, the winds of Mars had caked the ice lake in a veil of black dust and it fell to the surface like autumn leaves. Then, suddenly, something came back to him. Something about Isaac. In his role as a research chemist, Isaac Newton had often relied on taste to assess his creations. To a modern scientist, it seemed like a crazy habit but it made sense to David now. Though the light remained poor, there were lamps on his helmet and an inch or so below the dust, he could see the ground-glass finish of rock-solid ice. This close, he realised, it wasn't even blue. Then what was it? This thing that no man or beast had ever seen before, waiting through the eons.

Waiting for what? To become rocket fuel?

No, there had to be more to it than that?

Cutting in the power, David watched as his drill made progress. Not all their equipment, he reasoned, was crap. Pushing through to 5 metres, he was able to retrieve a quite professional looking core sample. Seconds later, Kazu arrived with a tube of plastic explosives and nudged it gently into the hole. It was the smallest charge on offer but Kazu had chosen to err on the side of caution.

"That's one hell of an ice cube," said David. "And this is a small bomb."

"We can always come back in. Get over to the buggy. Get warm."

The cold was on its way to their teeth and this one sounded rational. The bomb was detonated remotely with the buggy at 100 metres and the astronauts spotted a tiny flash through the forward observation windows and watched anxiously whilst nothing happened.

Inert for centuries, the mighty ice lake was reluctant to change its ways. A few minutes later, they spotted a crack.

"We can see an obvious fracture line in the surface," called Kazu, aware that their people in Houston would soon be discussing the same thing. "Nothing in the way of gross debris."

And for a few seconds, Commander Kazu leant forward, eclipsing his eyes with the palms of both hands. Maybe it was the perceived absence of an audience. Maybe it was something else about this planet, but this was a common habit in the village too. The man's hair had become wild and matted within his helmet and when his fingers slipped away, his face was blank.

Their explosives had failed. They would rest for a while and then go outside and repeat the operation. Feeling the need to defecate, David stumbled over to the latrine, pulling down the blind, wondering whether to ask for a delay in the next EVA. Throughout their recent struggles, the lip of his convene had been rubbing, severely, on the root of his penis and it was beginning to sting. He asked himself if Kazu was suffering from the same problem and if he wasn't why the hell was he so immune? David looked down. The light was bad but the abrasion seemed petty. He saw a second streak of redness to the right of his scrotum and he guessed – correctly – that it would worse by the morning. He glanced up at his other hand, clasping the base of the blind, lest the hook broke and the thing shot upwards and the world caught sight of him sat on his arse with his fingers round an injured cock. Closing his eyes in the tiny chamber, he escaped into blackness of his own mind and tried to refocus.

At the far side of the blind, Kazu had opened up a channel with the village. Although Hewish couldn't hear the response, it was clear that he was speaking to Rachael Callaghan. David Hewish felt an absurd desire to speak with his own abandoned woman in Washington and threaten to go berserk if she said no. He did not. This was dumb. The bitch had dumped him quite decisively and as he had already stated to his soul, he was grateful to her for that. In any case, he was starting to become distracted by the stench beneath his arse. Reaching for the air con with his right hand, he turned the thing up to maximum.

It was pointless trying to argue. They were going to have to go back out there.

So long to move into the airlock. So long to bound down to the steps of an ancient lake. So long to sneer at the puny efforts of men to refashion the face of another world.

"If that's all we're getting with the bomb, how are we going to get 150 tonnes?" David was stating the obvious and – given the stakes involved – doing little to improve their morale.

"We're going to be frigging shattered!" said Kazu. "Even if – CHRIST! RUN!"

But there was nowhere to run.

CHAPTER TWENTY-FOUR

Disgruntled by the earlier explosion, the ice lake was making a belated attempt to disintegrate. A gigantic sheet of material had sheared away from the main part of the cliff and was making its way to the surface in slow play.

The options available to the Ajax crew included death and running and as they had already discovered, running on Mars has never been an easy affair. Bounding like one of the early lunar explorers provides a better return on investment although on a planet with twice the gravitational pull of the Moon, the results are limited. Nevertheless, the astronauts were bounding now, traversing a good 20 metres before the ice could hit them.

Those villagers that were watching were able to see it all in real time, but Houston would have to wait a lot longer than that. Thirty minutes down the line, mission controllers in Houston would watch, open-mouthed as the pictures from the ice lake exploded on their screens. The central fragment was more than enough to end the entire mission. By sheer luck, it came down to their left, just short of the nuclear-powered buggy, casting off smaller chunks of ice around their feet.

Blacking out as he hit the ground, David Hewish remembered little of what would follow. The agonising slide across the sand, the fantastic challenge of hauling a grown man in a pressure suit to the height of the airlock: all of this would pass him by. Rolling bodily in an oxygen-rich cockpit, he began to whisper names from another world and as he rambled, it fell to Kazu to remove his suit.

"How long was I out?"

"Best part of an hour." Kazu was cross-legged in the opposite corner, his own filthy pressure suit slung out across the driver's seat. It was night time and the cabin lights were dim.

"I don't …" David Hewish made an attempt to sit up.

"They want you to rest," said Kazu. "The flight surgeons back in Houston want you to rest."

"Where's the ice?"

"Everywhere. We should be able to get everything from this one avalanche. That's what I'm calling it, an avalanche." And for a while the two men just lay there, serenaded only by white noise. Eventually Kazu added, "If you'd asked me a few hours ago, I would have said we were all dead men. If you're asking me now, I'd say we'll probably survive."

David's mind was moving on.

"Gotta torch?" he asked. "A mirror?"

The commander held up a small mirror to David's face and David checked each of his own pupils with the torch."

"What does it mean?" asked Kazu.

"It means I got a headache." He took a series of forced breaths. "And a few cracked ribs."

This news was reassuring. Physically, he was in better shape than he might have been but from a personal perspective, David had taken a different kind of hit. Ever since the outbound fire on the Ajax, Kazu had come to owe him a moral debt and deep down, David had felt that he was living in credit. Now they were even. Flat out on the floor of the buggy, he asked himself whether Kazu would see these events in the same way.

He couldn't say.

"Brought me out of Taiwan like this," David confessed. "On one of my own fucking stretchers."

"Didn't that save you?"

David had been wounded in Taiwan only hours before the nuclear explosion. Kazu knew this story too.

"I don't –"

"I was in the air over Taiwan," Kazu continued. "Thought there was still time to save the place." He shook his head, very slowly. "What a waste of time that was."

Hewish broke off for a bout of coughing, hoping to hell it was a one off and when he had finished, Kazu opened up again.

"Smith was on the Serpentine." This might have been a statement or a question. If it was a question then Hewish elected not to answer. "Met Smith in flight school," Kazu continued. "Told me nothing could ever be worse than that ship."

"Taiwan was worse than that ship, sir."

"Taiwan was just a flash. You lived or you died." Kazu clicked his fingers and returned to the present. "When this thing's over, Colonel, and the people in the village are safe, we'll come back to Mars. We'll go driving by the volcanoes. Out on the sand with the good stuff. And then we'll make some big breakthrough of our own. One day soon – one day soon – we'll walk round a corner and you'll spot something green in the sand …"

"Some kinda … extra-terrestrial daffodil!" They cracked up. "*Life on Mars!* They said it couldn't be."

"Then the naval aviator and the flight surgeon get to find it. Where all the Albert Einsteins screwed up … When this thing is over, Colonel. And the villagers are safe."

CHAPTER TWENTY-FIVE

In the States, the avalanche was headline news and the nation at large was suddenly aware of their existence. If the incident had taken the Ajax crew with it then NASA might have omitted to release the footage, but it hadn't and their survival was a triumph. The agency's popularity ratings were going into overdrive and a budget-sensitive management was delighted.

Far away in the Ajax buggy, an injured astronaut received strict instructions to rest for the next 48 hours and it was a telling reflection of the altered relationship between the ground and crew that a pair of mature career officers chose to ignore them.

"Hey!" said Hewish, loud and into the microphone. "This is Mars!"

This was Mars and their buggy was surrounded by a thousand chunks of ice. Soon, the astronauts were back on the sand, trawling for the raw material in person, dreaming of untold glories in another world. Hydraulic diggers shovelled the larger blocks of ice across to the trailers and by the afternoon of their third day in the crater, the Ajax crew were bedding down for an impromptu rest period that would drag on 'til the morning.

Rising with the Sun, Kazu discovered that their only kettle had disembowelled. His colleague had removed the element and placed it in a bucket. Checking out the bucket, Kazu saw a mass of ice surrounded by a muddy fluid. Further to the rear of this machine, the urine was still fizzing. Something special – Kazu reasoned – would soon be ready.

Over by the driver's seat, Kazu went into a rare monologue about the life of a naval aviator. Adjusting his water factory, David Hewish listened.

"Then you call to your wing man," muttered Kazu. "You call to your wing man and you pull. You pull on the frigging joystick and she just flips around." His face lit up and his hands went out between his knees, clasping the joystick that did not exist. "It's a beautiful aircraft. She always responds. Like a woman on heat."

Like a woman on heat.

This was one of those allusions that Hewish could have done without in the closed confines of the pressurised buggy. Turning round from the still, he held out his beaker.

"What is it?"

"Chateau de ice lake," said Hewish.

Hesitant on the floor, Kazu made a show of smelling and sipping the tepid fluid.

"Any particular year?"

"The hydrogen? I'd say around the time of the Big Bang. The oxygen, about four billion years after that."

Kazu's smile was uplifting.

"You know something, Toto?" he said. "With this lot on board, we might even see Kansas again."

CHAPTER TWENTY-SIX

Thirty klicks short of the village, the Ajax crew noticed something new. O'Reilly's people had driven down the road with the snowplough up front, sweeping a broad, boulder-free path to the north and breaking off to plant a fluorescent green flag every 500 metres. The change in road quality was palpable and the buggy picked up speed. Minutes later, they were safe within the footprint of the sail and their whole world was literally brighter.

After more than 20 days of total isolation, the naval officers were pleasantly surprised to be greeted by a small crowd of well-wishers. Eager to emphasise the changed atmosphere, the villagers had draped a variety of NASA and other flags around the airlock. All in all, four astronauts were out and about in pressure suits, ready to greet them.

Egressing in the southern airlock, the Ajax crew were again surprised to receive a helping hand from both Tan and Eliot, lowering themselves here to this technician-level task. The Chinese-American took care to remove the colonel's helmet first. Checking that Kazu was still encased he asked, "You in that thing with him everyday?"

By the morning, Colonel Hewish would not remember his reply.

"He's not an ordinary man."

Kazu was not an ordinary man and if you seek the presence of the exceptional, you have to be prepared to pay the price. Besides, Hewish had spent half of his life in one kind of floating institution or another. Mars wasn't all that different. The naval officers quickly retreated to the luxury of Smith's quarters and blacked out in their cots. Many hours later, they staggered into the dome and asked about breakfast.

Connolly and Erkhart had prepared a slap-up meal and they were served in an atmosphere of exaggerated politeness. Reconstituted eggs and, prophetically, mushrooms, seemed to dominate the menu. Uniquely for this settlement, Charlotte was wearing a skirt. It was nothing particularly flamboyant or inappropriate but it would have been impossible to wear such an item on the outward voyage and it had to have been a conscious choice. Glancing to his right, David saw Marnix by the breakfast bar and failed to recognise him. In another dramatic change of image Marnix had shaved his beard and gained the hairstyle of a test pilot.

"Marnix!" cried David. "You look like one of the Mercury Seven!"

"Like every space cadet should do," joked Kazu, slurping on the dregs of his freeze-dried coffee. "The looks of a rock star and the life of Cain!"

By now, all the players in this tiny world had gathered around the table and David sensed a plot. Seconds later, there was music, *Frank Sinatra music.* The patron saint of the USS Lexington had finally made it to Mars! All at once, a giddy, cheering crowd had hoisted them skyward and was carrying them down the corridor. Chanting lyrics from another age, they made a left at the entrance to the pool and kicked away their shoes. Hewish was itching for a swim but couldn't imagine how they could have made enough water.

They hadn't.

Climbing down into an all but empty pool, they saw the woman, Rachael Callaghan, 7 pounds heavier and substantially more shapely than the day they first met her. Her fascination for the Ajax crew had not gone unnoticed and she was waiting for them eagerly, draped in a white bikini and trademark smile.

And there, just beside them in this huge Kevlar-lined bubble, stood a pair of huge plastic tubs, each of them the size of a terrestrial oil drum.

On the floor and in the thick of it, Kazu and Hewish undressed without prompting. Leaping into the drums, they laughed hysterically as the water spilled over and the applause kicked in. Fred Weissman, who in other circumstances came across as a sad, brooding figure, took the opportunity to tease his superior.

"Nobohito Kazu!" he shouted, "You're reg- you're regressing to a lost childhood!"

And he was. Naked in a tub of cold water, Kazu had all but lost control. A Parkinsonian veil had been lifted and the muscles of facial expression were coming alive. Someone asked about his age and he responded with another man's line.

"Not so young as to love a woman for singing, nor so old as to dote on one for anything."

Visibly embarrassed, Hewish ducked for cover and gulped on the tasteless water. The villagers had been smelting the ice round the back and distilling it shortly afterwards, just as Hewish had done in the buggy. Bobbing up to the water line, Hewish coughed quite violently, and felt a knife-like pain in his ribs. Deep inhalation was still hurting but the villagers were getting wild and he decided not to show it.

Someone started the soundtrack to another Sinatra song and Weissman provided the words, his defining stutter banished by the mood of the day. Then, in an unplanned though widely appreciated move, the gardener had tore off her bikini. At the side of the pool,

David saw reconstituted milk shakes. There was even dancing. More than anything, there was a widespread conviction that within a matter of hours, a man would be able to take a hot shower on Mars and feel no guilt.

CHAPTER TWENTY-SEVEN

Five days elapsed. Discarding their more elaborate plans for the interval, the Ajax crew rested in the sidelines and watched the mortals toil. Soon, the entire American base on Mars was awash with power, water and sunlight. In particular, the pool had emerged as a new and unprecedented luxury. Such a large volume of water would change the thermodynamics of the entire settlement, buffering the micro-climate and ending the violent temperature swings that served to make life on Mars so unpleasant.

Leg ulcers notwithstanding, people took to wearing shorts. In the evenings, some of them even arranged figure of eight races through the corridors with individual fanatics clocking up 10 or 15 kilometres on the trot. The stick-like limbs that had first greeted the Ajax crew were soon to be reborn. Strolling down from the dining room, the colonel noticed the curves in a woman's butt and made no comment.

Meanwhile, Houston had agreed to the release of 10 cubic metres of liquid water for farming and there was planting in the greenhouse. In order to avoid radiation sickness, this task could only be performed at night. Uncomplaining but exhausted, Rachael Callaghan became a regular feature at the breakfast table, her tightly bitten fingernails stained by an alien soil. Rachael's unexpected capacity for hard work was almost shocking and yet it was her energy, combined with the irrigant and increased sunlight that looked set to see the desert bloom. The only concern in David's mind was *expectation.* Diving into clear blue water was one thing. Turning the stuff into rocket fuel was another.

Having alighted around 10 a.m., Colonel David Hewish reviewed his e-mails from the comfort of his cot and discovered that the forbidden zone was refusing to play ball. Research scientists at Marshall had been denied new data for a week and were beginning to describe withdrawal symptoms. Struggling to his feet, David found a pair of shorts and started thinking.

There was no transmission from the lab. Why? Foguet was meant to be dealing with this sort of thing. Maybe Foguet was busy with his maintenance duties.

Finally on his feet, David shaved methodically in front of a full-length mirror. His hair was long, his weight loss ongoing. In contrast, his skin quality was improving. Even the abrasion by his groin had gone. Further along that same thigh, the deeper scars of battle were as firm as ever.

Still thinking about the data streams, he decided to speak with Kazu and experienced the predictable embarrassment of finding the guy in the throws of passion.

"*Shit!*"

Having fostered another billion algae in the small hours, Rachael Callaghan was providing her own kind of early morning morale boost to their commanding officer. Slamming the door behind him, David decided to try a different plan. He would review his base.

Walking past Doctor Erkhart's quarters, he glanced through an open doorway and saw her, prominent beneath the bed sheets. The woman was lying beside another, obviously male figure. Stopping in his tracks, David felt the need to double back and take a second look. Thinking better of it, he walked on by.

So who was bedding Charlotte? This time? It certainly wasn't her bonafide husband, Pablo Foguet, and looked a lot like Marnix Gabanna. On balance, David reasoned, Gabanna was the most likely candidate.

In the States, Marnix Gabanna had been regarded as the nearest thing to a celebrity the agency could still muster and his sprawling career had included several encounters with the gutter press. Come to think of it, it was not inconceivable that Charlotte had actually dumped her own husband with the specific intention of bagging Marnix.

Showing no outward sign of alarm, Hewish soon discovered Fredrick Weissman and Pablo Foguet himself, kneeling over the very innards of the settlement. They were working on the electrical cables. Seeing the new arrival, Weissman became theatrical and raised his hands to the heavens.

"What in G-God's name are we doing here, Colonel?" he demanded. "Back on Earth, I was a professor at UCLA! I had technicians, research students, m-my own department! Now, I'm just the handyman."

David rested one shoulder against the wall.

"And do you see that as a good or a bad thing, Doctor Weissman?"

Frowning and with a similar mindset, Foguet picked up an item from his tool kit and held it up for teaching purposes.

"You see this?" David could. "This is a spanner! 'Two PhDs, Christ knows how many top-level publications and a spanner!"

"And the ice?" asked David. "How about the ice?"

"It's m-melting."

The colonel agreed.

"We've got a reactor on-line."

141

"Yeah, what d'ya think we're doing here?" Foguet, nodded to the wiring. "It's irregular!"

"The reactor?" asked David, with no outward sign of alarm.

"No! Your crazy mirror in space! The damned thing just wanders by every day! Takes an hour or so for Houston to tweak the gyros and get it back on target. D'ya think this place is some sort of theme park? Bullshit! D'you wanna know what this place really is? This is a dormitory for a bunch of post docs who wanted to make it big on Mars. Now, you're trying to turn it into a processing plant for rocket fuel. Well, let me tell you, Colonel, the electrical harness won't take it!"

The colonel's response was immediate.

"The people at the Marshall Spaceflight Centre say that it will."

"Well, I don't see anyone from the Marshall down here!" Foguet chanted. "This isn't the Lexington, Colonel. We don't do things 'cause people tell us to! We think things through and we act on our own initiative!"

"It'll hold!" said David, this time with real conviction. "Just stay with it."

"Your boss man humping the gardener now?"

He was, but David avoided the issue, progressing instead to the forbidden zone where he was greeted by the sound of *Rhapsody in Blue*. You didn't get this kind of thing anywhere else in the village and this passion for the classical could be mistaken for posturing.

The lab itself was reassuringly chaotic. The sleek lines and sterile, white environment of science fiction couldn't be further from this reality. Central to the whole affair was the mass spectrometer. Tan and Eliot were using this machine to determine the make-up of the rock samples they had gathered around the planet. It was one of the heaviest instruments ever to be flown to Mars but its arrival in the settlement had been seen as a sound investment by the powers that be. Data could be beamed back to Marshall for pennies, shipping the actual rocks would have cost billions.

Having checked out the scenery, David switched his attention to the two men here. Between them, Daniel Tan and Tom Eliot were 39 years senior to the rest of the crew and physical agility wasn't their forte. On Earth, they had both abandoned grown-up children. Earlier on in their careers, they had excelled in their own fields and gone on to fall foul of university politics. Flawed, but fantastically brave, they had all but starved to death with the best of them and had yet to regain their full health.

At 56, the Chinese-American, Daniel Tan, was the most senior citizen on Mars. Tan had a fetish for steel-rimmed spectacles, which he claimed to need for close-up work. Upon occasion, he had even been seen in this subterranean complex wearing the mirrored lenses of a naval aviator and it was harder to understand how these could be needed for anything.

His partner in crime was Tom Eliot. Doctor Eliot had gone prematurely bald as a freshman although the timely arrival of effective medication had returned a healthy head of hair and a slight refusal to have it cut. His choice of identikit steel-rimmed spectacles was genuinely annoying. With Eliot's head still engrossed in the eye-pieces of his binocular microscope, Daniel Tan looked up from his work and pretended to have only just realised that they had a guest.

"Spent three years prepping for this thing!" moaned Tan, pointing to the junk around his feet. "Now you've got us fixing the air conditioning!"

And a few weeks ago, thought David, *you were dying.*

"Well," he asked, trying to be helpful, "who should be doing the air conditioning?"

"Bose," said Eliot, without looking up.

David grimaced. He'd spent most of the outbound flight trying to memorise this kind of thing and the first time he needed it, his brain had failed him.

Predictably antagonised, Tan laid into his visitor.

"We've already tried starving."

"Yeah, well, breathing's a lot faster than that."

"And less hassle," mumbled Eliot, his eyes still out of reach.

"How about thirst, Colonel Hewish?" asked Tan. "How did you get on with the heat and the thirst?"

This time, David took several seconds to reply.

"What about the core sample from the ice lake? Have we looked at the core sample?"

"Yes!" said Eliot. "*We* have."

"It's water ice," Tan revealed. "'Less than 5% sand."

His patience depleted, Hewish clicked off the music and raised his voice.

"Look – Doctor Tan. *This* is a big deal. You may make out like it isn't, but in point of fact and as you are entirely aware, this is a *big deal*. Bigger than any of the research papers you've cobbled together in this unit. We're talking about the production of rocket fuel from an indigenous mineral ore on Mars."

"That would be ice?"

"Yes! The ice! It's the biggest thing since Sputnik and I expect you to play your part!" David pointed one finger and made the mistake of digressing. "And I expect you to get that mass spectrometer back on-line too. *Marshall,* expects you to get that mass spectrometer back on-line!"

Without knowing it, David had just walked into a minefield. In an effort to pull him free, Tom Eliot offered this, surprise, change of tack.

"So Colonel, which ship did you serve on? Prior to the Ajax?"

"In the navy? The Lexington."

Right on cue, Eliot broke into a smile.

"My kid is on the Lexington!" he cried. "Josh, Josh Eliot. Did you know that?" His shoulders sagging in despair, the colonel said something about the size of a typical aircraft carrier. "Well, Josh is in propulsion. You see, Josh did a lot of cryogenics in his PhD and the engine on the Lexington uses a super-conducting coil." Possessed by a vision of his first and only son, the man with the beard was more than loquacious. "You know, when Josh went down to the recruitment office, I told him he was nuts, but he went anyway! And them navy guys, them navy guys paid for the whole lot. An entire PhD and not a single dime from his dad! Can you imagine that?"

Having never forked out a penny for his own education, David could imagine that. At this point in time, however, he had other concerns. He had come here to inspect the all-new ice-processing factory and he asked them to show him round. Forgetting their earlier friction, Doctor Tan complied.

The only man actually working in the factory was Marnix Gabanna. Fresh ice was being shovelled into the tub whilst the previous batch melted. In the tub itself, David saw a dense slurry. The 5% sand content was building up. On the far side, he saw liquid water, over-spilling and decanting down towards the still. He checked out the man with the shovel. He didn't seem particularly breathless. If Marnix was the man in Charlotte's room, then he had, presumably, sprinted down the corridor in the last few minutes.

Another lump of ice crashed beside their feet and Tan winced as the spray hit his face.

"Hey, Marnix! Pack it in, will you." Marnix grinned very slightly and slung a little more. "Hey, Marnix! Are you listening to me?"

"Sometimes, you know. If I want to."

The scientist took a step back. For the first time, it occurred to David that Daniel was limping very slightly on his right leg.

"Most of the ice is outside," Daniel Tan continued. "At the far side of the cargo canister. They open the outer door on the canister and push some of it through with the bulldozer. Takes five minutes. Then we seal it in, open the inner hatch and use it like an airlock. Then you've gotta get it over here using men with shovels. That takes hours. There are no power tools inside the building. That's the big bottleneck in this whole goddamned plan. That's what this guy here is doing."

"It's a good set-up, Doctor Tan. You've caught on fast."

"'Didn't catch on to anything! I already knew. I read it all back on Earth. Why do you think they put the water reservoir in the blueprints?"

"You mean the pool?"

"Yes, the pool. Trouble is, this thing wasn't supposed to happen with ten men. The thing with the ice lake was meant to come in another four or five years, with like 50 men in the village, specialist equipment and a dozen or so people just here to make fuel. You're gonna struggle to –"

"And now that we have struggled," David Hewish interrupted, "how's the ice?"

Tan slipped off his spectacles and moved to polish one lens. Was this another trademark quirk, or a conscious break from eye contact?

"The ice is good. The ice comes in at -10°," he explained, studious and with no intention of picking up a shovel. "Incidentally, that's all thanks to the sail. 'Would have been -30 if it wasn't for that sail."

"Yeah," said David, moving to help Marnix. "Well it was a lot colder where we found it, Doctor Tan!"

Unnoticed by either man on the ice, Tan did something rather strange. He stood, amazed. "Are you going to move that stuff yourself?" he asked. David was. Clods of ice were already flying through the air. Tan moved to leave and as he did so, David shouted one last thing. "Daniel! Your data's late. Why?" The scientist failed to react. "It's not just the mass spectrometer. It's *everything!*"

That was enough for today and David began his hard labour, bathing in his own sweat. Within a few hours, he recognised the madness of exercise on Mars. Why the hell had he ever wasted time jogging when he could just as easily have shovelled rocket fuel? Then, with the latest batch of ice virtually clear, he broke off to rest.

"It's got to be good for you," laughed Marnix. "If it hurts this much, it's gotta be good for you." And this *was* good for him – even Tan could have seen that, had he bothered to stay. Marnix's body had come alive and the muscles across his shoulder and chest were taut for the first time in months.

Marnix was an oddball on Mars, and not just because of his willingness to deal with the physical. In this tightly sealed world, the competition between egos was undisguised and Marnix was one of the few people who made no effort to compete. That wasn't to say he wasn't visible. An older man like Tan might well have asked for attention at the breakfast table but it was Marnix who received it. The sheer speed with which his body had recovered from starvation was remarkable. His only competitor – Kazu – had actually arrived with over-worked deltoids but he lacked the natural athleticism of a man like Marnix. Women responded to him without inhibition and walked through the corridors of Mars, a richly plumed bird amongst hens.

Nodding in the direction of the lab, Marnix lapsed into his other sideline – humour. "Those guys are gonna be famous some day," he said. "But they're not gonna die of hard work!"

"No. No, Marnix, they're not."

"But Tan has a brilliant mind. For an idiot. I mean – as idiots go – he's pretty good with it." Their laughter was relaxed and really in synch. Then, after a few seconds, Marnix continued, perhaps a little more soberly than before. "I don't know whether you ever sat around wishing you might have a brilliant mind. But if you spend time with a man like Tan, there'll come a time when you realise you're not there yet. Then there's a day after that when you realise you never will be. And it'll hurt you. It always does."

A week or so later, David would ask himself why he asked his next question. "Have you nailed Connolly?"

"You know, before your boss man turned up? When Smith was still around and we weren't all shitting ourselves about dying every day, Mars was a different planet. It was like San-Fran-fucking-cis-co down here! Connolly, you know, she's out here again," he gestured with his hands to describe the rebirth of her breasts, "but it's not the same. Not like before. You know, like before, that woman had curves. She was an above-average height blonde ... And I've always had this thing about well-connected above-average-height blondes. I've had therapy for it but it doesn't seem to do any good. And you know, I said to myself, why not?" Marnix had the ability to make out like he wasn't looking for a response when he was. "But you know ... you know, Colonel, I'd rather be here than anywhere else. In spite of everything!

In spite of all the fuel that leaked out of the Von Braun. In spite of nearly starving to death." Something about David's face must have said *why?* "Time goes by, Colonel," Marnix replied. "We live and we die."

Time goes by. Walking away from the ice, the astronauts rested with their backs to the wall and wasted more time. Marnix had brought his own glucose water and they swigged on the bottle in turn. David would have used more powder and less water but said nothing. Instead, he became a student of Gabanna who spoke at length of his distaste for the world he had left behind, of his quest for adventure and his pain and frustration at the delays to their mission thus far. And then he said something else that might have been an attempt at manipulation but which managed to strike a reasonable chord anyway. "You take one hit in this life and it scares you," he admitted. "You take another and it scares you less. And then one day, you wake up in the morning and there's nothing left they can do to you that will make you bleed again."

This was enough. Enough to make David believe that he understood this man better than he understood doctors Tan and Eliot, Weissman or Foguet.

Then rather tellingly, other people started arriving in the ice room. The village was a busy place. Most of them were working in isolation and over a protracted period of time, isolation can become a burden. The ice room didn't strike David as the most dazzling place to hang out in. If there was a beacon of light here then it was human.

Kazu made a comment about all the good work they'd done and others did the same. Rachael Callaghan paused, bleary-eyed beside him, glancing from ice to Kazu and then back to the ever-youthful figure of Marnix. Sarah was suddenly fresh-faced too and neither of them were here to check out their future fuel supply.

Over by the entrance to the corridor, Pablo Foguet maintained a difficult stoop. All but invisible to his colleagues, Foguet was present and smiling but his smile – it seemed to David – was largely forced.

Leaning against the Kevlar, Sarah's looked to the future.

"When I get back – and you know, after watching you guys like that, I feel like I really am gonna get back – then I'm gonna go for Berkeley!"

"Berkeley!" gasped Marnix, almost laughing. "You have got to be kidding me! Berkeley's like the number one school, gal! Every doctorate and his dog will be making moves on Berkeley!"

Pausing by the exit, Kazu threw in an unwelcome remark about the state of their resumes. Perhaps because of his own career ambitions, Kazu had seen the flaw in her game plan very quickly. These days, he reminded them, thousands of people had been into space, even if it was usually only low-Earth Orbit. What's more, a couple of years on Mars had actually detached them completely from academic circles. Their chances of getting noticed by a top-flight university were a lot less than they wanted to believe. Seconds later, Kazu walked away.

CHAPTER TWENTY-EIGHT

Another day was dawning and David awoke in his cot. In the near distance, he could hear sobbing. Early-morning sobbing was almost as common as the sunrise in this place and had yet to be discussed in public. This latest voice was both androgynous and indistinct and David was grateful to have heard it when he was this lucid and this certain that it wasn't his own.

The sobbing stopped and the Sun rose higher. A brilliant white light was soon streaming through the UV filters in his ceiling and he sensed the need for action. Requesting his in box, he had a quick browse through his e-mails and then quickly closed them in a state of shock.

Action was coming his way. NASA had sent them a gift. An unmanned re-supply vessel was due to touch down in a mere 36 hours. This was the first time the agency had made any kind of reference to this event and he found this kind of caution alarming. Barefoot in his usual shorts, David rolled out of his cot and on to the office.

"What do you think?"

Kazu frowned and David Hewish checked his line of sight. The surveillance cameras in the office were all occluded. Kazu's junior had noticed this before. Previously, he had interpreted it as a barrier against sexual voyeurism. Now he wasn't so sure.

"Why have they only just sprung this one on us? The damned thing must've been out there for months!"

Squatting beside a wooden desk, Hewish racked his brain for an answer.

"Maybe they didn't believe in the machine," he said. "Like, the last two missed the planet. Some kinda quality control issue on the production side. Then they got worried it might be in the whole batch."

A pensive commanding officer nodded and read from his wall. "She'll hit the sand in 36 hours. Wait 'til the morning and then get out there in the village buggy, you should be able to bring her in."

Not so long ago, the colonel would have taken this as an order but Mars had changed them and he pushed for what he wanted.

"I'm more familiar with our own machine."

"They're concerned about the mileage."

In this context, *they* – presumably – meant Marshall.

"What difference is that going to make?" asked David Hewish, "if this thing comes down at 20 klicks and they call it a bad shot. We already got 20000 klicks on the Ajax buggy. First priority has got to be retrieval. What's on your –"

"The axle," said Kazu, with no apparent anxiety in his voice. Seconds later, he invited Hewish to choose his own crew and vehicle. It wasn't a difficult decision. Weissman was sick, Tan and Eliot were on the threshold of an advance that would re-define their epoch and in the scheme of things, Marnix Gabanna was the only serious candidate. The colonel found him collecting mushrooms from a cupboard by the dome.

This was dull, repetitive work and it wasn't easy to get anybody else to do it.

"I mean, I don't see Kelly going flat out like I am!" Marnix complained to David, filling his basket and stashing the tray to one side.

There were 200 such trays in the village, most of them tucked away in dark corners. Rachael had filled them with something unpleasant and seeded them in person. Since fungi don't care about photosynthesis, they'll never be troubled by the dark and mushrooms have been part of the staple diet on long duration missions for years.

"And when I finish this shit," said Marnix, "I gotta hose down the washbasins. I mean, the astronaut office's gotta have noticed that, haven't they? Where the hell is Daniel when I'm doing all this?"

"You're a brave man, Marnix. No normal guy would have come out here."

"Yeah, we were all brave once. But then we screwed up. Afterwards. After Smith ..." Suddenly, he changed the subject again. "They should have let you through the airlock."

"How come no one knew Smith was gone?" asked David, staying with Smith. "He can't have been crossed off the duty roster."

"We didn't have any roster. Besides, back then, even the big boys were going outside. What you've got to understand is that *this* ain't normal. I mean a guy like Weissman, a guy like Weissman had to be brainwashed to stay indoors and shit himself. It took frigging months to break him down! But look, I mean, if they were to ask you – if they asked you – I'd have your backing, wouldn't I? You'd say I was a good man?" David would but Marnix felt the need to gabble. "Like, when the hell do you ever see Tom and Daniel collecting the mushrooms?

"I mean, supposing Berkeley came up. If Berkeley came up and it was an engineering post, tenured and everything, and they wanted someone with an aerospace background, then I'd definitely go for Berkeley. Even though I know I haven't been productive enough out here, paperwise. I mean, as if risking my neck out here isn't enough already?"

"It is enough, Marnix. It is enough. You're a good man. Some day soon they'll come and ask me if you were a good man and when they do, I'll say that you were."

The boy from Montreal with the movie-star looks beamed through the half-light.

"You know, I think that will go a long way. Your word, I mean. Everyone knows that. Everyone says you're doing a good job here. And I'll be with you in the morning, in that buggy. And NASA will know about it. We'll be the ones who find that frigging supply ship and bring it in! Just the two of us? Right!"

David pushed him away and promised him what little he had to offer: a short break on the sands and a kind word in another world. The tedium of this place had been killing him for weeks now and the arrival of the supply ship should have been a cause for celebration. Somehow, celebration wasn't on the cards.

With Marnix gone, David rested alone beneath the dome, a transient surge of adrenaline hot in his veins. Anxiety and near total physical inactivity didn't go well together. He remembered the sentinel e-mail on the supply ship. In its desperate struggle to survive, America had evolved into a less than candid nation. Even so, this level of secrecy was shocking. He remembered the colour and the style of the text and wished he'd never read it. The supply ship was an unexpected distraction and neither he nor Kazu knew how to react.

The skylights darkened and the temperature fell. Over by the sapling, the Rockies remained vivid, the sunlight on those same projected mountains synchronised with the day-night cycle of the base. A nice touch, David accepted, and one of the few attempts to make life here bearable that ever seemed to work. Appearing on his left, Callaghan closed the door to the office and shuffled towards her greenhouse. He wondered if she had overheard his exchange with Marnix. The nights on Mars were getting predictable. Soon, he knew, the droids would become conscious and whiz through the blackness.

An hour or so later, David was awoken in his cot by the sound of a woman in his room. He looked up, hitting himself for reacting so sharply, because it could have been Callaghan and he devoted a lot of time and energy not telling her or anybody else how much he would have liked to lay her. The woman stepped forward. It was Sarah Connolly.

David ran the tip of his tongue along the inner aspect of his incisors. He was cold, concerned that she might see him with the tremor he was usually able to contain.

"Sometimes, Colonel," she whispered, "you gotta hurt people." The woman unbuttoned her blouse.

Cotton is a heavy material and most of the cotton on Mars had been run through the laundry machine a hundred times. Sarah's blouse was stained and tatty and he seemed to be able to see it in the dark. "Marnix wants too much," she went on. "He knows he's not Einstein but he doesn't want to be forgotten either." And she moved in on him slowly watching as he failed to fight her off and sinking down onto his torso to kiss him at length.

Doctor Connolly had been married twice and the act of the mechanical act of seduction was one of her core skills. Up close with the lights toned down she made him think of a much younger woman. *Of Christine.* Of a thoroughbred on the back of a fabled cigarette card that a man could lust over in a quiet moment. He recalled his last night in Washington, trying to decide how much time he had left before the Chinese would reunite him with his dead parents, hoping for something good from a woman he believed in.

She took him once, then again and through the course of a second or third bout of sex, Sarah began to slow down. Their breathing – initially frantic – was losing its pace. In the end, as Sarah sank to the edge of sleep, they heard something else. Sobbing. Strange and distant. Hard to pin down.

It's not you and it's not Sarah.

The woman was heavy on his chest but she was worth it. A stronger, more serious person than she needed to be, Sarah couldn't do frivolous. She couldn't not care what happened beyond the confines of this room and he sensed that there would be more to follow.

"Did you hear that?" he asked. It was the sobbing. Mars was a world where many people cried in the night but this was the first time he had mentioned it to one of them.

"You nut!" was the only resonance he could get from her and it was only in the morning, over breakfast, amidst the mundane and the virtual, that she asked another question.

"I'd really like to come out in the buggy with you. You know, when the supply ship comes in. That's if it's all right?"

Marnix was going to be pissed.

He might have lingered on this one for longer but within seconds he was receiving a new call from the forbidden zone.

The mass spectrometer was down and they were telling him about it. This was a familiar story with an unfamiliar tone. The device had no role in the process of life support and David had been plagued by concerns about its status for weeks.

"It's the accentuator," said Tan, with rare politeness. "It's failed three times now. We figure it's some sort of reactionary power surge rather than an individual component defect. Can't be three shit accentuators."

"Can't you get on with something else? Like some of the things Doctor Gabanna keeps doing in your place?" The colonel was on the point of disappearing when something about Tan's posture held him back.

"And when we've finished that?" asked Tan. "When we've done something else, will the accentuator start working again?"

"I don't know, Daniel! I don't even know what it does!"

Sensing a chink in his armour, Tan flipped over to attack.

"This is how quick you get to be human? One shot of the kryptonite and you're a mortal again?"

David waited several seconds before replying.

"Don't you have spares? Something we could cannibalise to keep the thing going?"

Tan stepped to one side, as if he couldn't decide where to run. His right leg was a little slow and once again, David failed to ask why.

"We already have," said Tan.

David's brain was beginning to tick.

"Where d'ya go?"

"The electrolysers."

"How many times?"

"Twice."

David left without comment, taking care to avoid the desperate sprint that his mission demanded, closing in initially on the ice room and beyond that, their improvised workshop for rocket fuel.

"Shit!"

Having not come here for a while, he was kicking himself for his neglect, for letting a woman and dumb games steal his attention. He looked up. The surveillance cameras were all disabled. Digital monitoring had been introduced to stop this kind of thing happening and now that it had been taken away, NASA had been blind to this latest folly. Maybe it was the kryptonite or maybe it was just his current mental state but by the time he heard Tan again, the guy was right behind him.

"What the hell do you think this is, Daniel? A picnic?"

Between the lab and the ice room, Tan had changed his glasses. He had donned the mirrored lenses of an aviator and David's blood was starting to boil.

"There are 11 lives at stake on this planet! Not to mention the near-term future of the entire American space program!" Tan's choice of facial expression was ill-judged. "You think this is some sort of game? Some sort of story? How the hell does killing us all fit into your game plan?"

"My dear Colonel," said the scientist, "how much longer will it take you to realise that on this planet, reality doesn't have to have a coherent narrative structure."

David was six months free of normal gravity and his upper body strength was on the wane. That been said, Daniel Tan was hardly short on momentum as he hit the ground. Shaking his right hand for the sake of his knuckles, David was suddenly returned to the days of his less than liberal naval boarding school.

There had been a place round the back, about a hundred yards into the woods and some nutty little bunch of cadets would often gather there. The doors were fragile but you could lock them with a sliding rod and those that wanted it, bare-knuckle boxing had been seen as an integral part of the curriculum. But that was then, when a hint of isolation and the right crowd could persuade a cadet to break whatever rules he had ever been subject to. This was now and the chief scientist on Mars was still on the floor.

"Hope they saw that!" said Tan, rolling around for a bit. "Hope your nannies in Houston got a load of that! I'll be playing shit like that at your inquiry when we get home!"

"*My* inquiry?" This was a pertinent question and it took all of David's anger to miss the response on Daniel's face. "They're down!" he shouted, pointing to the overhead cameras. "How else could they have missed this?"

The panels on the first two electrolysers were wide open. The accentuators were gone. In pursuit of his own research goals, Doctor Tan had disabled machinery that was crucial to their collective survival.

"Did you take them yourself?"

Tan shook his head.

"I sent one of the kids."

"Which kid?"

"So you can hammer them too?"

"How did they blow?"

"We don't know," said Tan, who had yet to get up. "Power surges. Accentuators on the electrolysers are the same size as the mass spec. It works for, like, a day then it fails again. So we gave it another shot."

Daniel Tan took a boot in his stomach, the rush of adolescence still thick in David's blood.

"Take one more and I'll kill you."

The colonel's name had been known to the villagers long before he got here. Daniel Tan took this very seriously indeed.

"We can fix it," he gasped, on side in a hurry. "We can fix them both. Just as soon as I've got the spectrometer back on-line, I'll –"

Rising to his knees, Tan took another blow, his mirrored spectacles skidding out across the floor.

"No, Doctor Tan!" shouted Hewish. "Much sooner than that!"

By this stage, people could hear them. Word had already gotten round about his antics with Connolly and it was hard to imagine that the bruising on Tan's face would be ignored. The villagers were an unpredictable, disparate crowd and Hewish was starting to see how Smith could have lost them. Minutes later, he managed to locate Foguet and dragged him back to the ice.

Once in position, the Spaniard was quick to see the problem.

"Are you an expert in this system?"

David Hewish was not an expert on this system although he had studied it for the best part of 30 minutes on his outbound journey. Sitting by the unit, he unhooked the remaining panels. The electrolysers were about the size of a household refrigerator and in many ways, he realised, less complex.

"What about the other units?"

"They're OK," said Foguet, trying to bring calm to the situation. "We just have to run them for longer. They'll be plenty. They'll be enough to produce our fuel, I mean."

"No," said David, his eyelids closing slowly. "It has to be a bolus."

The smile on Foguet's face was about to crack. Hydrogen is a difficult molecule to contain. Hyper volatile in its liquid form, the gas can seep through the tiniest cracks in a box. In short, each litre of hydrogen they produced would have to be used quickly before the previous litre had the chance to boil off.

David went through the device methodically, impressing the engineer more than he knew.

Even as he did so, Pablo Foguet's mind was moving on. "Are you gonna call this in?" he demanded. "To Houston, I mean? You see, this is why it's such a good thing we got a grip on those cameras. It means we get to talk these problems through before we pass them on. If you feed this back, if you feed this back to Houston, it'll be the end for those two guys. You realise that?"

David stayed on message.

"If they took this to fix the mass spec," he said, "then we can cannibalise something else to fix the electrolysers. What else do we have in this base? In this base or the cold supply ship? There's hardware in all of those places."

"Do you expect me to know that? Off the top of my head?"

"No, Pablo, I expect NASA to know when I call this shit in and screw those bastards over forever! What about the outriders? The European base? We could drive out to the European base and haul something in."

But Foguet was sceptical. The accentuators were exotic components and would not be easy to replace. Alone in Bose's quarters, David sought comfort from a beaker of distilled water. The ice lake, that had once tried to kill him, was helping keep him sane and the irony was clear to see. Dropping his beaker, he tried to think.

If two electrolysers remained off-line, what would that do to their chances of flying home?

The estimate from his own software was for one definite straggler, one possible. Strangling Daniel Tan would seem like a reasonable way to contain this figure.

With the lights out and his heart rate slowing, Hewish struggled to comprehend the mindset of a man like Foguet. A man who had actually attempted to defend his colleague, even though he knew that same colleague was close to killing all of them.

And although Hewish was doing his best to deny it, Chabod's long walk to the helipads in Texas was still hanging over him. Like Marlon Brando to Christopher Reeves, Chabod's voice was able to transcend time and planets without distortion. The option of following Chabod had been there from the outset and yet Hewish had chosen not to take it. Second from the top in terms of nightmare material was the lingering image of Bose, pulse free on his shitty mattress, a single plastic feeding tube hanging down from his nose. Whatever else he was prepared to do, David had no intention of meeting that man again. If the electrolysers couldn't be fixed, who else was going to die for it?

Then, just as his mind was about to go nuclear, there was a fantastic commotion by his door. There was only one room in the village that could be locked and this wasn't it. He felt an impulse to block the thing in person. He was too late. Exploding into the room, Daniel Tan began a cringe worthy spiel about life, his allegiance to science and the necessity of self-sacrifice.

"I've had my time," he wined. "I've had my time! Working in this unit has been the greatest achievement of my life, the one defining moment that all men dream of and few receive."

"Christ, Daniel!" David's head was throbbing. "I'm trying to sleep! Get outta here will you!"

But Tan had found a seat and sunk into it.

"I know I'm down there!" he reflected. "I know I'm holed up in that place all the time. But it's better down there. It's better for me there. Do you want me to hang around up here with all these kids around the place? Watching that smug bastard grope the gardener?"

The colonel gaped in the half-light. This reference to Rachael Callaghan was unexpected. Seconds later, his problems were compounded when Tom Eliot tumbled through the same door and threw yet another choked-up speech about the sharing of death. Holed up in the forbidden zone together, him and Daniel would slide pebbles into the mass spectrometer 'til the oxygen ran out.

Given the resilience of the life support system, it seemed more likely to David that they would starve but by this stage, all he could think of was the contact details for his psychology professor in Harvard and the correctional e-mail that poor bastard was about to receive. *Mars*, he would write in italics, *is anything but a personality-free zone!*

"Guys! Guys, get outta here!"

They got out. The door closed very loudly and David cursed his inability to lock it. He checked his wall monitors. The nutters were receding. After a slow return to the sac he struggled to lose consciousness.

He couldn't. He had to find a way out of this mess.

Grabbing a book from his bedside, he mumbled to the overhead lights and spent a few seconds with the lithograph. *Wuthering Heights* by Emily Bronte. Some poor schmuck in a previous century had nearly killed himself carving that thing. Now, David was going to wipe it out with the touch of one hand. Mars wouldn't even let him break off for a bit of quality fiction and he hated her for it. Calling up a technical manual with a desperate hiss, he watched, exhausted, as the very texture of the paper seemed to change as Emily was fading out and an idiot's guide to machine maintenance was coming to life.

His eyelids seemed to flicker and a few seconds later, he awoke with the Sun.

Shortly after breakfast, David found Marnix in the southern airlock, prepping a couple of pressure suits, ready for his big day on the sand. His heart was set on a clear-cut entry in the log and on this occasion it was going to be broken. David Hewish told him that there had been a change of plan and that it was Connolly who would follow him onto the sands. Marnix was pissed but the colonel's double flair for thuggery and sexual conquest had given him a new authority and the engineer backed down without a fight.

Ten klicks out from the village, David brought the buggy to a halt and waited for Sarah Connolly to give him an update.

"It's going into blackout."

The cargo ship had entered the Martian atmosphere. If it made it through re-entry then it shouldn't be too hard to find. Anything on Mars that could move had been built with its own radio beacon. Even if their new arrival landed outside visual range, they ought to be able to home in on the beacon.

The woman pointed to the sky.

"Do you think there'll be anything here for the big boys?" He asked her what she meant. "Tan and Eliot," she replied. "You see, Colonel, Tan and Eliot have been running this show since the day they hit the planet. Smith *thought* he was running the show but Smith was – well – you know, that kinda guy."

"And in reality?"

"You've gotta gain insight into the social fabric of this settlement. What are you? Like a doctor? And Kazu can fly a plane? The strings are all cut, Colonel. A pair of hotshots like Tan and Eliot were never gonna be content on your average campus. No more funding crises for them, no more grovelling in the chancellor's office. Out here, they're *free*." Connolly chuckled to herself. "Free to fight a war with Bose."

"Did you not get on with Bose?"

"Tan and Bose? You have got to be kidding me! Beijing wants the Horn of Africa and the Indians want to keep it."

"But Bose was born in Kentucky."

"And his folks were all outta Mumbai!" She shook her head, amused as always by his disconnection. "They had riots in San Diego last year. Did you not –"

"Down side?" David had stopped smiling. "Down side of being on Mars, I mean."

"They're stuck in a box on the edge of eternity. But that doesn't matter. You see, a scientist's ego – I'm sorry that's his reputation – is based on his output of published research. Out here, Tan and Eliot can write their own papers and post them to Marshall with a big *screw you* sign on the side. 'Cept Marshall don't want papers. They want raw data so their own people can write it up."

Over in the driver's seat, David stated the obvious: "Their instrumentation keeps going off-line."

"And their data stays on file. The shit stuff goes back the same day. The hot stuff gets put on hold 'til they can get it written up in the zone. Tan's pretty good friends with Foguet ya know." David cringed internally. Now he came to think about it, Pablo Foguet did spend a lot of time hanging out in the forbidden zone. Why the hell hadn't he seen this earlier? "Foguet filters the down-link, then Tan puts his name on a few of the papers. Some day soon, they all get to be famous."

"There'll be a price to pay for that when we get home."

"That's *if* we get home, Colonel. And let's face it, that's a big *if*. Besides, what are they gonna do to a pair of freaks like Tan and Eliot? Dock their pensions? Those guys are more bothered about their legacy than their lives. And believe me," she added, "Tan wasn't pissed about Bose."

Connolly's reversion to a platonic colleague wasn't surprising him though he did feel an awkward wave of sympathy for Marnix. This woman's demands were limited yet she knew how to get them. Looking through the forward observation windows, David caught site of the chutes.

Final impact was cushioned by airbags and they watched her bounce in the sand for a full minute. The dust settled and the supply ship came to rest some 12 kilometres short of the settlement. Not bad, David reasoned, for a 500 million-kilometre journey.

An hour or so later, the two astronauts were out on the surface, examining the craft in person. Having been initially surprised by its arrival, David was soon to be disappointed by its scale. Was this bucket of bolts really the best they could get here? And if it was, then why had they even tried? What if the Ajax had come down hard? None of the base-line crew would have been alive to retrieve this, their first successful re-supply mission in over a year.

Cranking the thing open in silence, he reflected on Connolly's take on his own role in this saga. For Sarah Connolly, he had been a means to an end. And for the village at large, he was a bell boy, an admin clerk, the Oscar nominee for best supporting actor with a respectful nod to the male romantic lead. David had been able to retrieve a core sample that no one else had retrieved. But there was nothing in his achievements as a medic nor even in that risible PhD thesis he'd been able to bang out in the constitution that would ever make Tan and Eliot blink.

He soldiered on. Eight hours later, the last of their new goodies were safe in a pressurised cargo canister. Powdered milk, freeze-dried beans. It was all much of a muchness. Then, just as he was starting to think of the sac, he saw something else.

"Pablo!" he hollered, "Pablo get down here!"

The village was about to be blessed by its second miracle. A supply ship that had been loaded more than seven months ago had arrived on Mars with the very spares that they needed the day after they recognised the urgency of that need. David was holding an accentuator.

CHAPTER TWENTY-NINE

With hindsight, there was a secular logic to it. Beside their haulage vehicles, the electrolysers were the most vital pieces of equipment on the planet and mission planners back in Marshall had thrown in enough spares to knock together two.

In the morning, there was no shortage of smiles around the breakfast table and as an additional bonus, some of them were about to become famous.

"Retrieving their new supplies from the Martian desert, Dr Sarah Connolly secures them for the benefit of ..."

The television networks had caught on to their achievement. What's more, the heroine of this particular story was actually pointing to her own TV image over coffee. Seconds later, the pictures faded and Charlotte said something reconciliatory about David's absence from the piece. Evading eye contact, David asked Pablo Foguet for some help in the ice room. Foguet nodded and offered no resistance whilst the pair of them fixed up the electrolysers. Later that day, David broke the news of their malfunction to Kazu with the corollary that the crisis was over before it had actually begun. Aware of how close they had come to disaster, Kazu shrugged calmly, saying, "I already saw his black eye."

This was an endorsement. David skipped down to the ice room, grabbed a shovel and listened half-heartedly whilst Marnix exposed him in the kind of casual vulgarity that could make a man feel 20 years younger.

"You should have told me it was Connolly," Marnix gabbled. "If I'd known you were nailing Connolly, I wouldn't have, you know, I wouldn't have been so pissed. 'Bout her taking my seat. In fact I'd probably have gotten a band."

Connolly had paid for her privilege with a currency that Marnix could understand. This was his way of showing empathy.

"Marnix," said David. "Is there anything that goes on in this base you don't know about?" Marnix dropped his shovel and answered to the effect that no, there wasn't. "Did you know about the accentuators?" He'd heard about the failures but just assumed that Foguet would figure out a way to fix them. This kind of shit was happening all the time in the village, he countered. The fact that Tan's ego had nearly killed the lot of them was barely worth a mention in the log and if had been Marnix's job to write the log, he would have just written *typical day*. Losing interest in the matter altogether, Marnix returned to that topic that was most dear to him – ass.

"She wanted the seat," he said, as if David didn't know this. "That's why she gave it to you. She wanted that seat and she got it. Big deal! In the scheme of things, what's one more EVA in your log book? Even if she does get to see herself on TV."

David wasn't hurt to hear it in these terms, but he wasn't particularly heartened either.

"That's what I like about you, Marnix," he concluded. "You've only got one area of specialist interest."

Marnix Gabanna was all smiles.

"There had to be one!" he grinned. "One guy whose only real focus was on tits and ass!"

Which wasn't entirely true. Quite apart from his passing enthusiasm for Berkeley, Gabanna had already

169

liaised with his agent back on Earth and was on stand-by to front some new kind of sales campaign just as soon as he got home. Even on Mars, his name had been submitted alongside S Connolly and C Erkhart on an original seismology paper although he had yet to collaborate with the older men.

David knew all this shit but he didn't care. He sank down on the Kevlar, his smile frozen on an open mouth. If Gabanna was responsible for a breakdown in team morale, then he was loath to blame him for it. Connolly and Erkhart had gone down on this guy of their own free will and if there was blame to be apportioned on Mars, then as far as David was concerned, it could be done on Earth.

CHAPTER THIRTY

David's remit for the settlement spilled over into the field of nutrition. Though he had avoided detailed discussion of this matter, he had a reasonably clear idea of how long they could hold out in the base. If he classified the contents of the recent supply ship as emergency rations, he would be able to keep them all breathing for an additional four months on normal intake and up to ten with protracted weight loss. Long enough for the political situation on Earth to right itself? Long enough for America to get a grip on her problems overseas and return her attention to the sky?

Sifting through the rest of the inventory from the supply ship, he noticed another batch of spares. Their existence amidst the edibles was starting to feel like a nod to fallibility. In the immortal words of Antonio Chabod, *"It's fucking madness!"*

Well, Chabod was still in Academia, tearing his hair out because he was stuck there and not out here with the dumbest man on Mars. Because for all the trials and tribulations of this mission, the Ajax crew were making progress and the arrival of their new supply ship had only strengthened their hand.

What's more, David felt that he was beginning to understand these people and the animosity that had characterised their earlier conversations had largely gone. What's more, life in the settlement was gaining a veneer of respectability. Every crewmember had been assigned a list of daily maintenance tasks and it was common knowledge that Tan and Eliot did none of them. Most of the hard scrubbing had been handed over to a pair of nocturnal droids, their scurrying paws being barely audible in the early hours of the morning. By day, the droids made themselves scarce in the corners and the floors and the walls to shoulder height were spotless. From time to time, the ultraviolet filters on the skylights were wrenched open and the humans expelled from the room until dusk. There were microorganisms on Mars that could survive this kind of exposure but there weren't many and the smell that had once defined this settlement was long gone.

In the evenings, the villagers would gather together in shorts and T-shirts and other items that the young might choose to wear beside the beach. Sprawled out in a spacious dining room, they recalled the days of thermal underwear and woollen hats with undisguised pride.

After dark, they watched old movies. When they were done, the engineer, Fredrick Weissman, took to playing his guitar whilst the occasional astronaut with a voice led the half-forgotten lullabies of a near-forgotten world. And as the night wore on and as the villagers prepared for bed, David Hewish would read from his collection of terrestrial paperbacks.

"Why," asked David, "is Socrates is a hero? Why does Socrates remain a hero, so many thousands of years after his death?"

"Socrates ain't no hero!" said Callaghan, flippant between an older man's legs. "That guy is a loser."

"Socrates," said Foguet, rather defiantly, "remains a hero because of the way in which he chooses to face death. He evades –"

"Socrates evades *nothing!*" called Nobohito Kazu. "The only thing Socrates ever did was save the bad guys the hard work of doing him in."

"Well, Socrates was an old man," said David, who was defending a personal hero. "The big question is – is this a disaster that Socrates brings upon himself? If Socrates had minded his own business, if he hadn't gone around polluting the minds of the young –"

"Socrates is a hero *because* he speaks to the young!" insisted Foguet, vocal in his own little corner. Then, almost pompously, "When *I* was a young man in Barcelona, I too spoke to the young!"

"And then you watched them die!" laughed Kazu, kicking the guy where he least wanted a kicking.

"I have no need of a lecture on death! Not from you, *Commander* Nobohito Kazu. Those of us that escaped the carnage in Europe know enough about war –"

"The men on the Lexington won't make that mistake."

By now, things were getting out of hand. Foguet was on his feet, raising an angry fist.

"I did everything I could!" he yelled.

"There are children who might have lived in Europe now who have never been born ..." Everyone was looking. "... because of *your* fuck up!"

David Hewish made an effort to get on his feet but Kazu was already moving forward. Seconds later, they collided in the middle of the room and quickly made their way to the floor.

"They're fucking you over now!" spat the Spaniard, who had been watching the latest news from Japan.

Nobohito Kazu, who had used his time on the planet to good effect, was 14 pounds more massive than David, but David was agile and sober with it.

"Foguet!" David shouted. "Foguet, get outta here!"

The others were all on their feet.

"Jeess!" someone squealed in the half-light. "We haven't had this much fun since the last Big Thaw!"

Since the last Big Thaw was well over 100 million years ago, it seemed reasonable to suppose they were taking it all in context.

"Foguet!" called David, "that's an order! Get outta here!"

David Hewish went down on his commanding officer, breaking their fall with both of his knees. Kazu's skull hit the deck with an alarming thud but the gravity on Mars is low and the Kevlar soft.

In any case, Foguet had already gone. Ignoring the order to release his own superior, Hewish rested bodily on a man who could have easily broken free when he was sober.

"Beat it! All of you!"

The last of the villagers dispersed. Kazu desisted and David rose to his feet.

"You've had enough now? *Commander Kazu?*" Something in the commander's breathing suggested that he had. "This is supposed to be an *all-American* base." David sighed, falling back on the kind of blunt patriotism that was common on the Lexington. "Ahhhrrr, fuck it! Let's get outta here!"

CHAPTER THIRTY-ONE

The villagers were not distressed. Far from it, the skirmish in the dining room had actually raised their morale and there was a widespread sense of anxiety that it might never happen again. David did his best to dismiss the incident as a passing phase. In truth he knew better. The authority of the Ajax crew had being permanently undermined.

In the morning, their leader was sober. Making no reference to the night before, Kazu started prepping for another trip to the ice lake. Having mapped out the route on their first visit, he believed that the second one ought to be easier. Their nuclear-powered buggy would depart in eight days and if the Ajax crew could obtain as much cargo as last time, then another four journeys ought to see the Ajax home.

The wild spirit of optimism was further enhanced by the promise of fresh eggs. Charlotte and Sarah had retrieved a box of chick embryos from the Ajax and had thawed them out in the laundry room. Just around the corner, Weissman had constructed his very own alcohol still. The garden had been producing fresh fruit for weeks and at least half of the stuff was going for fermentation. Soon, the villagers realised, a new kind of happy hour would be upon them.

Conscious of this new optimism, David Hewish became cautious. David's father had drowned when David was only 12. It would be misleading to suggest that the man had had a great influence on him. All the

175

same, the occasional exchange had stayed with him and one such moment was with him now:

"Life goes wrong. Remember that. When you think it's going good, it'll suddenly go wrong. It doesn't matter. That's what life does. It's about picking yourself up when you've hit the ground."

Things were getting better, so – in accordance with his father's doctrine – they were bound to get worse. It was just a question of which setback hit them next. Sometimes he feared this prospect, sometimes he ached for it. Your average day in the village was boring and the doctor was actually relieved when Fred Weissman walked into his quarters and asked for a medical opinion.

Weissman had developed an unfortunate ulcer in his natal cleft. This was not good. Having photographed the guy's rear end at length, David tracked down the last jar of dermatological cream on the planet. Natal cleft condition in the village had been disappointing when the Ajax crew arrived and mission planners back in Marshall had not foreseen this need.

"You know," Weissman was shuffling into his pants, "you know, this sort of thing doesn't make it easy for me in a suit." The man's tone was strangely altered. "And they're asking me to get in a pressure suit. They want me to start digging in the sand."

"Who's they?"

"The people at NASA, that naval aviator you dragged out here from the Lexington!" he groaned. "They're saying we all have to suit up and get out there."

"We're stranded on an alien planet, Fredrick. Someone's gotta do it."

"But why should it be me?"

Weissman requested a 'medical note' restricting him to light duties. Since there was virtually no paper on Mars, the note would take the form of a brief liaison with David's counterpart back on Earth followed by an internal memo to the base commander. Weissman's pathology was real but so was his lack enthusiasm for hard work. Pausing by the doorway, the engineer added another line.

"Dreadful time," he said. "When you know you're gonna go …" His eyes creased over again, the skin across his temples suddenly showing his age. "I think that's maybe what *he* did. I think maybe he just sat down in the sand …" Remembering Smith some more, Weissman petered out. Finally, "How do *you* plan to go, Colonel? When the time comes?"

"I'm not going to *go*, Doctor Weissman. I'm going to get through this and get out of here in one piece."

"That's what I heard about you, Colonel. You always get out." On the edge of the corridor, Weissman found himself on the receiving end of a new request.

"Do you mind staying out of the pool?" asked David. "'Til this has settled."

The ulcer touched a raw nerve in Houston and David received a long-winded e-mail demanding a more elaborate review of his crew. The doctor was due to board the buggy in a less than 72 hours but he was obliged to obey orders. This base was equipped with its own medical facility but the place was packed with all kinds of imposing equipment and he had never felt comfortable in there. Having improvised a couch and a desk in Bose's room, he soon posted a duty roster by the horseshoe.

Practically every tooth on the planet was synthetic and oral hygiene was excellent. On a similar note, the widely anticipated symptoms of scurvy were nowhere to be seen. Describing their own mental conditions, Connolly was "fine" and Callaghan "overworked". Weissman offered the sobering revelation, "I shit a lot."

Confronted with the issue of his wife, Foguet came out with a short rant about Callaghan and her ongoing misdemeanours in Major Smith's office. Trying to stop a riot, David reminded Foguet that Smith had been dead for months, that lots of guys on Mars weren't screwing anyone and that some things are better left unsaid.

"And there are some things," Pablo warned him, "that can never be undone."

Daniel Tan was suffering from sciatica in his right leg. David had noticed the limp a few times and failed to appreciate its significance. The chief scientist had suffered from this before and his latest attack was only a shadow of his former bouts.

"It's not the strength," he explained. "The muscle strength is OK. I can stand up but it doesn't feel right. It's numb and it hurts and it feels like I've been pissing down my leg for the last three weeks." And then he tried to laugh. "Some day soon, when I stand up and find out I really am pissing down my leg, that's when I'll start worrying." David gave the man some painkillers and a brief lecture on the natural history of the disease. *You'll get better. Give it time.* "Yeah …" added Tan, perhaps a little too irreverent, "… that's what your buddy told me."

The buddy in question was Major Smith and it seemed likely to David that Daniel had mentioned this name purely to grind him down. Even at this late stage in the mission, the villagers retained the ability to shock. Halfway through the clinic, David found himself returning to the medical room in a hurry and tracking down the ultrasound scanner. Not having used the thing for years, he tested it on his own gall bladder, then carried it back to his patient.

Last but not least came Nobohito Kazu and David Hewish was dreading the conversation that would follow.

In an effort to calm his own nerves, he reviewed Kazu as he had on the others.

Apart from a modest degree of weight loss, the commanding officer's body was doing OK. His pulse was regular, his urine vintage.

"How's things?" asked Kazu, which was a reference to the crew.

"They've come a long way since the cavalry showed up. First the food, then power." David decided to skip the dermatological angle. "Now the pool."

"What about the thing with the surveillance?" said Kazu. "Their refusal to smile on camera?"

"Have you covered up the lens in your office?"

Waving this one away, Kazu spoke as if in passing, "Since Callaghan. Only those two."

"As far as I can make out they were concerned about being humiliated by the guys back on Earth, poring over their dodgy habits whilst they died slowly of hunger."

"Anything else?" asked Kazu.

"Diarrhoea."

Kazu leant forward, gesturing with cupped hands around his face.

"Christ, tell me about the diarrhoea!"

But David's mind was moving on.

"Sex."

"Actually, don't tell me about the diarrhoea. Just tell me about the sex."

"We've got a pregnancy in the village." David knew of no other way to break such news. "It's Charlotte Erkhart," he went on. "She'll deliver in 31 weeks."

Kazu was visibly shocked.

"But Charlotte gave up on Foguet before we got here," he said.

David shrugged.

"This is Mars."

"Then you'll have to perform an abortion."

"She's refusing."

"What the hell difference does that make?" Getting up from his chair, Kazu raised his voice. "My orders are to get this crew home."

"Maybe we still can."

"How? Do you think it's realistic to deliver a baby on the Red Planet? Keep it fed and watered until it's physically strong enough to survive the voyage home? Like, for example, 15 years? Even assuming that a child reared on Mars would *ever* have the physical strength for space flight!"

But David had already discussed the matter with Houston.

"There's another plan," he said. "I downloaded it in the last few days."

"What plan? I haven't been updated on any kinda plan!"

If Kazu was confessing to his own distraction, David made light of it.

"We could fly them back in the Von Braun."

"The engines on the Von Braun were built to run on methane," said Kazu as if his colleague might not know this. "Methane doesn't boil. And there's still methane in the tanks."

"We could bleed off the methane and refill them with hydrogen. Four people could make it home on a high-thrust trajectory. That way we can cut the personnel in the base from 12 to seven. Concomitant savings on –"

"Do they tell you to send Callaghan?"

Kazu paused in the corner and slid down against the wall. Aware of the discontent within the village, his facial expression stabilised.

The doctor spoke again.

"Now, I know we don't get this crap on the Lexington."

And then, David saw something else. Something that he could recognise because he felt it himself. A passing memory on a haunted face: "Not any more."

"With this pregnancy, you could make a case for –"

"A termination?" said Kazu, his mind returning to the present.

"Not if we get her home," David insisted. "On a high-thrust trajectory, we can get her home before she delivers. Hydrogen makes for a better fuel. Send Charlotte – not Rachael. Rachael's good with the farm. The rest of them are planetary scientists. What are they good for?"

"Humping!" Kazu jeered. "These guys are humping all over the place!"

Leaning over his superior in person, David Hewish became firmer.

"Get the pregnancy outta here, sir! We'll all be better off without her."

The boss man got a grip.

"Who else would we send?"

"Somebody cockpit qualified. Two of them, case one of 'em flunks out en route. The two women are more science based than propulsion – astro navigation types."

"Can't they train in mid-flight?"

"Not everybody's a naval aviator."

Kazu lightened up. His junior had gotten to him.

"Alright, O'Reilly and two others take off with Charlotte and maybe Gabanna."

David nodded in agreement.

"If they go straight to escape velocity, Marshall thinks they'll be OK. Even if there isn't enough fuel, they can aero brake on the Earth's atmosphere."

Kazu peered up from his patch of the floor with real scepticism. "Aero brake? How much delta V can you bleed off in the Earth's atmosphere?" he asked.

"All of it if you want to," said David, without cracking a smile.

"Then signal Houston." Kazu had seen the joke. "Tell 'em we've read it through and we're on for the ride."

CHAPTER THIRTY-TWO

As soon as they got the concept across to them, the village was alight with excitement. It was a response that only seemed to harden Kazu's view of the place. Virtually no one on the planet wanted to stay here. From the relative privacy of Major Smith's quarters, the base commander recalled a memorable incident in the story of the Alamo, where the senior officer – *Houston* – offers every man in his outfit the chance to step forward and run away. "Best not try that here," he warned. "We'll have a fucking stampede!"

"It was a tough time," said David. "Waiting to be rescued, I mean. If their mission had gone as planned, they'd all be free of this. With their families." Trying to find some common ground, Hewish tried a different angle. "Tom's got that son on the Lexington."

"And I'd be with that son today, if I hadn't spent three years trying to get to Mars!" Kazu protested. "I'd have been the captain of that frigging aircraft carrier! I jeopardised my career in the navy trying to get out here! Did you know that? And at the end of it, they sent me right back into combat!"

"There's nothing I can do about that today, sir. We're stuck out here 'til we find the ice and a launch window to get us home."

Seeing sense, Kazu cooled. "You're right," he agreed. "Go see if their ship is OK. Get over there in the buggy and see if she's fit to fly."

The very next day, David set off for the Von Braun. To his rear, Marnix Gabanna, Kelly O'Reilly and Rachael Callaghan were strapped in the gap where the Ajax crew had once slumbered. Up front, Sarah Connolly had found the co-pilot's seat and with his eyes fixed firmly on the road, David asked Sarah how long she had spent on her own outbound flight.

"Seven months."

Seven months.

Although aware of this number, hearing it out loud seemed to make it worse. How the hell could anyone stay sane in a can for seven months?

"And on the Ajax," said O'Reilly, "it was just the two of you? For a full 17 weeks."

Ever so slightly, they were taunting him. It took the mindset of a man like Gabanna to pull them away.

"Hey, Colonel!" he cried. "Hey, Colonel!" Through the corner of one eye, Hewish could see the smile on Sarah's face. Marnix was like that. He could make people laugh. "Don't get disheartened by these Einstein types. These old men that think they're Einstein. Think they're gonna make some great scientific breakthrough like Albert did. You know, the miracle year."

"And they could be right," came another, softer voice.

"Well let me tell you!" Marnix wasn't easy to subdue. "Let me tell you, you gotta remember Roentgen."

A collective groan engulfed the cockpit. The astronauts had heard this story before.

"You remember the Roentgen story?" David did, but Marnix decided to tell it anyway. "Roentgen was in this lab on his own. And the lights were out. And he had this machine that was making X-rays, but nobody knew it was making X-rays, 'cause they're invisible and all the hotshots in the world were just irradiating themselves merrily, without even knowing all these rays were flying round their labs. And then Roentgen leans forward and he sees this glass plate glowing on the floor. And he thinks, *hey – what if there's some invisible rays that no one ever saw before, coming out of this machine and making that plate glow?* So he puts out his hand to block these rays and he looks at the plate and he sees like this moving X-ray picture of his own hand! And he's just discovered X-rays. Can you believe that? In the space of ten seconds, a guy who was regarded by most of his colleagues as a nobody gets to win the Nobel Prize!"

The telling was crass, but his audience was buying it, largely because he had screwed more than one of them. In the end, Kelly made this attempt to shut him up.

"It was luck, Marnix. Luck like that doesn't come easily!"

"It comes to them who deserve it!" Marnix declared. "You see, Colonel, fortune favours the brave. 'Sometimes, anyway. Like – OK – very occasionally, fortune favours the brave."

They had stopped listening. The vehicle drew to a halt and all eyes turned to the Von Braun. Up close, she was a fine looking vessel, towering some 15 metres above the sand, stubby, with two external fuel tanks latched on to each side. The big idea was to load these tanks with liquid hydrogen and oxygen and use this propellant to break free from the Martian gravity. If their plan succeeded, then the crew would be able to ditch the external tanks as soon as they cleared the stratosphere. With luck, the Von Braun would be back in Earth orbit in a similar timeframe to the outbound journey of the Ajax.

Like that ship, the Von Braun had arrived on Mars with a thirst for electrical power and an array of solar panels lay splayed around her foot pads. After a year or so in the wind, those same foot pads were covered in sand.

"The photo voltaics are going under," said Hewish. "Do you want me to clean them up?"

"Sure," replied Connolly, calm and self-assured in her pressure suit. "Feel free."

The villagers made their way across the sand, egressing in the Von Braun as a group. Alone in the buggy, Hewish activated a spider-like robot in the cargo bay and watched it dance between the boulders. For a while, this eight-legged creature seemed hell bent on destroying his faith in autonomous navigation. Finally waking up, the robot deployed a very low-tech-looking sweeping brush.

"Eight legs good, two legs bad."

He read a little Auden and did a few sit-ups in the back, his own fitness report still fresh in his mind. A handful of e-mails zipped down from their mother planet and he scanned them briefly from the cockpit. Then, about three hours into his isolation, Sarah Connolly emerged from the Von Braun and adjusted the solar panels. Seconds later, a sparking neon tube light confirmed the renaissance.

The Von Braun was anything but a dead spaceship. She had merely slumbered, these last 12 months, in the shifting sands of Mars. Now, at last, her unwitting hibernation was over and from the perspective of the doctor in the buggy, it looked like a full recovery. An hour or so later, he received a message on the com, asking him to suit up and stagger over.

Removing his helmet inside the spacecraft, David was quickly introduced to the latest thing in smells.

"What the hell is *that*?"

"She needed a good cleanout," said Sarah, which was her own way to acknowledge the state of the latrines.

"Kelly wants you in the cockpit," Rachael added. "Can you get there in that suit?"

David was about to answer in the obscene but decided to show restraint. Glancing up at the flight deck, he saw the rungs of a narrow ladder.

"Help me off with these gloves?"

Minutes later, he was reviewing the flight deck in person, a cloud of frozen mist erupting round his lips. This scene was an all too predictable: the smell, green shit that seemed to have etched its way round every pane of glass, the cold.

Kelly had booted up the onboard computers and was trying to coax the operating system back to life.

"It's sure gonna be tough on you guys," she said, clearly at ease in the captain's chair. "I mean, watching us blast off home and all."

Reluctant to show any kind of feeling on the matter, David stayed on an even keel.

"We can hack it."

Minutes later, his worse fears were confirmed when Callaghan unveiled a vat of semi-solid gunk she had discovered by the latrines. Almost immediately, there was talk of salvage, "for the greenhouse".

"You have got to be kidding me!" David hollered. "We've got 160 tonnes of water in the pool! What the hell do we need this for?"

"*That's* rocket fuel!" said the gardener, defiantly. "*This* is bio-mass! Show a little backbone will ya! In another two weeks, you'll be eating mushrooms outta this."

"Well get it in the *back* of the buggy!" he fumed. "And make sure it's properly sealed. I don't want to find that thing effervescing by the breakfast bar!"

CHAPTER THIRTY-THREE

Even as one group of astronauts prepared to leave the planet, a second was ready to resume its exploration. Freed from the constraints of mission salvage, Tan and Eliot had reverted to type. Detailed instructions from the Marshall Space Flight Centre were analysed at length and then ignored whilst the men in the forbidden zone dreamt up their own.

Along the corridor and beside the UV machine, their only credible rivals were making progress of their own. Their seismometer array was on-line and the data streams were excellent. Weissman and Foguet had assembled a robotic rover in the gymnasium and this machine had already driven some 600 kilometres across the dunes. Since driver and robot were both on Mars, real time control had been possible and the village was littered with new data.

The astronauts were soon discussing their next sojourn across the sand. Much to the distaste of the naval aviator, the villagers were planning to launch a winged flying machine.

The 'Gossamer' wings in storage consisted of two sheets of transparent polymer, stretched out across the very flimsiest of frames. They could get off the ground with the help of a drop-off rocket motor and maintain altitude with a small propeller. Though the matter was rarely discussed, it was a machine of this kind that had been used to locate Smith's frozen body.

Meanwhile, doctors Tan and Eliot were examining the core sample from the ice lake. Having nearly died in their attempt to retrieve this sample, the Ajax crew were interested to hear what they had found.

"So what can you see?" asked Kazu, relaxing to a bit of Schubert in the forbidden zone.

Eliot tossed the offending sample in one hand, as if to judge its weight. "Like 110 PhDs," he said, "assuming we can get the thing back to JPL."

"Any signs of life? Any fossilised ferns? Something we could hand over in Montreal and bag the Nobel Prize for?"

The scientist's gaze was scornful.

"You guys amaze me!" he laughed. "Half the time you're begging us to throw in the towel, the other half you're dreaming up some kinda bug hunt of your own! Well let me tell you, Commander, Edison is dead. Research on Mars is for the professionals. If you wanna make it here, you've gotta live for it. And whilst we're on the subject and like I keep telling your medical friend here, *Mars-is-a-dead-plan-et*!"

Lacking the status to be afforded a chair, Kazu's medical friend had taken up position on top of the mass spectrometer and was about to raise a query of his own.

"But if there *were* anything?" he asked, "if there is some sort of legacy from another age, wouldn't that core of ice be the best place to find it?"

Tom Eliot swung idly on a carbon-fibre seat. "My dear Colonel," he mused, "I can't believe that life – even if it did exist – could have survived at those latitudes. It's just too goddamned cold."

And then Eliot gave way to Tan.

"You see, guys, a chemical reaction goes faster when it's warm. That's why they made you stick a Bunsen burner under a test tube in your chemistry class. So, if it happened, it happened *here*. On the *equator*. Look, we gotta dedicated geological drill in this base. We could get a core sample anywhere we like. In fact that was the plan right up until –"

And for a moment – just for a moment – Hewish saw something else: eyeball contact between men with a secret.

"Until what?" chirped Kazu.

Had he seen it too?

"Until Major Smith turned up dead and our troubles on Mars began."

"And before that? Before that, everything was hunky-dory?"

The conversation faded, just as Beethoven came in with more than the usually pretentious fifth. Once again, Hewish wondered if this passion for the classical was real or a carefully contrived. Perhaps it belonged in the same category as their collection of reflective spectacles. Whatever, the Chinese-American eased himself away from his work and Hewish sensed a new wave of defiance.

"Is this your interrogation chamber?" asked Tan. "Or a research lab?"

"At the top of that ramp," Kazu told him, "they call it the forbidden zone."

The scientists made no comment and the commander left. Meanwhile, on top of the mass spectrometer, David Hewish had outstayed his welcome. Just in case he had any doubts about this matter, Tan picked up a large volume from his desk and flipped it open. David's heart missed a beat. It was his own PhD thesis, available on-line to the very few that might have an interest.

"Yeah, I looked through this thing last night!" said the chief scientist, sliding one finger across the page.

"You dreamt this thing up with this thing in the constitution?"

"How would you know that, Doctor Tan?" David Hewish brushed the dust from his thighs, ready to run.

"You wrote that on the front cover."

David had expected to be stung by his thesis eventually but not this quickly. Reaching the ramp, he heard this call from Tan. "Ah – I wouldn't worry. No data, no economic resources; I've seen worse than this!"

David ran to his own medical room and closed the door. He would have preferred to have locked it but locked doors were few and far between on Mars. Having said that, since he was the only doctor on the base, he was unlikely to be disturbed here. He thought about the thesis and he thought about the idea of having Daniel Tan read it and heard the sound of fingernails scraping on a very traditional blackboard.

The patronising bastard!

Looking for distraction, David found a box of dirty instruments and decided to get them clean. On the Lexington, his scalpel blades and needles would have already gone overboard but out here he was obliged to keep them safe in case his core supply ran dry. The sharps had been washed but they were far from sterile. Arranging them in a glass box, he carried them over to the airlock. He'd take the thing outside in his next EVA and leave it on the sands beside the pilot light. A few hours in the Sun and the ultraviolet would have sterilised the lot.

It wasn't enough. His heart was still racing. The airlock was as good a place for rumination as any and he crouched there, gazing at the needles and thinking about his recent conversation in the lab. Tan and Eliot were habitually awkward, but they had never performed in quite this way before. Why? Could they be tired? Antagonised?

He thought for one hour and began to feel bad about the time he was wasting. He knew from experience that there was nothing to be gained from inactivity.

Jogging through the settlement was starting to feel like a cheap fairground ride where the passenger himself sat still and the rest of the world spun around him. Every few minutes, the mildly comic figure of Eliot shot by in Bermuda shorts, mouthing some kind of crap about exhibitionism. Marnix Gabanna made a cameo appearance in the ice room whilst Sarah Connolly was his sole admirer, resting in a well chosen corner of the same room. The latest couple on Mars were an open secret, flaunting their feelings in every nook and cranny of the building, as if the world had never seen love before.

Sarah's gain was Charlotte's loss and the widespread conviction that Marnix had fathered Charlotte's child had led to mixed feelings in this closed, incestuous community. One man's light relief had landed the rest of them with a new kind of pressure and their entire strategy for survival had been re-written because of it. "That is what happens when you send women on a high-risk mission," said Kazu to Hewish, flat out in Major Smith's quarters, largely naked with Rachael Callaghan beside him. "The navy spotted that eight years ago. NASA's still living in a dream world!"

Meanwhile, approaching his billionth orbit, David became aware of Charlotte, alone with her machines, pressing her brow against the seismometer kit and doing little else. Like Marnix kept telling him, Charlotte was not an unattractive woman and her habit of wearing the same deep blue skirt was – presumably – a request for attention.

Through with his exercise, the doctor feigned interest in the data streams and got a response. "That's *ours*," he heard her say, as if the issue of possession mattered more than the achievement itself. "Just remember that. Not one single byte of this stuff came out of *that* place." She nodded in the direction of the ramp. "These are some of the most sophisticated instruments ever to be flown to Mars. We actually picked up your avalanche, all those thousands of miles away." Tearing off a sodden vest, David missed her eyes as they shot across his torso. Then, he heard her say, "Do you know what I miss?" Expecting something vulgar, David was taken aback when she mentioned her youth. "I miss the intensity of feeling."

"What feelings?"

"When I was a teenager."

"Doesn't it get intense here?" he asked, suppressing a manic laugh. "I mean, it all seems pretty severe to me."

Charlotte shook her head, all the more vulnerable beside these vast machines. "It's not the same," she told him. "Not now. Mars is a dead planet. When you were young, that's when it got to you. When I was, like, 12, maybe 13, saw things I'd never seen before. Colours. Words between the music I'd never heard before. Like a dagger. Like ..." She gestured again with her hands. "Like a bullet through the side of your brain. That's all gone. That's NASA for you. NASA hasn't recruited a guy on a high for getting on the last hundred years."

He wanted to hear some more. More about her break-up with Foguet? Verbal agreement that it had been Gabanna and not some other sex maniac who had caused this mayhem. From where David stood, Charlotte's life didn't seem short on intensity at all.

"You think you're some kinda hotshot flight surgeon?" she asked. "Pitching up here with a pile of mess kits and freaking us out?"

"I was acting on orders."

"But you got off on them." He did not deny it. "You and that crazy aviator from the Lexington."

"You were dying."

"Well we're not dying anymore, Colonel. We're back on schedule. Pretty soon, even Weissman might give up on that stutter! Rachael's got her green shit going. Tan and Eliot have found a freedom here they never knew on Earth." He couldn't see what they were free of but she was quick to inform him. "Free from … the act of subservience to lesser men."

"People have different strengths," he reminded her.

"And weaknesses."

"Like Weissman," said David. "Weissman's a good engineer. Why doesn't he go outside the base?"

"Because the convene rubs on his dick," she revealed. "When you bury Weissman – and my guess is that you will bury Weissman – don't waste your time on a suit. It takes hours to put a dead man in a suit. Believe me, I've already done it. A spanner and that guitar will do it for Weissman. That's all he's gonna need."

"And Tan? Eliot?"

"Eliot, I mean, Christ, *Eliot.* Do you know Eliot?" He did. "I mean, did you know that Sarah and I actually worked for that guy?"

David didn't, which was worrying because he thought he'd studied the background to this mission in some depth.

"Tan supervised my PhD at Stanford," she continued. "The data used to come down from the satellites around Mars and straight into our computers. Tan was the hot favourite for the Nobel Prize. Everybody said so. Then they fucked up Sweden and there wasn't a prize to win anymore and Tan started wandering round the place really pissed. Then all these Scandinavian types turn up in Montreal, saying, hey, this place looks a bit like Europe! Let's restart the Nobel Prize thing in Montreal just to give ourselves something to do! And he cheered up a bit but it was too late. Tan had lost sight of the pure faith."

"How come?"

"Politicians." She tossed her hair, doing her best to show him why Gabanna and Weissman and God knows how many others had tried to nail her thus far. "You know, *university politics.* Then – out of the blue – Eliot pitches up." Charlotte smiled inside herself, as David Hewish often smiled when he thought of Alice. "Fresh from his bare-knuckle fight with MIT. Plenty of hair, some brain. Trying to lead the big guy astray."

"How far did he get?"

"About ..." She made a show of arching her neck. "Three hundred million miles." David allowed himself a smile. "Kept telling us all how data in itself would never be enough. How we had to get out here in the flesh.

"So we came. Sarah and me? We hit this planet six months after those idiots and it's really just the same down here as it was in Stanford. Difference is, the politicians are harmless. Something bothers you out here? Push it over. This is Mars, bro. What the hell is going to happen to you?" She smiled some more. "Sarah was already a post doc when I got to Stanford. That was right after Taiwan?" He nodded. "Kazu's commanding officer in Taiwan was a woman. Did you know that?"

"Yeah, I knew that."

"Why does that not surprise me? A nerd like Tan thinks that women are only here to serve him data. Over breakfast we give him some muesli and in the daytime

195

we gotta serve him his data. Tan and Eliot haven't donned a suit in the best part of a year! Did you know *that?"* David did. "Even Smith couldn't get them in a pressure suit – 'cept for the day he died – and they were all out there then. Afterwards, Daniel tried to stop us looking for the body."

David sat up.

"How?"

"He tried to stop us flying the Gossamer wing for reconnaissance. He said it was too important a thing to waste on a guy that might be dead! Then Pablo started going on about the wind speed, saying how it might just come down anyway."

"Wait a minute, wait a minute!" David was suddenly baffled. "How do you mean *might* be dead? Smith disappeared on foot. He can't have had more than eight hours of oxygen in that backpack."

"Yeah, but – you don't believe it 'til you see the body." Charlotte shrugged. "Smith didn't come back. Time goes by. They said his oxygen was out. Then we had this big meeting under the dome and we all got asked what to do. That was like the shittiest day of my life. The rest of us thought Smith was this great man. We said he deserved to be found, wherever he was. Then – then when they found him." Without any kind of pre-emption, the woman broke into a sob. It lasted five seconds. "We said he had to have a proper burial. He deserved to be laid out for a real Viking funeral, in a long boat with his frigging sword and his armour if we'd had any armour. Not ditched in the sand for the wind to get him. Do you see what I mean?"

"Yeah," said Hewish, sober beside a defunct UV machine, "I see what you mean ..."

CHAPTER THIRTY-FOUR

Later that day, the crew assembled by a horseshoe-shaped table for supper. A strange, disparate group of individualists, the collective act of eating was one of the few things that drew them together.

"OK," said Kelly O'Reilly, seated at the far right of the table. "OK, it's all about ice now."

"Yes." Just this once, O'Reilly and Kazu were in agreement.

"And you're planning another trip to the lake?" This wasn't random. O'Reilly was going somewhere. "What about using our own vehicle? Here at the village?"

"You haven't the range," said Hewish, pushing in from the opposite end of the horseshoe.

To his immediate left, Fred Weissman and Pablo Foguet were much too quiet. Wherever O'Reilly was heading, they were in on it. Sensing a trap, David Hewish turned to Eliot, a big shaggy dog of a man, tight-lipped beside his trusted accomplice. This was not good. The Ajax crew were outsiders within a group, nominally in control but still distant from the team.

"Using the pressurised rover from the village," said Kelly, "we ought to have an operational range of 1000 kilometres."

"And it's 3000 kilometres to the ice lake," snapped Kazu unnecessarily.

"But if we dump re-supply canisters at 1000 kilometres, and pick them up on the return journey, we might be able to get out to 2000 kilometres."

"Which would leave you 1100 klicks short of the lake. Both ways. You'd still be coming home empty-handed. Besides, you can't match our speed."

"Alright," said O'Reilly, "so here's a plan. We set off in the village rover and get out to 1000, maybe 1500 kilometres. Then you guys drive out to the lake, bag some ice and come and meet us half way. Then we switch trailers. You hook on our empty trailers and start driving north again. Meanwhile, me and the boys head back to the village. In the end, we both make it home with 500, maybe 600 tonnes of ice between us. Enough water to fly one Von Braun class spacecraft back to low-Earth orbit."

Kazu frowned, visibly frustrated that the villagers could change his agenda. Finally, he gave them this answer.

"We'll have to run that past NASA."

"They're on-line now," said Foguet, "listening in on our every spoken word."

And then Kazu conceded another point.

"That's not always a good thing, is it? Alright, Kelly, download this shit to Texas. See what they come up with."

CHAPTER THIRTY-FIVE

To Kazu's undisguised dismay, Mission Control Houston approved of the plan. What's more, Houston had come up with a new idea of their own.

"They want them to fix the snowplough to the village rover," said Hewish.

"Who's they?" asked Kazu, indignant in the office.

"Marshall. Marshall figures O'Reilly and Weissman could do it."

"Weissman shits himself near a suit! What's the rational behind this one?"

"The road surface," said Hewish, not enjoying himself. "If they can flatten the road surface for the first 1000 klicks, then we can push up our speed."

Kazu made an effort to pace and was quickly defeated by the size of the room.

"It makes sense," Hewish persisted. "Percival Lowell said the Martians would build canals. We're gonna build a road."

If this one pressed any buttons in Kazu, he didn't light up. Instead, he reminded his junior of their recent past.

"You're going to build a dirt track, slightly flatter than the one they had when we first got here. Look – Colonel! When I landed on this planet, I risked my life to save these people. They tried to kill me."

"I know that," said Hewish. "I was there. I was with you on that day. But you told me in Texas – in front of Hutchings – *we can't get home without a crew.*"

Kazu's head was shaking.

"I just don't buy it. How about Eliot? The other day, with that other professional fruitcake, Daniel Tan? What was he on?" Conscious that his colleague had seen it too, Kazu went a little further. "There's more to this shithole than starvation. There always has been."

Seconds later, Hewish found himself forced to speak again.

"It gets worse," he said. "There's an abandoned ESA base about 1000 kilometres north of here. They want to use it as the refuelling station for their vehicle. Kelly thinks she might be able to break into one of the habitats, salvage some goodies. European stuff. Maybe find some kinda science angle –"

"If they wander off the path, if they go off message, things will get bad. Fast. Even *Roger* knew that."

"Never stray off the path," echoed the colonel.

"And never go outside alone."

The detour had the support of the agency. The naval officers had little choice but to comply.

"Alright," said Kazu. "Lemme get the fuel dump for the Von Braun running. Once I got that done then we can get the buggy ready for the road."

Again, David Hewish had a different agenda.

"Houston wants me busy," he explained. "I'm going to check out the greenhouse, make sure this place will still be breathing when we get home."

CHAPTER THIRTY-SIX

Shortly after sunrise, Kazu went off site with Gabanna. Two years ago, an earlier crew had established a fuel dump some 1500 metres from the base and Kazu wanted to confirm its viability before starting electrolysis. Within seconds of their departure, Kelly O'Reilly was tugging the doctor's arm and asking for a private consultation.

Expecting the worse, David was only mildly disappointed to discover that she was only complaining of back pain. He hadn't actually noticed any changes in the woman's posture but Kelly was about to lead an expedition north and the idea of a crippled astronaut in the village buggy didn't appeal to him. Following a brief physical examination, he agreed to prescribe a course of painkillers and started to worry when Kelly wouldn't leave.

Something else was nagging her. Toying with her crudely painted fingernails, she started to slate her own boss.

Kazu!

This was just an essay title. Once she got going, the bitch was practically sneering. How the hell had Hewish made it through 17 weeks in a can with Kazu?

Like a lot of military personnel, Kazu was famous for his dismissive attitude towards the fairer sex and this character trait had not been lost on the highly sophisticated population of the village. The only woman in the base that the commander had any time for was the one that was giving him sex and the only woman who could still abide the man was the one that was getting it. On Mars, she garbled, as in that other outmoded universe, the United States of America, women had been sailing in the wrong direction for too long. After nearly a year of abuse from Daniel Tan, O'Reilly was now being abused by her own successor.

"You managed to run the village single-handed," David reminded her. "No one in the village actually slashed their own wrists and with a little less leadership at the top, they might have done." It was a reasonable point that achieved little in the way of pacification.

"How the heck does a man even end up like that?"

"Are we still with Kazu?" And his pre-Cambrian attitude to Taiwan," said David, which was in danger of becoming his answer for everything. "Look, Kelly, it was your idea to use the illage buggy. It was a sound idea. Even Marshall thinks so. If you're looking for a place to show your wares, this is it. All you got to do is meet us on time and on target and there'll be smiles all round."

"And if I don't?"

The doctor answered frankly.

"Kazu will break your neck."

Kelly nodded and walked away, clutching the double wounds of low back pain and professional frustration. Had the village been equipped with a more generous complement of men, David might have asked for a different leader for the forthcoming trip. In the circumstances, there was nobody else to ask.

That was Kelly. Later that day, he found Rachael and told her that he wanted to check out the greenhouses. Never averse to male attention, Rachael said yes, even offering a specific time.

"Dusk."

Dusk made sense. Since the ice had arrived in the village, the plants had had water and Rachael's working life had become nocturnal.

A half-hearted airlock separated the carbon dioxide-rich atmosphere of the greenhouse from the rest of the settlement and Rachael handed him a lead-lined jacket to block out the radiation. The Sun had dropped under the horizon an hour ago and the crops were just discernible beneath the occasional bulb. Oxygen masks, not dissimilar from the ones Hewish had worn during the Ajax fire, would protect them from the CO_2.

"We're talking 2000 square metres of land here." The gardener's voice was crackling on the com. "Five basic crops. Fourth-generation GM. I only ever see it by flash lamp. You can't come out here in the day."

"Why's that?"

"The Sun," said Rachael, which was another way of saying *the radiation*.

"They've got pills for that."

"Gives me the squits!"

The greenhouses consisted of a series of plastic tubes, each of them overlying a shallow trench on the north side of the village. A group of purpose-built robots, unrecognisable amidst the surrounding hydroponics, were aiding her every move. With the help of the water from the ice lake and the extra sunlight from the sail, Rachael had been able to run the greenhouse at a frantic new pace.

Under everything that was green lay a tray of hidden mushrooms. Mushrooms, the gardener told him, needed space but no sunlight. You could stack them under just about anything and they could thrive in the kind of crap nothing else could thrive. Trying to keep this one out of his mind, Hewish concentrated on the sharper, greener stuff. Genetic engineers had provided the astronauts with plants that their forefathers could not have dreamt of and he couldn't resist the temptation to touch.

"Oranges are not the only fruit." The colonel squeezed a peach between a finger and thumb. The peach was nearly ripe but the oranges needed more time. "How much longer for this one?"

The woman looked down at the bush.

"The apples'll be good in another ten days. The oranges, another week or so."

Intrigued, David asked another question.

"Will the oranges grow any faster? Once you've picked the apples and plums? When the same plant only has to feed one kind of fruit, I mean?"

She shook her head.

"They're on an internal clock."

"And the oxygen?" he asked. "How much oxygen are we getting out of this stuff?"

"That's the Holy Grail. Or at least it was the Holy Grail 'til you guys pitched up with your trailers full of ice. You can turn oxygen around with green stuff, but you haven't got the surface area here to keep 11 people breathing."

"What about a smaller crew?"

This was a leading question. The gardener's manner changed abruptly.

"Four men might just make it," she said, after some delay. "With a farmer on site. And no crop failures."

He saw some raw sewage, all 500 litres of it. Its bubbling surface was shrouded in darkness and on the whole, David decided, this was a good thing. A little further afield, they found a second and then a third tub of the same stuff, each a little closer to fermentation than the last. He wanted to ask her what she was doing with it but couldn't quite face the discussion that might follow.

204

Ten metres later, some kind of hideous pea soup became prominent on their left.

"Algae," explained the girl. "I got this thing up and running as soon as you got back from the lake." Was this the final destination for the sewage? He didn't want to know. "You can forget all your nth generation citrus fruits. If you just want to keep breathing, this is the way forward. Primitive plants are the best."

"And Mars is a primitive environment?"

"Too right, Colonel. You're catching on."

Their tour was over. In all the months he had been on Mars, he had never once stepped foot in this building and he was glad that he had been here now. At the far side of the airlock, Rachael took off her jacket and her oxygen mask and David did the same. He thought they were done and was about to thank her but there was more to follow. She led him down from the greenhouses and over to the yawning gap behind the laundry machine. There, Rachael introduced him to another first: a Martian chicken run.

"We wanted to give them names," she said, grabbing a ball of fluff. "Then Kelly stopped us."

"Is Kelly running the show?"

"Kelly's on the ground, man, every day. Kelly doesn't vanish in a truck every few weeks. Besides, she's got a point. What if we end up putting these guys in a pot? Nobody wants to eat something with a name?"

Several weeks after incubation, there were two fully-grown hens and a fair cluster of chicks. David hadn't set eyes on a non-human species for the best part of eight months and in other circumstances, the animals might have had him gripped. But today, there had been something else stealing his attention and he found it difficult to look anywhere else.

"What about …" he stumbled on his words. "What about the future? Someday, I mean. Couldn't we grow plants outside the greenhouse? Find something that could grow in the Martian soil. That's if we could get the temperature up? Keep the place damp?"

The gardener was unimpressed.

"That's science fiction, Colonel. No cover at all and your crops will dry up. The ultraviolet alone would kill them. What d'ya think is saving us from the bugs in this place? If you're asking me, could we breed something that might survive in some kind of new pressure low, I'd say yes. But what's the point? If you want a crop that shoots up fast and gives you something to eat, why would you want to disable the thing by leaving it in a low-pressure environment?"

"Terra-forming," said David, running through his options in turn. "We know there was liquid water on this planet."

"*Was*. Past tense. That time is dead and gone. Like Australia." The gardener's patience was fading fast. "Colonel, is yours a science mission?"

And he drew breath. Because she was beautiful and because nothing else in the village really was. Mars truly was the shithole she had once called it but Rachael wasn't.

"No," he accepted, "this is not a science mission."

"Not for you, maybe," she laughed, with an unexpected change of attitude. "But the rest of these idiots are hell bent on it!"

CHAPTER THIRTY-SEVEN

Come the morning, Kelly was taking her own expedition towards a pre-determined rendezvous point on the dunes. The stuttering figure of Weissman had been slated to steer with Pablo Foguet as his back-up and Marnix Gabanna on standby for light relief and macho tracking shots. Their crew compartment was only marginally bigger than the one in the Ajax buggy. It was hard to imagine how they could cope in there but O'Reilly had asked for four personnel and Houston had agreed.

"You could have said no." David overheard Rachael speaking to her lover. "Houston's miles away, you can do anything you want!"

But Nobohito Kazu didn't do anything he wanted. He obeyed orders as and when they came through to him. His orders for today were to sit around and wait to set off in their faster, nuclear-powered vehicle in the next 48 hours.

With O'Reilly out of the picture, Connolly gave names to the poultry: *Tolstoy and Dostoevsky.* During the period of extreme rationing, NASA had ordered the villagers to stay in their cots and read Russian literature. By delicious irony, a pair of Russian novelists would soon provide their eggs.

Kazu retreated to his office and David became frustrated by inactivity. Craving an omelette, he made a bid for the laundry room. There he found Sarah and Charlotte, doting over their new prodigies and quickly denying the existence of eggs. Marnix was off campus and this, presumably, was what these idiots did when their instruments were working and Marnix wasn't.

There was still time to kill and David had to find work to fill it. NASA had made a special request. It was low-demand activity but it would serve to keep them occupied. The only risk involved was that of failure and he decided to face it anyway.

Dragging Kazu down to the laundry room, David Hewish stood him in front of a well-positioned electrolyser. Over to his left, Eliot was rigging up a camera and saying downbeat about the likely number of takes.

"We haven't got time for that, Tom," said Kazu. "Just get me a board and we'll get going."

Right on cue, a digital blackboard sprang up behind them and Kazu used his finger as the chalk. Their target demographic was the American high school student and as David had foreseen, the thought of playing to this crowd had brought them back to life.

On full throttle, the process of electrolysis would be hidden from view. Today – and for the benefit of the cameras – Eliot had dismantled the panels and exposed the liquid water to the air. Kazu was already scrawling his intimate knowledge of chemistry across the board.

$$H_2O + energy = H_2 \text{ and } O_2$$

Kazu grabbed two plastic beakers, plunged them into the water and turned them upside down. With the power rating set at 1%, Eliot pressed the button and ordered his cameras to zoom in. Seconds later, the electrodes were all sound and fury and the two beakers were full of bubbles.

Though the performance was unplanned, word had spread throughout the settlement like wildfire and to their rear, in the corridor, most of the population had come to watch.

Holding a flaming strip of card in his right hand, Kazu did a set piece to camera about the chemical composition of water. Kazu wasn't much of a scientist but he understood the principles involved. He blew on the twisted card and waited for the flame to die. Finally, with one tiny corner still glowing, he lifted the beaker from the water and introduced the card from below. The flame was rekindled.

"Pure oxygen," said Kazu. "Pure oxygen ignites a glowing stick."

Kazu took the second beaker from Tom Eliot, keeping the thing inverted so that the gas would remain inside.

"Let's see what the other electrode came up with."

The second taper went the same way as the first and when the flame got close they heard something good: a sharp, loud pop that lit up every face in the room.

"Hydrogen!" Kazu turned to Eliot as if his findings were some kind of surprise. "See if you can get me 50 tonnes of that stuff."

There endeth the lesson. Three hundred million miles away, countless American high school students would soon be watching the edited highlights. All around them, the educational establishment would be praying that their nation's youth might yet find the brain cells to defeat Beijing. Out here on Mars, the performance was over and the villagers were drifting back to their stations, grinning only with the memory of their own lost teenage minds. Soon, the Ajax crew were alone again and with the entertainment over, they returned to the more practical issue of hair.

By tradition, hair on Mars had always been cut beside the laundry machines and it was time to do some now. Leaning forwards in his chair, Kazu waited whilst Hewish ran the clippers through his scalp.

"The buggy's good," said the commander. "Two trailers lined up. Food and water for two months if we need it." And then he added, "You were with Callaghan?"

"Checking the crops."

There was a brief hiatus. Stepping back from his scalp, David watched the man run his fingers through his hair. It was a poignant image. This was how they had cut David's hair in high school. Fresh off the boat as an orphan in the States, they had dragged him into a naval boarding school and issued him with a crewcut and a pristine uniform just as soon as he had sworn allegiance to the stars and stripes. Years later, during his relationship with Christine, he had sometimes let his hair grow longer but in essence, a regulation haircut was all he had ever known.

Rising with good posture, Kazu found his voice.

"Houston wants a line-up. What do you think? Should she go home on the Von Braun?"

"We need her for the farm," said David, uncertain of his own motives. "We've already got the expectant mother slated in for the seat. Kelly wants to lead something. Get her to lead this. Give her a second cockpit-qualified man."

"You're right." Kazu had made his mind up. "Marnix Gabanna can do it!"

"Marnix is screwing Sarah," said David, who had screwed Connolly himself.

"That's right," said Kazu, "and before that he was screwing Erkhart. But Marnix can fly and Sarah can't. Marnix gets the seat."

CHAPTER THIRTY-EIGHT

Marnix got the seat and was grateful for it, grinning idiotically on the data link from the village buggy as soon as the message got through. Watching the parade of teeth, David's mind returned to the Alamo. Whatever Marnix felt for the people on this planet, it wasn't love.

Meanwhile, with all preparations complete, the Ajax crew set off for the ice lake in the best of spirits. A thousand klicks down the line, Kazu vomited, once after food and quickly responded to a shot of intramuscular Ondansetron. Having felt it coming on, he had been able to grab a vomit bowl and the mess was well contained. Retching aside, their latest adventure was a brisk and straightforward affair. The tracks from their earlier journey were clearly visible and the man in the driving seat need only follow them.

"Daniel Tan," said Kazu, as if reading out a banner headline, grabbing David's attention in the process.

"What about him?"

"You gotta stay calm," Kazu explained. "You gotta stay calm when you pick up on that kind of behaviour and realise it's all coming from a Chinese guy. 'Member when I was on the Lexington. Just before you caught your shrapnel. This guy turns up from Washington and he starts telling us not to hate the Chinese. Some do-gooders in DC were worried that we might all hate the Chinese and it might spill over onto the streets. You know, into a riot or something down the Chinese cultural centre. So he gives us this speech 'bout how it was our patriotic duty to go kill them. Blow the slanty-eyed little bastards out of the sky, he says. Before they could bomb out troops but don't actually hate them. Like it mattered. And I had this man in our squadron. Little short guy – a lot of aircrew are below average height – but I guess you already knew that. And he goes out to use the latrines halfway through his speech. Wanted to do his business before we got onto the flight plan for the sortie. And he misses the political spiel. So we take off and shortie gets it over Taipei. Gets this heat-seeking missile up his ass. Releases flares and all – but it's no good. No chutes. No nothing. He's gone. And that night in the officers' bar, this dick from DC comes up to me and asks if it was him. You know, the one who walked out of his lecture and took a dump rather than listen to why we shouldn't hate the enemy. And I said yes, it was he. The Chinese killed him today. And you know something? It really bothered that little bastard. It mattered that shortie had missed his lecture. That he got killed when he was only 25, maybe with an idea in his head that he was supposed to hate the people he was at war with. But if he hadn't gone to the latrine, he might have been enlightened. He might have died not hating them."

"Did it matter to you?"

"No."

"What happened to the man from DC?"

"The man from DC went to Taiwan. After he'd done lecturing us on how he wanted us to feel about dying, he went to Taiwan. Got there just in time for the big one! No one heard from him again!"

The buggy erupted in a protracted blue-collar laugh that surely reached Houston and would, presumably, see more than one mission controller begin to cringe.

"Like it matters to them ..." Kazu concluded, looking out at the planet with his back to his colleague. "Like it matters to them, how you feel when you die."

The rendezvous with the village buggy occurred on schedule with grown men waving to one another like excited kids. For a while there was even talk of donning pressure suits and trekking out from one machine to the next, but in the end, Kazu ruled against it. Half an hour later, the nuclear powered buggy was driving north.

Away from the wheel, David fell back on Dylan and attempted to read some poetry to his bemused boss.

"Dead men naked they shall be one
With the man in the wind and the west moon;
When their bones are picked clean and the clean
bones gone,
They shall have stars at elbow and foot;
Though they go mad they shall be sane,
Though they sink through the sea they shall rise
again;
Though lovers be lost love shall not;
And death shall have no dominion."

And death shall have no dominion.

David had first encountered these words in Taiwan though he neglected to share this fact today. Within weeks of reading this poem, he was medi-vacked off the island with a lump of shrapnel in his thigh. Over on the Lexington, things were happening to Kazu too. Kazu had been elevated to the dizzy height of squadron commander. Whilst physically uninjured, the aviator's promotion would prove a two-edged sword, his predecessor having disintegrated on her third day in the skies. Poetry can mean different things to different men and one of the things that determines this is the time and

213

the place where we he reads it. Having found Dylan in Taiwan, Dylan's work meant more to David than some.

Suiting up by the ice lake, the Ajax crew found a cheering abundance of water ice, still scattered across the permafrost. On this trip, the massive and treacherous lake itself would be avoided and the astronauts felt better for it. With another 40 tonnes in the trailers, they turned around and followed their own tyre tracks back to the rendezvous point.

When they arrived, the villagers were somewhere else. Orbiting an abandoned trailer in the sand, the Ajax crew saw tracks that led out to the desert and conversed in the obscene. Speaking directly to mission control, Kazu asked for an explanation and as soon as the speed of light, Houston obliged.

"They've run off on some sort of clandestine *science mission*," said David, reading from his computer screen. "There's a riverbed down there. Kelly's got an interest in riverbeds."

"An *interest* in riverbeds? Does she ever wake up in a morning and wonder what happened to Bose?"

Evidently she did not, for Kelly had digressed from her duties and in doing so, had threatened the viability of the entire operation. By now, the Ajax crew had fought long and hard and suffered much. On his knees and in the back of his own vehicle, Kazu spouted his latest list of grievances to a diffident lens. He looked, for all the world, like a man of piety before a distant God and in a sense, David Hewish realised, that's exactly what he was.

"Kazu!" cried David, his voice unaffected. "Got a call from the buggy. They're in the canyon."

"Which canyon?"

"*The* canyon. The biggest canyon in the known universe." David was pointing west. "And it's that-a-way!"

CHAPTER THIRTY-NINE

"So, they went on a science mission," David continued, "ski-ing off piste more or less as soon as we waved goodbye. That way, they figured they could make it back in time to meet us by the roadside."

"And now they're in the valley?"

"Mariner Valley, the world's – I'm sorry, that's the biggest single geological structure in this solar system. If I wanted to do science on Mars, that's where I'd do it!"

"But they were under *orders* to stay here!"

"They're under military jurisdiction, but this is not a military crew. The villagers are actually selected for individual initiative. Military personnel are –"

"And our cargo?" asked Kazu, throwing something at the airlock. "What about our cargo? Screw 'em! My orders are to get the Ajax off this planet. I'm heading back to the village."

"We can't. There's been an accident."

The commander's shoulders sagged abruptly. Then after the briefest delay, he spurted, "Who?"

"Weissman."

The story emerged as follows: at some stage in the last few weeks, the villagers had taken it upon themselves to go looking for rocket fuel. After so many months of being cooped up in their own base, they had been able to formulate a plan whilst evading contact with Houston and the Ajax crew. The plan centred around the supposed existence of permafrost in the desert.

Trapped within the rigid confines of the buggy, Kazu's anger lacked the physical space it required.

"How were they are going to do that?" he hissed.

"I'm not sure. Fire something hot down it, I guess."

"This is the water that's been hiding on Mars for eons? Just waiting for some jerk from the village to turn on the tap?"

But prospecting for water on Mars can be a hazardous business, as the Ajax crew had already discovered. One of the power tools in the village buggy had exploded inside the cockpit and Weissman had sustained a head injury.

"So he's *not* dead?" asked Kazu, unable to hide his disappointment.

"No," said David, "but he's barely conscious. Gotta Glasgow coma scale of 12, dipping down to 10."

Hewish was reviewing a series of images coming over from the second vehicle. In the background, anxious voices were describing the scene. The doctor began to summarise,

"It happened three days ago. He was out for a minute then he came round. They didn't call it in. After that he stayed lucid right up until this morning then he flaked out. Blood pressure's up. Slight asymmetry of pupils. They're a day away from us, that's if we drive flat out."

"We're *not* gonna drive there at any speed!"

"Even if we get there, we haven't the gear to save him with. We gotta re-group at the village." This time, it was the doctor's turn for piety. Raising his face to the overhead cameras, he asked this question: "You getting all this?"

They were, although it soon became clear that Weissman was unlikely to make it as far as the village. Kazu began to discuss the consequences of his death.

"Even with Bose out of the picture, it was always going to be a tight fit in the Ajax. If you check the numbers and then you take out one man, it makes for a precipitous saving in food and fuel. My home is a fighting ship. If we were still at sea, if we were still at sea and we saw ten men in the water, and we only had room in our boat for five, do you think I'd just leave them and all sail on by? And say sorry, I couldn't fit them all in? Do you understand what I'm saying?"

"Yeah, I understand what you're saying, but what I'm saying to you now is that we aren't at sea, this isn't a battle field and Weissman's still alive."

"And there's nothing you can do for him?"

"No. That's not true. We could drill his skull. There's a burr hole set in the village."

"Yeah, but he's not going to make it as far as the village. Even the brain surgeons in the States are telling us that. Look, look, tell me honestly. What did Weissman actually *do?* On this planet? Apart from strutting that guitar?"

By fantastic coincidence, the answer to this question was about to arrive in style.

"Boys, boys ... Like I told you in Texas, this is no ordinary mission."

It was the emeritus good guy Hutchings, wheeled out from some half-forgotten basement for one more lecture on the com. Though the distances were huge, the signal was good and the image was clear. Gunning for Weissman and their own survival, David Hewish omitted to pass comment on the old man's features. And yet the changes were there to see. Maybe it was fate, maybe it was the stress of the mounting strategic crisis in the Pacific, but these last few months had not been kind to Hutchings. His tweeds seemed stiffer and more bulky than when they had last met, his hair thinner. He was one of the very few constants in the organisation that both men would have recognised and his presence here alone gave weight to their orders.

"Weissman is your resident authority on the electrolysis kit. On top of that, we've had him browsing through the literature in that field, more or less as soon as you hit the planet. Sure, there are a lot of people on Mars who can turn their hand to anything, but the fact is, it's not going to be easy to jump in that pool and turn it into rocket fuel."

"So what do you want us to do?" whispered Kazu.

Tapping into the same logic, Hutchings replied as if in real time.

"We need to get David over to their vehicle. David's gonna have to board that thing and put some burr holes in this guy's head. Your patient isn't going to be easy to move, so they'll have to stay put whilst you drive over to them. The surgeons here are giving you two days."

"The instruments are in the village," said Kazu.

"The burr hole kit's in the village but we can get it out to you on a Gossamer wing. We've got Connolly getting that last remaining wing rigged up, even as we speak."

"*The Gossamer wing?*" gasped Kazu. "It doesn't have the range!"

"We think the canyon is just inside the range of the Gossamer wing ..." This time David actually laughed out loud. The anticipation was uncanny. "But if it isn't and if the wing comes down early, then your orders are to return to the village and offload your ice. The surviving wing offers some further potential for data acquisition but we're willing to sacrifice that potential on the off-chance that one life can be saved. That's the

218

deal. If the Gossamer wing fails, then Weissman fails with it. Just drive on by as soon as it hits the ground."

And Hutchings faded out.

CHAPTER FORTY

In its fabled past, Mars had been thoroughly drenched in liquid water. These days, the planet was practically bone dry and like most planetary scientists, Kelly O'Reilly had spent the best years of her life trying to figure out what had happened to all the water.

For some years, there had been speculation that a dense permafrost had survived in the sand at a modest depth, just waiting to be uncovered by mortal men. And if permafrost existed anywhere, then – Kelly reasoned – it ought to exist in the valley.

In pursuit of this dream, Kelly had led her crew far away from their pre-determined path and out onto the uncharted sands of Mars. And whilst many in the agency might see this as reckless, for others – and especially for those with insight into crew selection – it was highly predictable. Passivity in a time if crisis is an ignoble act. Being rescued by a couple of naval officers didn't fit into the game plan for the villagers and if they could discover an indigenous fuel source on their own initiative, they might just be able to convince the world that they had saved themselves.

Daybreak on a Red Planet.

The nuclear-powered buggy had been in the canyon for over an hour but Mars is a low-horizon body and many a surface explorer has found himself lost in the middle of some immense structure with only a few surrounding boulders and grit for company. In any case, this particular morning, visibility had been further impaired by something else.

Fog.

Early morning mist is a well-recognised feature of the Martian landscape, although this was a fresh experience for the Ajax crew. Kazu experimented with the headlights, only to groan deeply as the beam bounced back in their faces. It was time to stay put and wait for the air to clear.

Restless in the back, David Hewish took an interest in the overhead exercise beam whilst Kazu rested. Having nearly killed himself, he broke off to watch some dumb-assed Technicolor comedy where Frank Sinatra danced but didn't actually sing.

Two hours passed by. Black and white stills buzzed back home whilst their impotent leaders in Houston struggled to maintain the same degree of composure. Every minute that they sat here, an already large haematoma was swelling by osmosis and squeezing the life out of Weissman's brain. What's more, their ice was not being delivered whilst the launch window for the Von Braun was inching closer. Having declined the option of physical exercise, Kazu remained inanimate for this interval, squatting instead in the far corner of the buggy with neither eye contact nor verbal communication. David Hewish had seen this kind of behaviour on the constitution although the scale of this vehicle seemed to amplify their effect.

Finally, just when he was thinking of looking for the next in-flight movie, the mist cleared and the village buggy found shape in the west. The northern barrier of the canyon – itself some 6 kilometres high – was still out of range. In the opposite direction, the southern wall was clearly visible.

"Even if he comes round …" Kazu was helping the doctor into his suit. "Even if he comes round, it could be months before he's good for the job. What if he's not fit for the launch window? What are we gonna do then? Bury the little bastard with Bose?"

David was not impressed.

"We came here to save these people," he insisted. "We will save them."

"Yeah, you're always so keen to bring them home! Leave no man behind, huh? Where the hell did you hitch on to that idea?"

David Hewish hit the surface and bounded out onto virgin sand. Fifty metres short of the village buggy, he performed a brief survey of the site. Their drilling equipment had been assembled to his left and he could see two abandoned core samples by his feet. Seconds later, he found himself distracted by hands waving from the cockpit.

"The gossamer's on its way," they called, trying to sound positive.

"You got an ETA on that?"

"Erm, yeah – they launched at sunrise."

Switching his attention to the sky, Hewish checked his head-up display.

"That's five hours ago," he said.

"Connolly's on the joystick."

And for a moment, Kazu's voice flashed across the com.

"Another fucking PhD thesis in the making!"

David Hewish checked his oxygen. The gas cylinders in his backpack would be good for another four hours. His on-board fuel cell was solid and the soles of his feet – at this stage – were playing ball. All he needed now was a box of surgical instruments and then he could get on with some real cutting. If the wing came down hard, there would be no burr hole set in the village and none in the valley either. If the wing came down hard, he would walk away and know that Weisman would die. It would cause him pain but he could do it.

"Village com," he demanded, trying to find a link with his voice. The computers were on form and a string of messages leapt up in his face.

The Gossamer wing was approaching from the south.

CHAPTER FORTY-ONE

In the beginning, there had been three Gossamer wings in the village, two of which had already been launched. The first had been sacrificed in an effort to locate Major Smith. The second had been flown on a recent research mission to Mons Olympus and the third was being held in reserve for that dim and distant day when a clear set of mission objectives could be identified. When news of Weissman's injury came in, delivery of the medical package became that objective and wing number three was quickly bolted together.

They launched after sunrise, with 8 kilograms of life-saving equipment strapped beneath the engine. It wasn't much of an affair to look at, just a couple of guys in pressure suits, trying to hold down a winged flying machine in an ill-defined breeze. If there was a terrestrial analogue here, it was Kitty Hawk.

Sarah had set herself up in the forbidden zone where the view from the wing had filled the wall. Having served as pilot on the first two flights, it seemed reasonable that she should fly this one too.

"Hang on tight," she called to Tan, who was already hanging on to a reasonably large object. "This is going to be one hell of a ride!"

And it was! Their wing soared through 2000 metres in the first five minutes. Although launched into the wind, she quickly turned around and headed north, imaging their outpost in the process. It was a view that seemed to emphasise the fragility of their existence and the tiny patch of colour that was the greenhouse evoked a cold silence in the lab. Only when the wing flew past them and the village had faded did conversation return.

Several hours later, the Ajax crew were waiting in the valley.

"You should be able to see it from the south." This was Rachael Callaghan's voice, loud and unmistakable on the com. From her lip mike, David caught a short burst of Brahms.

He looked to his left.

"I'll stay out here 'til we have a visual," he said. Then, "I have a visual."

To the south and at an altitude of less than 300 metres, the Gossamer wing was coming around. In the first instance it flew directly towards the two buggies. Seconds later, it banked west, skirting just above their heads. It was a fantastic sight and David's body responded with an unexpected surge of adrenaline.

I'm standing in the middle of the biggest canyon in the known universe, waiting for an outsized butterfly to scrape down beneath my feet. Thank Christ for Weissman and his frigging brain.

Steering north again, the villagers became mute with the spectacle that awaited them. Mariner Valley is probably the most dramatic structure in the known universe and an opportunity of this kind would never be repeated. The scientific community was already lobbying for a hold on the landing and a complete circuit of the site, just for the additional data this might provide. But any machine can malfunction and there was a man down in the village buggy.

Sweeping around for a second pass, Connolly bled off altitude and touched down about 100 metres short of the vehicles. There was no dust. The surface here was solid rock and the portside wing crumpled – instantly – as it hit the ground.

The on-board cameras had survived the impact and within minutes, his audience in the village could actually see the colonel's feet, pottering around the wreckage, eager to retrieve his new toy.

Back with the village vehicle, David Hewish pushed that same set of toys into the airlock. Re-pressurised and de-suited in the cockpit he assessed the situation. Four people had set out in this machine and their cots and their kit and the ever-present toiletry smells were predictably awful. Flat out in the back, Weissman's head had been propped forwards by a bundled towel.

"Blood pressure's holding up really good," explained O'Reilly. "A while ago, I thought he was going to fade out on us. I've never really nursed a sick guy before. Have you nursed a really sick guy before?"

This was a dumber than average question and David chose not to answer it, crouching instead beside a patient that was on his way out. Weissman had blown a pupil. Rising blood pressure was actually a bad thing although again the doctor didn't tell them. Scalding himself for his indulgence by the Gossamer wing, David realised that Kazu had been right all along. If Weissman was about to meet his maker, it might have been more sensible to let him go.

Away from his patient, doctor examined the rest of the crew. The room was baking hot and what struck him hardest was the near total absence of clothing. Upright in one of the cots, Marnix Gabanna came across as anxious, unshaven and essentially naked, the jet-black margins of his crotch merely adding to the adult nature of this scene. For his part, Pablo Foguet had stripped down to his boxer shorts. The Spaniard – who was also sporting a full five days of stubble – had knelt beside Kelly who was herself draped in a similar outfit, combined with some kind of very basic bra.

David Hewish was grateful for the bra.

"We've made some progress in the valley," said Kelly.

Was she trying to excuse the accident?

"Like what?"

"Permafrost," blurted Foguet. "Permafrost at 18 metres."

David controlled his line of sight again. An obvious yellow stain was erupting from the front of Foguet's shorts.

"You were sent here to deliver ice!" he reminded them.

"Ice coming down from 2000 kilometres further north!"

David Hewish stood upright, his thoughts returning to the job in hand.

"Depressurise the airlock!" he ordered. "Do it! Fifteen minutes empty."

"What for?"

He stepped over to the hatch, ready to slam the thing in person.

"I'll drill him in the airlock. We should be able to get him flat in there."

"Why?"

His butt went down on the driver's seat, his face seeking refuge amidst both hands.

"Get the air out and the ... You gotta a drink or something?" They had. "Thanks ..." He swallowed. "And the low temperatures, the bacteria count will fall in the airlock." He gestured towards the cabin and pushed his head against the wall.

"Are you good, Colonel? Are you alright?"

The colonel nodded to Weissman. "Shave his head. Down to skin. Just the right side will do."

Foguet found himself a razor and bent over, revealing an extended natal cleft to David, who quickly felt the need to look elsewhere.

Why had they asked him that question? He glanced at his right hand. There was no discernible tremor. Could it be his face? His weight loss?

He looked around him some more. There was another surprise waiting for him in the corner.

"Whisky," volunteered Marnix, checking his reaction. "I think it's Scottish. We got in the European base first. It was eerie. There was a whole crate of whisky on the dinner table. Like the last guy to leave had left us this hand-written note. Must've been the boss man. I guess he figured there'd be another relief crew in six months. Not 15 years."

"I ... did you read it?"

"It's in German," said Kelly, meaning no.

Weissman's scalp had begun to glisten but his breathing was ever more laboured. It was time to get cracking. Hewish dragged him into the airlock and knelt down beside his head. The package from the Gossamer included local anaesthetic and he injected a couple of patches of exposed skin. As a token gesture to the bleeding, there was adrenaline in the local. Iodine prep, a single incision down onto bone and most of the eyes by the portal disappeared.

The burr was manual. In Taiwan, he'd used specialised power tools for this kind of thing but this was Mars and on Mars, a man had to make do with what he had. It took him five minutes. Bony shavings littered the floor like snow and his biceps began to ache. Suddenly, he was through to the inner plateau of the skull. Bone wax to smear against the oozing cancellous bone, then a stellate incision through the bulging dura.

In the end, it rushed out like diesel oil, as he rather suspected it would do. There was even a crazy kind of irony to this find. Just as Weissman had hoped to find fresh water beneath the sands of Mars, Hewish had found a liquefied haematoma beneath that same man's skull. Seconds later, he caught sight of something else. It was the organ that had persuaded Kazu to come out here in the first place and they weren't even sure it worked any more: it was Weissman's brain.

Resting in the cockpit, David spoke directly to O'Reilly.

"Did you clear this with Eliot?" The woman went blank. "Did you clear this shit with Tan?"

"No," she said, after some delay. "I acted on my own initiative. And it was worth it. We've got good data in the computers. Did you think men like Tan and Eliot were the only ones with any initiative?" The colonel had never thought any such thing. "Ever since the bastards nuked Taiwan, it's been the pits for women in this country! Well, let me tell ya, a woman thought of this one! *There is water in that sand!* And I've seen it!"

Giving up on her completely, David crawled back to his patient, where he performed the unenviable task of urinary catheterisation as another voice called out, unhelpfully, through an open hatch.

"Sometimes, Colonel, this is the price you have to pay."

Weissman survived. All in all, their diversion to Mariner Valley would cost them seven days in real time and a lot more than that when the patient's sick leave was factored in. It was true that Kelly had discovered permafrost in the valley but it was true also that the majority of the scientists on Earth remained sceptical as to its credibility as a fuel source. In any case, the woman had acted without authority, all but killing one of her own crewmates. Kazu was incensed and would probably have beaten her physically had he been able to get close enough. As far as rocket fuel was concerned, the Ajax crew had already filled a swimming pool and the mainstream opinion back on Earth was that rocket fuel on Mars was best gathered by the ice lake.

Regrouping at the original rendezvous point, the crews prepared to go their separate ways. First there was the matter of the trailers. The honour of exchanging trailer hooks fell to David Hewish and he soon disappeared into the airlock. Thirty metres away, his counterpart from the village buggy was doing much the same thing.

"Don't egress 'til you see the little bastard out there!" shouted Kazu, still venomous in the driver's seat. "Start dying slowly on the sand and you'll be out there on your own for the first 20 minutes."

The trailer exchange took 50. When David next removed his helmet, the Ajax buggy had been gripped by a familiar tremor.

Kazu was driving north.

CHAPTER FORTY-TWO

Over *400 tonnes* of liquid water. Mars hadn't seen anything like this since the last big thaw. The pool was positively brimming over and there was another 500 tonnes of ice round the back. It was time to cut in the electricity and start making rocket fuel.

The decision to power the village using photo-voltaics had been taken two decades ago. Its fundamental flaw was the difficulty in maintaining an electrical supply after dark. To this end, a small reservoir of liquid water was electrolysed on a daily basis, producing hydrogen and oxygen. When night fell, the two gases were reconstituted in a fuel cell system and in this way, power would continue 'til the dawn.

If the astronauts wanted to fly home, they would have to run the electrolysers around the clock. The explosive gases thus produced could then be liquefied and stored in the fuel dump prior to their transfer to the Von Braun. Nobody had raised the matter for a while, but if either the electrolyser or the liquefaction kit broke down then they would all starve to death.

What's more, their resident expert on electrolysis was bed-bound and out of action, his bizarrely shaven scalp a daily reminder of their predicament. Humanitarian issues aside, Weissman had been saved for the sake of his technical skills and in spite of this, their rocket fuel was nowhere in sight.

Enlisting an all-female team of orderlies, David slid Weissman's body into a magnetic scanner and performed an optimistic scan of his head. By the following morning, the image reports were bouncing back from Houston and doing little to improve their morale. Weissman would be out of action until well after the next launch window.

Someone else would have to take over his duties.

Having psyched himself up in Smith's office, Kazu stormed into the forbidden zone and ordered Tan and Eliot to pick up where Weissman left off. Foguet, who seemed to be part of the furniture down here, felt the need to answer back.

"For an immigrant," he sneered, "you're very American!"

"And for a refugee," barked Kazu, "you're an ungrateful bastard!" The base commander thrust one finger in the direction of the dynamic duo. "Just do it!" Then, "Pablo, give them the power."

Later that day and in a private conversation in the office, Kazu would confide in Hewish in biblical terms. "I am a soldier and I give an order and the order is not obeyed."

Which was not entirely true. The problem – as David saw it – was much more fundamental than that. The problem was that these were simply not the uniformed patriots that this particular naval aviator had been trained to lead and their tendency to obstruct and query their own orders was wearing the man down. Moving to leave, David looked back at Kazu with real anguish. This hunched, desperate figure seemed about as far removed from the officer he had met in Texas as a man could get.

For a few seconds he recalled the pilot's briefing room in the bowels of the Lexington, a modest 10 x 10-metre little theatre of their own where men in flight suits lined up to hear their orders. To the regular crew of the Lexington they were a breed apart, too special for them to even look upon. Just once, David had gotten in at the back, behind the curtains, peering long enough to see a man in white ascend the lectern and a hoard of followers rise to their feet in recognition. Kazu pleased them to be seated and David escaped unnoticed. That – David knew – was how Kazu liked it. Not a bunch of mavericks in their own little bunkers.

Escaping from the office, David Hewish tried hard to escape the same kind of introspection that was hammering his boss. It was dusk. In his time on this planet, David had never benefited from the warm darkness of a relationship. He was reluctant to turn to the limited supply of alcohol on site and the transient endorphin rush of exercise was losing its appeal. Wandering back to the dome, he sensed the vice-like grip of a decaying mood. It felt like an old friend, returning without invitation, uncertain as to how long he would stay. It was bad news and it might have gotten worse had it not been for the spectacle that awaited him there.

Marnix Gabanna and Kelly O'Reilly were doing press-ups by the sapling.

"Ignition!" Kelly's voice had never been shriller.

"All engines rolling!"

The unlikely looking double act was rehearsing their roles for the launch of the Von Braun. Blinded by their virtual reality specs, the astronauts completely failed to notice their guest. What's more, the rehearsal had an air of real spontaneity to it. Looking to his left, Hewish saw the draft copy of a new paper, blown up on the wall.

PERMAFROST LEVELS IN MARINER VALLEY:
THE OUTCOME OF A NEW SURVEY.
K O'Reilly, F Weissman ...

He scanned the provisional list of authors. Tan and Eliot were absent. Was that a deliberate slur?

"Three thousand metres!"

Pumping herself off the floor, O'Reilly showed no sign of flagging. Far from it, her upper body strength was actually improving. Inches to her left and pumping twice as fast, Marnix Gabanna was going through the motions.

"Roger that!"

Reluctant to laugh out loud, David climbed up onto the table and gazed out at the night. A bright green pilot light was flickering from the mast above the village and by this and by the light that spilled out through the dome itself, he could see the first row of dunes. Beyond that, there was only blackness. He felt the need to drive out there, to pass through this wasteland and on to the next settlement, to the next town. But there was no next settlement and there were no other towns. This tiny collection of Kevlar bubbles was the sole oasis of life on the planet and there was nowhere else to hide.

CHAPTER FORTY-THREE

Total rocket fuel volume was now an issue. Even allowing for the low temperatures on Mars, everybody knew that liquid hydrogen would boil off first. With this in mind, Sarah Connolly and Marnix Gabanna had busied themselves with the bulldozer and had buried the two storage tanks beneath a healthy head of sand. Insulation of this kind was going to make them all feel better and the mission planners foresaw a 20% reduction in evaporative losses. Sadly, the fuel tanks on board the Von Braun would lack this kind of protection and if the mission succeeded, they would quickly be exposed to direct sunlight. Millions of miles from the nearest planet, there would be no night shift and no sand dunes to hide behind.

What's more, the launch schedule was critically dependent on their ability to pump cryogenic fuel out of the storage tanks and over to the Von Braun. In order to avoid an explosion during transfer, Kazu had elected to pump the liquid oxygen and hydrogen on separate days. With this task completed, they would then come under pressure to launch the spacecraft before the hydrogen had time to evaporate.

By now, Hewish had been trapped underground for the best part of a month and was visibly pissed that Connolly and not himself had been asked to cover the tanks. How the hell did she get that job? Had she offered to seduce Kazu in the latrines? In his quarters or some other place? Who could say? From the outside, Kazu's relationship with Callaghan seemed kosher although it lacked the in-your-face blatancy of one of Gabanna's adventures. Consuming himself with another round of medical errands, Hewish was taken aback when Charlotte Erkhart approached him with a face as long as he felt and a hand against her gut.

Without any kind of verbal communication, the two of them acknowledged the potential seriousness of the situation. Charlotte looked down at her abdomen. It felt wrong.

"How?" he asked.

She couldn't say. It just felt wrong.

He lay her down, reverential, conscious of how she might be. His heart was racing and his concerns went beyond the fate of her unborn child. If the products of conception were gone, then Charlotte's seat on the Von Braun would be in jeopardy and a war would break out in the settlement as to who should take her seat. He glanced at her abdomen. This case was like a binary number, a one or a zero. If the foetus existed then they were all in business. If it was gone then the story was over. It's still unclear whether any of the medical interventions on offer can ever change the outcome in a threatened abortion. Reluctant to discuss her bleeding directly, David went looking for the ultrasound scanner in the medical room and found himself pausing by the exit to that room to check for onlookers. There were none. Back with Charlotte, he picked up on a pounding foetal heart. He tried not to sigh. Listening to the rhythm with her eyes closed, Charlotte failed to react.

"He's OK," he told her. "He's right there. Look."

She turned her head. Very slowly. Like she couldn't face the thing inside her and it took her some time to go for a mainstream smile.

And he smiled with her. The kind of smile that comes with a break of tension or the end of a battle. It was easy to smile with Charlotte. Charlotte had no pretensions and was undemanding. Not that there was a lot that anyone could really demand on Mars and maybe, David reasoned, maybe that was part of what Marnix had seen in her – apart from her more obvious attraction. Charlotte never made demands of your soul.

"You see," he said again. "He's alive and kicking. The first intrauterine explorer on Mars. Even Daniel Tan can't put in a claim on that one."

Her smile broke – just as abruptly as it had arrived and she said, "Think how much easier it would have been for you if he were dead."

"Well, he's not dead." David searched for the message in this one and failed. "And he's not going to die."

He was afraid, perhaps, that she might lead into a conversation about families. She didn't and he felt better for it. Growing up as an orphan wasn't his favourite party piece and after a brief hiatus, Charlotte sat up on the couch and agreed to return to her quarters.

"Why don't you come with me?" she asked, standing by the door, one hand on her yet to be distended abdomen. Was this why she had come here? "What if he gets sick on the way home?"

"On the Von Braun?"

She nodded.

"Who'll care for him then?"

"I can't," he reminded her. "My orders are to stay in the base."

"We never had a medic since Smith died. Nobody stopped breathing. Why don't you tell 'em you gotta stay *with him*?" She was talking about her unborn child.

"What about Fred?" she went on. "He could get sick again."

"Weissman's out of the woods."

"There's no one medical on –"

"I'm not leaving!" he said, very deliberately. "Not until the last man –"

"If you come …" Charlotte was trying say something else, "… it won't crash."

"What won't –"

"The Von Braun. If you're on it, we won't die."

Suddenly, he felt the need to embrace her, and whisper in one ear.

"Anyone can die, Charlotte." They had signed up for a high risk mission.

"No," she breathed. "You will survive."

She left. Still with child. Still many months from term. David shuddered to think what would happen if she went into labour in zero gravity. Trying to block this one out, he ended his day in Weissman's room, sitting down beside their resident trauma case, trying to decide how he felt. He felt better. His urine had been clear for days. The headaches were gone and Fred was able to answer a string of simple questions with nothing but a trademark stutter to slow him down. Even his hair was making a comeback.

He asked for the urinary catheter to be removed and after a few seconds of hesitation, David agreed, deflating the balloon with a syringe and sliding a smooth, 20-inch Silastic tube back into daylight with his other hand. There were no obvious signs of infection. The catheter was good and the doctor made a mental note to clean it out later and hold in reserve for later use. If Weissman failed to pass urine normally, the damned thing might be back in his bladder by the morning anyway.

He checked Weissman's face. His neck was arched and his eyes screwed up but in a second he seemed to exhale and return to the world. Seeing Weissman as a man emerging from confusion, David told him some cock and bull story about Kelly and how gutted she'd been for taking him over to the valley in the first place.

"You don't have to t-talk shit about Kelly," Weissman protested.

"She nearly took your life."

"Sometimes," Weissman told him, "sometimes Colonel, that's what it takes."

And then Weissman started to ramble about something else. About Jerusalem and the aesthetics of a society now lost to the world. At first sight, there was nothing odd in this. He had a head injury and in David's experience it was common for New Americans to romanticise their dead countries.

"I had family there," Weissman continued. "More than family, f–" He seemed to find this word harder to say. "F-friends. It's not easy to love one country and know that it's dead and your other country's still living. I'd already lived in the States. I already lived in both worlds. It wasn't so tough …" His mind drifted further and Weissman offered a vision of a mythic afterlife that the doctor would have been better off without.

"There are people there."

"People where?"

"People there waiting for us. People we used to know."

Standing to leave, David slung the catheter to the wall and let out this explicative: "Bullshit!" wishing, before he had even opened his mouth, *There is no such place.*

"I guess that one doesn't work for you?" said Weissman. "Does it?"

It did not.

239

CHAPTER FORTY-FOUR

At last, the Von Braun was ready for blast-off.

As had once been the tradition at the Cape, the flight crew dined on fresh orange juice, grilled steak and scrambled egg. It was a low residue diet that would minimise their need to defecate as they entered zero g. The steak came out of a can although by sheer chance, their departure from the planet had coincided with the arrival of fresh eggs in the settlement. Had it not been for the gravity of the moment, the fact that there were fresh eggs on Mars at all would have created a sensation.

NASA had requested that the pre-launch breakfast should be televised for the benefit of the North American networks. Not every astronaut is a natural on television, but Marnix was. Having spent the first part of the morning laughing and waving to the hidden lenses in the walls, he decided to tear off his T-shirt in the middle of his eggs. Little, if any, of the fuel in the Von Braun had been shovelled by the older scientists and it would have been unfair to restrain him now.

"If you were out there," he asked David, sliding one arm around each of the women beside him, "if you were out there, in the Von Braun, with both of these lovely ladies, which one would you want to have first?"

Marnix wasn't the only man on the planet to have asked himself this question although he was the only one to have actually voiced it over breakfast. Chipping in from the sidelines, the Ajax crew mentioned something about the agony of choice and the smiles and the streaming hair that followed would later delight the terrestrial press corps.

For the veterans in Mission Control, kind of play-acting was all too predictable. This was gallows humour and it was sufficiently commonplace in modern America to have become boring. Hunched by the dining table, David saw it a different way. What they were looking at here was simply normal behaviour for Marnix. There was nothing underhand or sinister about this guy and in a way that's what he liked about Marnix. In a wave of inner sadness, David reflected on just how few people there had been in his life he had ever been able to indulge with such little worry, with so little concern that they might turn on him suddenly and try to slit his throat. Kazu? Probably. Smith? Yes. But Smith was part of a different era and David was trying his damndest to forget Smith.

And how might this day end for David? Was there any sort of outcome that they were not prepared for? A launch scrub? A disaster on the pad? Success for the Von Braun followed by a lingering death in the village? Would he be able to put a bullet through his own head when he had to? Yes. He could do anything. If the Americans should ask him to write his own epitaph then he would write this: *he had become invulnerable.* He had become invulnerable and he would draw strength from that fact. Because there was no one or nothing could hurt him again. People would try – he accepted that – but they would fail. David had been tested in the very darkest of places and he had not – could not – break.

The party broke up. Most of them retreated to their quarters. Only Charlotte Erkhart remained at the table, prominent in a welcome smile and a deep blue skirt that ended above her knees.

"There's still time to change your mind." Charlotte had gotten his attention. "If you were on this flight … we'd make it back." He must have looked surprised. "Everybody knows that."

"Why?"

"Why do you think that ice lake missed you?"

"It didn't. I nearly died. Kazu dug me –"

"They didn't even kill you in Taiwan. A frigging H bomb! A frigging H bomb and it didn't –"

"The shrapnel got me first."

"And before that? That ship in the Pacific. The Serpentine! Do you think that was chance? You're not gonna die on this mission, Colonel. Believe me. *You're a survivor.*"

He said something about luck and time and began to feel superfluous as the flight crew assembled beneath the dome, progressed to the airlock and bid their farewells. David, who sometimes shared Nobohito's snobbery towards the women on board, reluctantly acknowledged that women were actually much better than the men at this process. Even a Latin figure like Foguet could only manage a firm handshake and the persisting embrace of Erkhart on Connolly was a drama that would stay with him for life.

One step short of the inner hatch, Tom Eliot moved to block their exit and deliver a farewell speech. His actions had an improvised feel to them, but his speech was well structured and it seemed reasonable to suppose he had prepared it in advance. Tom remembered Smith by name and offered a belated eulogy for Bose. And then, Tom's closest colleague, Daniel Tan, produced a lovingly gift-wrapped package and handed it over to Tom so that he in turn could wave the thing in the air and pass it on to Kelly.

Tom Eliot's son was on the Lexington and Tom was under no illusions as to the risks that his son was taking. But the men and women in Viking Village were involved in a battle of their own. The difference here was the cause they fought for. Just as Josh fought for a strategic cause, the villagers fought for scientific knowledge and progress. Even in these desperate times, Eliot argued, such work retained its value. He offered a generous smile to Kelly O'Reilly and then Kelly opened the package and produced the glass cylinder that contained the remnants of the core sample that David had recovered from the ice lake. David himself had never regarded it as being particularly important and yet its presence here today brought a strange hush to the proceedings.

The central thrust of Eliot's speech had achieved a real resonance in David's brain. At the academy, he had dreamt of making some wild discovery in outer space. Having gotten this far in person, he accepted that that dream was over. No matter how hard he worked, the joy of instant discovery would never be his. If there was a riddle in these sands then it was Daniel Tan who would solve it, struggling as he was to decipher the soil samples and every other scrap of data he could dredge from the surface of this planet.

The talking was over. The crew of four packed themselves into the buggy and were chauffeured by their only doctor along the well-worn tracks that led out from the village and down to their sturdy rocket ship. It was a predictable line-up. Kelly could command, Marnix could fly, Charlotte was pregnant and Fredrick Weissman could walk in spite of everything.

Inside the Von Braun, their seats were clean and ready for them. David followed the crew inside and waited to strap them down. Securing an astronaut for blast-off was a crude step on a complex journey. And as he checked, and as he nodded to each living, breathing creature in turn, he began to feel something else. A deep foreboding, a sixth sense that had walked with him on other days and that seemed to scream of death. Every seat on this ship had the feel of a coffin and David had been sent here to nail them in.

Kelly was checking her monitors. Charlotte had barely spoken since they entered the airlock. Someone said something to David about shutting the door on his way out. Over on the flight deck, Marnix Gabanna told him that a woman could never be truly beautiful unless she had height, style and legs in proportion that she knew how to walk on. It didn't even sound like goodbye. It sounded like the same conversation he'd been having with David since the day they first met on the ice.

Having returned to the village, the colonel entered via that same airlock that he had first encountered with Kazu. On that occasion, he had felt the need to break in quickly. Today, things were different. Today, he took time to kick his feet and unclamped his helmet, running a damp cloth around his boots and resting them gently beside the bulky suit. Too long a delay might have drawn attention to his mental crisis but too brisk an entrance would only lengthen his ordeal.

On the floor, beside a row of narrow lockers, he saw a loosely folded skirt. It had once belonged to Charlotte. Charlotte had been permitted to bring so few clothes to Mars that she had chosen to wear this one item again and again. Stripped from her body, it had lost all shape and the fabric over her butt was noticeably discoloured. Charlotte had been the only woman in the base to have ever worn a skirt and though he had failed to react at the time, this return of the conventional had meant something very real to him. Like the distilled water. Like the vivid projections of American panoramas, Charlotte had made his existence on this planet all the more bearable. Now she was gone. Most likely, to the same fate to which he had just delivered Marnix Gabanna. The colonel's eyes dewed up. He felt an irrational impulse to dash back to the spacecraft and untie her, to cradle this woman in his arms. Why had she chosen to leave this thing behind? Why –

"We'll do better without her!"

It was Daniel Tan, sitting directly opposite him and watching his every move. This was the last man David Hewish wanted to meet at the end of this corridor and his irritation was clear.

"*Smith,*" said Tan, like he found it hard to say. "Smith is responsible for all this shit. Yeah, he's dead an' all but it was Smith that set the ball rolling! Shacking up with that gardener, so the rest of us had to lie there and hear her squealing in the dark. Letting this girl …" He nodded towards the open locker. "Letting Charlotte wander round in that fluorescent blue. How do you think Pablo felt about that? Being forced to watch his own wife pushing it in some other guy's face whilst he tried to chew his oats. Now she's pregnant with another man's child. I stopped going up there …" Tan waved one hand at the ceiling, as he might have done below decks. "… what? Like months ago. Best to stay with my work! And don't come at me with your sneering and your faith in the atavistic! We're just human down there. Can't you see that? Look at me! You can't run the village like a prom night! It's too small. We're too old. We've all bled too much." He shook his head with genuine contempt. "A boss man has to rule by example, not self-indulgence! Look at the mess we're in now! Half his crew locked up in some bucket of bolts that they built to run on methane! Fifteen minutes 'til we find out if it works!"

Daniel Tan's plea was uninvited and it wasn't at all clear what he expected to gain from it. With blast-off so very close, David led the scientist back along the corridor, towards a dome that had become Mission Control Mars. Over by the wall, the remnants of their crew were lining up to watch.

Ninety seconds to go. Kazu pressed the com link onto mute.

"The Ajax is a better ship," he informed them.

This line did not go down well with the senior scientist in the settlement.

"Then why the hell are we flying this one?" he grumbled.

"The Von Braun's been out there for over a year. If she blows, that doesn't mean we won't make it." Kazu was offering them reassurance in the face of imminent disaster and in the process, he was scaring them shitless.

The clock ticked on. Barely visible in the projection beside the sapling, the engines on the Von Braun were chomping at the bit. For everyone in the village, this was to be a life-affirming moment but for the Ajax crew, this day was particularly poignant. If they could send these people back to Earth and nothing else, then their mission to Mars would be deemed a triumph.

Zero!

Leaping up in the low Martian gravity, the Von Braun rose briskly through a pink and cloudless sky. Silent and with no discernible flame, she gained momentum at a fantastic pace.

Like God and Robert Heinlein intended.

Liquid hydrogen never makes for a particularly bright exhaust flame, although on this planet, it did offer an additional bonus. A fine trail of water vapour had crystallized in her wake and she seemed to draw a line in the sky.

"That's our ice!" called the colonel, his voice lost in the mayhem.

Lest the planet felt cheated of its long-held water, most of what they had gathered by the ice lake was falling back to the surface. On this day, and for the first time in a hundred million years, it would rain on Mars.

Twenty minutes into the flight, the spacecraft shut down her engines and discarded her external fuel tanks. Her present trajectory would see her home in seven months. If she could re-ignite her engines in the near future, that figure might fall to four.

People ran in and out of the dome. Someone handed out hot chocolate. Cameras onboard the Von Braun had captured a bird's eye view of the ascent and they watched enthralled as a dazzling video sequence played out again and again on the screen. Maybe someday soon they would follow the Von Braun back to Earth.

The Ajax crew had already flown a spaceship to Mars in almost half the normal transit time. Today, they had gone a step further. Today they had launched a return mission using an indigenous fuel source.

The limits of the possible had been redefined.

That same night, the remaining villagers assembled by the pool and prepared to celebrate. The music was already playing. Imitation Viking helmets were thick on the ground. Having been plundered for rocket fuel, the pool was barely packing 13 inches of water but in this gravity, 13 would be enough to break their fall. As far as solid food went, the dynamic duo had set up a barbecue in the corner. The first chunk of meat went in the pan and everyone heard it sizzle. In David's mind he might have been back in Oz, but there was something else going on here, something very strange.

This meat was fresh.

"Tom? Where in the hell did you get that from?" Kazu queried. "You got some kinda buffalo round there in the lab?"

"At home on my very own ranch, Commander."

David munched on his burger and smiled politely, not realising that there was more to come. A large vat of fluid had been wheeled over from the forbidden zone and in an affected gesture of excellence, Eliot sliced away another sheet of tissue ready for his acting assistant, Foguet, to fry.

Looking up from the pan, Pablo Foguet spoke to the Ajax crew in hushed tones,

"*This ...*" he waved one hand towards the pool, nodding his head firmly in the process. "This is brilliance ... This is real courage ..."

But David wasn't listening. His mind had latched onto the meat and its extremely odd behaviour. Dinner, he saw, was a lot more than fresh. It was *still alive*. Slowly, very, very slowly, something white was crawling out of the vat.

"It tastes like chicken," said David. So, the mad professor had been able to synthesise poultry on Mars. Big deal.

"It *is* chicken."

If it hadn't been for the chewing, the doctor's jaw might well have dropped.

"Muscle tissue from the chicks," Eliot told him. "Cultured in our vats. One giant rhabdomyosarcoma, with a few extras for taste. No need for battery farming. No need to even slaughter a Russian novelist. And why should we? All we ever wanted from them was the meat?"

"It's sick!" gasped David.

"My dear colonel," beamed the scientist, perhaps a little churlish, "you've never been truly hungry. This is the answer to every vegetarian's dilemma. Should I eat the stuff, knowing that they've shot some hapless creature? Or should I sit here and be anti-social? Well, worry no longer."

"I never did," said David, who was finding it hard to swallow. "I'm a committed omnivore."

Meanwhile, the music was getting louder and spirits were on the up. If they could do all this, if they could grow their own food and harvest ice from an ancient lake, maybe – just maybe – they could do *anything*.

The music skidded, suddenly rebooting with a slower, sweeter rhythm: Glenn Miller *"In the mood!"* a great track for a small community in a state of triumph. Poised on the edge of elation, Kazu leant forward as Daniel Tan caught his ear.

"Fantastic, Commander Kazu. I didn't – I didn't think you could do it."

"Well, we will," said Kazu, pointing to the pool. "This stuff is gonna unlock the whole universe. For the price of keeping 12 people alive on this planet, NASA can keep 1200. Not just a village, maybe even a town and then a city. Think about that!"

It was a conversation that would have lasted longer had it not been for their latest distraction. Whisky! Whisky that was actually old enough to have been distilled in Scotland, salvaged from a dead European base and concealed again by a thoughtful Marnix Gabanna. In times gone by, NASA had actually banned this kind of stuff from space missions but those days were gone and in any case – this was Mars! Lest the surviving villagers were able to finish it all too early, Sarah Connolly produced a barrel of Weissman's very own moonshine, brewed beside her poultry in a modified plastic bucket.

David Hewish took a sip of the stuff in person and let the music take him. The fear in the airlock was behind them now and restraint was a thing of the past. His world was spinning but his world was like that and he'd been trained to stay calm in a stressful situation. Whatever, he would feel no pain. The first avalanche had missed him and so would the next. Moonshine would not weary him. He was a rocket ship, he was a satellite, he was out of control. He was in-des-truck-ing fruct-a-ble and there was nothing and no one and nothing that could take him down.

He could out-dance Sinatra and if he'd felt the need, he could have fired up the Ajax with the stroke of one hand. On Earth – he knew – they would try to portray him as a hero and he would hate them for it. He would spurn media attention and refuse public accolades. He would do battle with the Chinese People's Army and wipe them out single-handedly, armed only with his father's light sabre. He would hunt down that quality broad from the jet copter and caress her butt gently through the course of a long weekend in Seattle.

And then, before they even realised she was gone, Doctor Sarah Connolly dashed back to their world. The woman had covered herself up with a wet T-shirt and a desperate shroud of pain. Nobody heard her scream, but she hollered some more and soon they were all listening, cutting out the music, just in time for the headline news.

"THE LEXINGTON HAS BEEN SUNK!"

PART FOUR
NEMESIS

CHAPTER FORTY-FIVE

There were few details. Initial reports suggested that the disaster had occurred within Chinese air space making a large-scale recovery operation impossible.

Nearly 3000 men had been lost at sea.

The sinking had an immediate impact on the village and their feelings were not entirely noble. For one thing, their own predicament had been placed in a new perspective. With this kind of trouble in the Pacific, what sort of emphasis would Washington place on Mars?

Even the name Lexington carried the inescapable connotations of midway. In tandem with this came the sickening realisation that a major power might have surpassed the United States in both its tenacity and its technical expertise.

For the Ajax crew, this was a particularly bitter blow. China had already savaged their nations and they loathed her for it. Half of Kazu's family would spend this day under martial law in Tokyo and there was nothing the Americans could do to stop it. If those people had ever dreamt of a moment of liberation then that dream must have seemed as far away today as it had ever done. But for the colonel, the past was even more brutal. Homeless and orphaned at the age of 12, he had fled to the United States on a cargo ship. It had been his father's fate to stay and fight and it was not without coincidence that as a young naval officer, David Hewish had repeatedly volunteered for the struggle against China.

The party was over. Dispersing to their individual bolt holes, the villagers fell silent and hoped to hell it wasn't true. David got as far as his own quarters and quickly found comfort in his tangled bed sheets.

The Lexington was dead, swallowed up by a vast and awesome sea. Of all the ships he had ever sailed in, this one had meant the most to him. The Lexington had been more than an instrument of war. She had been the stage upon which the greatest dramas of his life had been played out and she had sailed on that same ocean that lay between his nations. She had been a kinder, gentler lover than that bitch of a publicist in Washington could ever be. Now she was gone.

A deep wave of malaise swept through his soul and he curled up in his cot to fight it. Five hours passed by. He supped on clear fluids and felt better. Creaking up off the sheets, David went looking for Nobohito Kazu and found him in the only place he could have been: alone in Major Smith's quarters, open-mouthed, foetal, without tears.

The colonel slid to the floor, his shoulders propped up against the Kevlar, the palm of one hand slapped loosely across his brow.

"I should have been there," said Kazu.

It took his visitor several minutes to respond.

"What could you have done? What could one more naval aviator have done?"

"Been there."

The Ajax had been a ship manned by converts. Perhaps because of that, her crew had been willing to take risks that the likes of Antonio Chabod would not countenance. Now, they had a new vision in their minds. Now, they could see a vast fortress in the sea, slipping beneath the waves, more 3000 of their shipmates trapped below decks. Prior to this disaster, Kazu and Hewish had lived with the conviction that they had nothing to lose. Today, they were bereaved.

Suddenly, David leapt up from the floor.

"Eliot!" he exclaimed.

He ran down the corridor, checking each room in turn, eventually finding Eliot in his underground lair. Tom Eliot was searching for details on the sinking and although he had access to the civilian net, his search had been hampered by propaganda and the sheer distances involved. Tan, who had no history of military service in his family, was docile beside the mass spectrometer. Picking up on his oriental features, David resisted the temptation to open fire.

"Can they swim?"

David stopped in his tracks. It was a sad reflection on his own mindset that he had yet to consider this possibility. Ships can be rebuilt and a large number of men might yet have survived.

"Yes!" he said, his relief undisguised. "The Lexington's covered in life rafts. You just punch a button and the whole damned thing jumps out. And there are jet copters on the deck. If we had other vessels nearby … if she went down in a breeze …"

Such optimism was ill received.

"Don't give me any of that shit!" screamed Eliot, getting up from the screen. "He's down in the fucking engine room! It's below the water level!"

"Not necessarily." David was clutching at straws. "What if it wasn't his shift?"

Eliot broke free from his corner, racing down the space between desk and spectrometer and eventually ending up in a pile in the colonel's arms, the wildest of hair crushing up against his cheeks. Hearing the commotion, a fourth villager was making an appearance in the doorway and it might have been Callaghan but by this stage, David didn't care.

"He's the only one I've got!"

CHAPTER FORTY-SIX

In the morning, David found himself alone by the breakfast table with only Sarah Connolly showing up to meet him.

"Did you hear that, Colonel?" asked the woman, slurping her coffee and sneering very slightly, as if the entire fucking war was David's fault. Over in a corner, one of the sanitation droids was shutting down. It was 5 a.m. and like the irate blonde before him, David had found it difficult to sleep. Chewing slowly on his muesli, he did his best to ignore her.

"He's the only one I've got!"

He swallowed.

"Yeah, I heard that."

"I've got a pair of them," said the woman, as if David ought to feel bad about this too. "I've got two sons and if one of 'em goes down I'll be holding the second one in reserve. Not that they will go down. Neither of them were dumb enough to join the navy!" The officer remained silent. "But Eliot's got nothing else!" she went on. "Eliot's wife? Dead for five years. His laboratory back on Earth? Given over to some dick with a passion for fossils. Did you know that?"

"Yeah, I knew –"

Movement by the office. Rachael Callaghan was escaping his bed, as David knew she would, wrapped in a body warmer and not a lot of anything else. Stealing his attention even in grief, Rachael trotted along the corridor and over to her room.

And for all the pain of this moment, David tried to gain perspective on this woman's brain. What the hell was keeping her going? All the fun of the farm and the bedding rights to the toughest man on Mars? Daniel Tan treated her like dirt, although he almost certainly wanted to nail her too. The other women, David realised, chose to shun her.

Raw and unshaven, the base commander soon staggered through the same door, consciously evading his audience. Straight after breakfast, he was back in the office, talking to Houston on a secure link. By the time he returned, the rest of the crew was waiting in the dining room and in a polite and matter-of-fact way, Kazu proposed *another* expedition to the ice lake.

"Yesterday," he told them, "we demonstrated the feasibility of refuelling on Mars. We did that using the Von Braun. Next, we need to find fuel for the Ajax."

The disaster in the Pacific was not mentioned. Instead, the discussion centred entirely on Mars. Logistically, this was to be the most daring journey to date. Kazu and Hewish would perform three successive runs to the north, each exchanging a cargo of ice with the second vehicle at the halfway point.

"Can we rely on you to back us up in the village buggy?"

With O'Reilly between worlds, it fell to Pablo Foguet to reply.

"We already looked at this." This was a bad news. Kazu was looking for a pledge of obedience – not a lecture. "We're hoping to get some soil samples –"

If the villagers had had any doubts as to the temper on Kazu, his next statement would erase them.

"This is a life and death struggle on an alien planet!" he shouted, "I expect to see that vehicle in position."

Six feet across the table, Pablo Foguet remained implacable.

"We will be, sir, but there's time to do our work along the way."

Then, unexpectedly, Tom Eliot came out in support of a colleague. "Pablo's got a point, Nobo! What the hell is the point in us sitting here, waiting for you? If we're not otherwise engaged, we might as well do the things we came here to do. And if we've all bought it by main engine cut-off, then at least we can say there was a purpose to our lives."

"Last time you tried this kind of shit, you nearly killed Weissman!" This was Hewish, realigning himself with his shipmate.

"Americans are infantile!" spat Foguet.

"Well at least we still exist!" said Kazu. "What future did you give *your* children?"

And the room hushed as every astronaut reflected on the great issues of this day: lost children, lives without purpose and the call of the wild.

CHAPTER FORTY-SEVEN

The buggy trundled north towards the ice lake.

"You can't herd cats." Colonel Hewish was preaching from the back. "These people came here to make some kind of contribution to mankind's knowledge. Let them find a little dirt."

"They've got their dirt! They've got more dirt than we know what to do with! What if they have a mechanical malfunction? It could happen! There's a limited life expectancy on this hardware!"

The Ajax crew were 27 days out from the village. Twice now they had shuttled between the rendezvous point and the ice lake. So far, Foguet's people had exchanged trailers on schedule and without delay. Everyone was upbeat except the naval officers. Not for them the luxury of space or community or indoor volleyball. Acting on orders from a distant command post, they had become inmates in a cell of their own creation.

Many times in this mission, Hewish had envisaged a mass of attentive faces in Houston, poring over their every waking move. This was a fantasy. Most of the time, the Mars office was undermanned. The majority of the images returning from Mars were neglected in Houston with the sheer scale of the throughput being impossible to review. In the last few days, that situation had changed. Events in the Ajax buggy had become compulsive viewing and conditions in the vehicle were starting to make their mentors gape.

With the ice in tow, the buggy was crawling southwards at a pitiful pace. Other than the day-night cycle of the planet, their days lacked any kind of structure and around sunset, Kazu had taken to speaking to Callaghan on the voice link. Initially, they conversed on a private channel, later on the com. The transition to open mike passed without fanfare and for a while, David Hewish became troubled by this change. What was the boss thinking? Had he stopped caring? Had he deemed himself beyond judgement? In any case, his voice was impossible to ignore and from the beginning, David had heard most of what he said.

The mission commander was anything but a poet but there was a warmth and humanity to his feelings that had been sorely absent from their outbound flight. And in spite of everything, David began to see a kind of virtue in their love. He began dreaming on their behalf of a different future. He dreamt that one day soon, he might visit this offbeat couple in some idyllic town. Somewhere south. Somewhere rural. Somewhere that would free them from all the pain and the filth that would surely blight the future.

Part of the life support let them down and it had to be the toilet. Sloping out became an integral part of their job plan. Houston advised them to chew on something new and secret that had been tucked away in the medical kit and was meant to block out the olfactory nerve but it only made them want to puke some more and in the end they decided to do without it.

Neither man had showered in a month.

Closing in for the final leg of their outbound journey, Hewish began to feel it in his gut. A few minutes later, a new round of stomach cramps saw him creasing up beside his cot, a strategically placed bucket tight between his thighs.

"It's all shit," he told Kazu. "I never once threw up on the Lex!"

Five hours short of the ice lake, it struck him again, this time much more severely: desperate, steady retching. It wouldn't stop. The volume of fluid spewing out through his lips began to fall. There had to come a time, he reasoned, when there was nothing left in his innards for him to lose and he thought it would stop then. He was wrong. His upper GI was in the hands of a psychopath and the bastard wouldn't let him go. Exhausted, practically choking on the stuff, David escaped to the floor of the buggy and began to squirm there steadily whilst Nobohito Kazu drove on, saying nothing 'til the engine cut out and their cockpit became gripped by a familiar haze.

"Is it the Pacific?"

"No." Kazu was going through the medical kit. "You gotta get up. I can't do it on my own."

"It wasn't supposed to be us …" This whimper must have sounded pathetic. "It was supposed to be like 50 or more men. A dozen or so just for the ice …"

David Hewish felt a cold and alcoholic swab on his shoulder. Seconds later, a brief stab in the deltoid. "Ondansetron," said Kazu, who couldn't really say this word. "You've got 20 minutes."

It had to be done and there was no one else to do it. Tan's mythical crew of 50 did not exist. Suited up in the airlock, Hewish followed Kazu out of the buggy and on to the freezing waste. The debris from the avalanche was all around them and they swept the stuff up in silence.

It took 12 hours. Halfway through the proceedings Kazu became concerned about one of the tyres on the rear-most trailer. Trying not to gag, Hewish bounded over to take a look.

In the course of this mission, the Ajax crew had asked their machinery to perform miracles. To date, this particular machine had yet to disappoint. Whilst the absence of liquid water had saved them from such earthly concerns as corrosion, the exploding mileage had finally taken its toll. The reactor was still solid but some of the tyres were starting to show their age. Hewish had noticed this before and in the cold blue light of the ice lake, he saw it again as if for the first time.

"What do you think?" Kazu was down on the floor, inspecting the underbelly of the rear-most trailer. In a matter of seconds, the cold was going to make it to his knee. He had to be nuts. "The axle's bad. We're gonna end up trying to fix the thing halfway to Borelius."

Pensive in the sidelines, David Hewish retracted his hands from his gloves and clenched both fists in the sleeves. "She'll hold together," he said. There was no attempt at eye contact. "Think about it. She's come this far."

"I know ..." said Kazu, his face hidden, his voice clear on the com. "That's what worries me."

Kazu circled again, this time checking the starboard tyres. He began to think out loud, confident that his message would be received and understood.

"Do the boys back in Houston have anything to say about this? I expect you to actually come up with something real. Not some worthless shit."

Night fell by the ice lake and David took some solid food in the rear of the cockpit. Conscious of his physical condition, Kazu pushed the air pressure towards sea level and they supped together on steaming tea.

"It's good," mumbled the doctor, his view fixed squarely on the lip of his mug. The water temperature had reached 100°. This was the warmest drink they would ever share on Mars.

Reaching down for one of David's paperbacks, Nobohito Kazu toyed with its tattered leaves.

"I never saw you read my stuff before."

It was Plato.

"Socrates is such an asshole," said Kazu, as if in passing. "He should have broken out. Gotten himself a knife, taken the bastards down one by one."

There was a case for spending the night by the ice lake but for reasons that neither man could express, they were unable to relax in its presence. Departing by floodlight, Kazu built her up to 6 klicks. They were heading home and they should have felt better. Then, without warning, the doctor went down again from the gut.

Two days passed by.

His diarrhoea waxed and waned with the racing moons of Mars. The bizarre thought passed through his mind that Nobohito Kazu might actually shoot him although this one never materialised. Kazu took amphetamines and stayed at the wheel. The axle on the rearmost trailer showed gradual deterioration and the spectacle of impending disaster began to seize them both.

CHAPTER FORTY-EIGHT

Bent double beside a filthy washbasin, David Hewish groaned deeply with the morning Sun. It was 6 a.m., and the pains in his gut were beginning to fade.

"We'll be on the flat soon," he said. "She'll make 10 klicks on the flat." And with one hand sliding towards his belly, he added, "How far are we from the village buggy?"

"Four hundred and nine."

Unshaven and dishevelled, the doctor surveyed the cockpit. There were mess tins everywhere. An untouched back-up suit had been hung to the rear and was swinging, like a headless torso from the door of the latrine.

"We've really let the place go," he said.

"Look!" Kazu's interjection was abrupt and abrasive. "Look, Colonel, I think we've got to make a decision here. The axle's bust! That wheel is failing! Where are we going?"

"OK." David was comfortable on the floor again. "OK, let's ... ditch the second trailer."

Over in the driver's seat, Kazu had grabbed a flask of lemonade. "No." He took a swig from the flask. "We've got to fix it."

"We ought to check in first." David was playing for time. "What about the village?"

"The village doesn't have a clue. If the village had a clue, they'd never have got us into this mess in the first place!"

"But then … then we'd never have come to Mars."

"I know." Kazu slid one leg into his grimy suit and his junior reached out to stop him, one more time.

"I've let you down," he whispered.

"You've never me down," said Kazu, cranking open the inner hatch. "You don't know how to."

Kazu was silent in a closed airlock and David Hewish was sick. Watching on the monitors, Hewish began to cough. "God!" he spluttered. "*God, help me!*"

And from where he was now, there seemed to be something inevitable about this whole affair. An infernal momentum that had become more blatant as the mission wore on and from which there was no escape. He thought of the jet copter flying out of DC. He remembered Antonio Chabod, and the fear and loathing in that scream: "*It's fucking madness.*" Curiously, David had grown to hate that man. David had agreed to this mission for one reason and one reason only: *because it was impossible.* Because no matter how awful he felt today, this pain was as nothing to the pain of staying behind, of enduring life with the knowledge that some other man had gone and that he had not.

Twenty minutes passed by. He wrapped another tourniquet around his forearm, pumped up his veins and tried to slide an intravenous drip into the back of his left hand. He missed. He pulled it out and a purple stream of blood began to flow across his fingers and he tried and failed another three times, until the cannula found a home in his cephalic vein. He grabbed a bag of crystalloid and linked himself up, squeezing the fluids with his sticky right hand, hoping to hell the next slug of anti-puke stuff would find its mark.

The bag imploded. The crystalloid was through. He felt better for it and began to kick himself for not having tried this technique earlier. Struggling to his feet, looking out of the cockpit window, he watched as a monstrous dust devil homed in on them fast. The dust devil smashed directly against the forward observation windows and resumed its journey at the far side of the vehicle.

Seconds later, the buggy jolted. Then nothing.

"KAZU?" he shouted. "KAZU!"

There was no reply. The biometrics were flat-lining but that was just as likely to be due to the instrumentation as it was death.

He tapped into the village. "The buggy's stopped for repairs! He's not responding on the com! I'm suiting up."

Through the airlock and onto the sands, Hewish orbited the vehicle and saw – as he reached the second trailer – a fallen astronaut.

The rear wheel had buckled on its own axle, spilling ice and dust across the bulk of a man. Hewish scraped some of the ice away with his heavily gloved hands and leant over the victim's face, coming close in a bid to see through the visor. Though the silver was dense, he was able to persuade himself that there was something still twitching behind the plexi-glass.

He looked up again and saw 50 metric tonnes of ice in a trailer leaning over at close on 40°. It was a frigging miracle it hadn't buried the guy completely. One corner of the trailer was impinging on Kazu's pelvis and the fabric of the suit was indented.

"Kazu? Can you hear me?"

He could not. Kazu was pinned down. Hewish couldn't pull him free but he had to get free, even if it was only to salvage the components of his suit.

"This is Hewish. We have an emergency situation here. We have a failure of the rear trailer, portside, rear wheel."

He bounced round to the opposite side of the vehicle and started to inspect the other tyres. Here and there, a streak of carbon fibre had worked itself loose and started to sprout from the surface. Overall, however, tyre pressure was good and they were still 3 metres tall.

There was facility to reduce the pressure from the cockpit, but in the circumstances he decided to do it on manual. Deflating each tyre in turn, he watched anxiously as the weight of the trailer began to spread itself more evenly across the sand.

He spoke to the village.

"You're going to have to get the village buggy out here as fast as you can. I've lost the rear trailer. Kazu is trapped. We need the village buggy out here!"

Running back to his injured colleague, he pulled him free from the ice, waiting as he did so for the villagers to call and tell him why they couldn't do it. Kazu was too heavy to carry. Even in the limited gravity of Mars, an injured man in a suit is an appalling burden and Hewish quickly found himself climbing into the airlock alone, not just because he couldn't formulate a plan but because his feet were freezing.

What hope was there for Kazu? Even if the initial injury hadn't killed him, he was days from the limited medical facilities that could be found on this planet. Death following major trauma occurs most commonly in the first 60 minutes and they were already through that window. Sifting round the airlock, he gathered up some ropes and cables and some other bits of kit and convinced himself that he could rig up a pulley.

Suddenly, an audio signal came down from the Earth. The voice was human although his visor was displaying written text for the mentally deranged. "This is Houston … we recognise a major situation. Be advised, Nobohito Kazu has *died* in this incident. I repeat, all bio readings report death within three minutes of the initial event. We recommend recovery of the body – only if that act of recovery …"

Like people, medical instrumentation can malfunction and Hewish chose not to heed this warning, struggling instead with a rope and a sling around a dead man's chest. Kazu had never explained how he got him on board after the avalanche. Whatever, the colonel's own technique worked well enough and Kazu's body was soon inside.

Secure aboard the vehicle, Hewish removed both helmets and discovered a noxious fluid swilling out across the inner aspect of Kazu's visor. This was a good sign. "You've got to be alive to puke!" he shouted, triumphalistically.

An emergency airway. Mouth to mouth, Kazu's stubble was sour but on his lips, you could still taste the lemonade. External shock leads. Sub-cut adrenaline and an IV line, most probably in the cephalic vein followed by abandonment of the whole damned process, much sooner than he had intended because David *knew*, from everything, from the feel of the crumpled pelvis, the dilated pupils and the sound of a hollow chest that this was a man beyond all hope of salvage and that everything he had done in the last few hours had been in vain. It was time to rest in the cockpit beside a dead body and reach for a plastic bucket that might collect his own vomit. One last time. For old time's sake.

In the background, villagers were barking on the com.

"Be advised …" It was a woman's voice. It was *Rachael Callaghan,* totally unaffected. "You are out of range. You are out of range." Was this, he wondered, how she sounded when they first saw Smith from the Gossamer wing?

Don't say it. Don't feel it.

269

"I repeat-you-are-out-of-range!"

David was having a different conversation

"Don't leave me!"

Do not go gently into this good night.

But he had already gone.

"You're still 400 kilometres too far north for us to be able to reach you. If you think we can come out to get you, it means you haven't been listening to anything I've said. We *do not* have the range!" Then, in a different tone, she blurted, "How much ice did you lose?"

Commander Nobohito Kazu was not the first man to die on this planet, nor would he be the last. Colonel David Hewish had no intention of being the next. Whatever it took, he was going to get himself off this rock.

Quietly, the doctor unhooked the bag of crystalloid from Kazu's IV line and switched it over to his own arm. As he did so and for reasons he was unable to explain, he caught sight of the storm shelter in the Ajax with Kazu 15 feet beneath it, shielding his brain with a mosaic of mess tins. The storm shelter had been built to handle six. It could easily have taken two. Why the hell had he asked this man sleep down there with the gamma rays when he could have given him a place behind the lead?

"What do you want me to do with the body?" he asked. Wait another hour or so and the Olympian words of wisdom would stream down from the skies. Until that time, he was trapped in a cold and pressurised chamber with a pile of human remains.

Why waste time doing one thing?

He reached for a mop and wiped the place clean on his hands and knees: the misted windows, the pools of vomit, the discarded soap and sweat and human hair. The latrine. And after that, he found himself collecting the brown gravel that was Mars, scattered across the corpse and through to the airlock, tainted in places by his own venous blood.

Time mattered. He had to get going and he began to curse himself for his emphasis on aerobic exercise, for not pushing his body every waking moment since they left the Earth, that he might have had the physical strength now to pull a dead man from an airlock and out across the sand.

He re-attached the gloves and the helmet to the body and wrapped it in the same bed sheets that had lined their stinking cot. Bleeding the rear tyres of their gas, he opened the trailer gates and watched in silence as the pressure suit disappeared.

It would not melt. Not until man had won and Mars had lost and the frost that sealed this barren landscape had died away. Hewish had thrown other men overboard but none had meant this much to him. The only man harder to leave behind would have been Smith.

Some day. Some day, Kazu. The ice shall melt.

"... and death shall have no dominion."

And maybe kids will sit down to eat with the parents and friends and their elders and betters will tell them that a man such as this once lived.

They won't believe them.

"Dead men naked they shall be one
With the man in the wind and the west moon;
When their bones are picked clean and the clean
bones gone,
They shall have stars at elbow and foot;
Though they go mad they shall be sane,
Though they sink through the sea they shall rise
again;
Though lovers be lost love shall not;
And death shall have no dominion."

And David Hewish crawled back into the cockpit, bleeding, ever so slightly, from one nostril. His heart was bleeding too but his ride was hardly bothered as the control panel was quick to remind him.

"Strapped to a wheel, yet they shall not break ..."

In the space of ten minutes, she was up to 14 kilometres per hour, gaining speed with the smaller payload.

"And death shall have no dominion."

If he had a soul then it was already out there, rushing past Phobos and making its way up to the fabled afterlife where Weissman so loved to frolic. Their dead aviator was loath to waste time and in any case, though David had missed it, there was already somebody waiting for him.

CHAPTER FORTY-NINE

He would later be criticised for his abandonment of the body. It was, however, almost certainly the right thing to do. Another service in the sand was the last thing these people needed and having spent a further week in isolation, Colonel Hewish was more than prepared for the discussion that would follow. De-suited in the village, he recounted the loss of his superior to an audience of five.

Having obtained command by default, Hewish proceeded to issue orders.

Find your own shovel. Bring in the ice. Stand by for Marshall to calculate the likely fuel requirements for the Ajax.

He'd lost one trailer but their weight at blast-off had been downgraded too and they might just make it. Failing that, he would break for a few days and then return to the ice lake.

Turning to face a somewhat dynamic-looking double act on his right, he queried their preparations for the Ajax launch.

"Yes …" muttered Eliot, reluctant to meet him in the eye. "We've had a few days to work on it."

They'd had a few days to work on it. Hewish checked their faces for signs of bullshit and saw something else. Hostility. Hostility like the day that Kazu had breached the news on the ice lake. What kind of shit would they try to pull on him next? If he wanted to survive, he was going to have to push them. "We've got a new launch window from Marshall." His voice was clinical. "We should regard that launch window as our only realistic opportunity for a safe return. Stand up, march out of this room, get to work!"

The women left as a pair, sharing some new kind of secret with a sultry glance. In contrast, Eliot and Foguet departed alone. Only Daniel Tan chose to stay by the table where he tried to distract his new boss with some complete bullshit about the Greeks.

"*Ajax,*" he hissed, as if it really mattered.

"I'm sorry?"

"I checked him out," said Tan. "Ajax was a hero to the Greeks. He was the son of a king." David Hewish nodded whilst Tan continued. "After Achilles, Ajax was ranked as the second bravest man in the army. But Achilles bought it at Troy." The scientist gestured to his own heel. "They got him in the ankle with that arrow thing. The second bravest man was down to inherit his armour."

"Did it happen?"

"No. They couldn't decide who should get it. So they had this battle just about the armour. Ajax ends up killing Agamemnon *and* Menelaus. And they were his own guys. In the end, this Ajax character loses it completely ..." He tapped his forehead. "Ajax wasn't so strong up here you see."

Not for the first time in this mission, David Hewish glanced at the scientist and reacted adversely to his oriental features. These were the words of a colleague and the face of his enemy and in his judgement of this man at this time, Hewish placed emphasis on his face.

"Don't you want to know the rest?"

"No, Doctor Tan. I want you to walk down to the ice room and pick up a shovel." He stood up, providing a hint. "If we've got to go back to the ice lake, I've got to go quickly. I need to know what we've got. Fast!"

"We don't need to! I've seen the ice!"

"We can't predict the dust content. It might not all be water. Christ, Daniel, they didn't send me here to discuss the Iliad."

Daniel Tan glanced down the corridor, a distant wary look on his face. *"Athena."* His mood had changed. "Athena was this goddess who hated Ajax. She pushes him right to the edge. In the end, he falls on his own sword. You know what I think, Colonel? I think that sometimes we think we're in control, but we're not. Sometimes, a man doesn't get to say how or even when."

Hewish walked away from the table, finally out of patience.

"Daniel! For God's sake!" he shouted. "Pick up a fucking shovel!"

And then Tan came out with another line, a line that stopped David Hewish in his tracks.

"David, David ..." he said. "I love you dearly. *Be careful.*"

They went about their business. David Hewish roaming the base, checking each unit, asking for reassurance that the pool was still viable and that the fuel pumps and the electrolyser would see them through. Having got what he wanted, he returned to the smelting room, snatched a shovel from Tom Eliot and started to shift the stuff in person. Collapsing by the wall, Eliot's face was almost blue. "Rest for five," David yapped. "Rest for five then come back in."

Tom rested. The others worked. Rachael called up some heavy rock music and this seemed to calm them. Two of them had stripped to the waist; others were building up a sweat for the first time in months.

Within the hour, the blonde mop across David's forehead was black and wet and begging him to break off and rest. He felt the need for flavoured glucose water and was on the verge of fetching a bottle in person when Tom Eliot went over again on the ice, taking the impact with the palm of one hand. Incredibly, the fracture was actually audible above the rock music.

David ran over to his stricken colleague. The wrist was bent. Tom was off the field. Looking to his right, David saw Sarah Connolly, her mouth open, her eyes half closed, her endless hair drenched in sweat.

"You've broken it!" she wailed.

Kicking himself for all the time they were already wasting, he helped Tom Eliot back up the corridor and into the medical room where a simple x-ray confirmed the worst.

"Christ!"

He cast the limb in soft plastic, telling the guy to keep the thing elevated and offering to share a flask of his ubiquitous flavoured glucose water. Finding strength from the fluid, David darted back to the ice with a 100% conviction that he could fill in for both of them.

As soon as he got there, he became aware of something else. His workforce was on the verge of rebellion. Only Tan was actually digging and their newly appointed commander felt the need to speak. *Drink from this thing!* They passed the bottle around. *Dig!*

Checking them out in turn, he fought back despair. The heavy mob – the muscular figures of Marnix Gabanna and Nobohito Kazu – were long gone. Kelly O'Reilly, by far the strongest woman on the mission, had been taken from him too. David was trapped with two ageing, able-bodied men, a cripple and a pair of angry women.

Reluctant to give up before sundown, he ordered them to rest for one hour and then return. His team dispersed. Alone in Major Smith's office, David doused down his brain in a tiny basin. He was burning up. To some, he knew, he was expressing a new kind of brutality but within his own mind, he was more than human. As with the other astronauts on Mars, he could only give so much. Putting his inbox onto verbal, he looked for more fluids.

FOR YOUR EYES ONLY
Political situation deteriorating rapidly. NASA is unable to guarantee access to low-Earth Orbit into the New Year. For this and other reasons, your forthcoming launch window should be regarded as your only realistic option for survival.

They'd told him this before but it was good of them to remind him of it now. Over by the latrine, David pressed a bottle to his lips with his left hand and aimed for the pan with his right. His mouth was parched, his facial hair sharp against his wrist. If he had still had the energy, he would have given himself a shave. He needed a shave.

Oblivious to the state of his body, the computer persisted. Not every bit of news was bad. Assuming they could get the stuff inside, there was more than enough ice to launch the Ajax. Even allowing for small losses during electrolysis, NASA regarded a return journey to the ice lake as unlikely. Of more immediate concern to David was the timeline for blast-off. With the reduced demands of a smaller workforce and the current output from the garden, he could have held out here until the Martian spring. Instead he was being asked to fly home with all due haste. It wasn't hard to understand why. The

Ajax had been designed to fly through deep space and would be unable to enter the Earth's atmosphere. If NASA couldn't get a shuttle into low-Earth orbit, then the crew would perish, a stone's throw from their final destination.

His 60 minutes were up. Striding back to the ice room, David looked for the scientific community and found them, doting on one another in a lonely corner. Eliot was beaten by the wall whilst Tan attempted to soothe him with some kind of steaming hi-tech beaker. They looked like an ageing couple, deprived of a much-loved grandchild, seeking comfort from each other in their hour of need. Closer to the actual tub, Foguet, Connolly and Callaghan were already at work.

It might have been more sensible to pack in but this particular batch of ice was almost in the tub and he kept them behind to finish the job. Untrusting to the end, David sealed the inner hatch to the cargo canister in person and initiated the process of depressurisation. Pressing his forehead against the bulkhead, he let out a fantastic sigh.

The job was done and he made his way back to the ice room where Kazu's former lover was waiting to perform. Doing a double take in front of him, he watched her go down on one knee.

"We don't have to do this!" she argued. "We don't have to do this!" Rachael said something about Eliot and his broken wrist as if the fracture was an act of malice. "I got food coming out of the greenhouse. We can keep going 'til the spring."

"Give it up!" he ordered. "Go to bed. We meet here again at 0600."

Alone in Smith's quarters, David rested beside the great man's desk. He took up a fresh banana and began to peel it. Maybe Rachael was right. Maybe they should hold out here for longer. After all, she'd grown this frigging thing on Mars.

The sack. He had to hit the sack.

Then, just as his body was ready to give in, Eliot burst into the office with an entirely new request for sanity.

"Do you realise what we have achieved on this planet?" In point of fact, David did realise what they had achieved on Mars although Eliot had only come here to describe his own progress. "Doesn't that mean anything to you?"

"Tom!" Lost in a shroud of white cotton, David's voice was indistinct. "We've gotta get outta here."

"The body of work on those machines, the body of work on our computers? It is without precedent. What else could it be? No one's ever done this before. Relocating the scientific community to the point of investigation and letting them to run the show from there."

"Did they let you do that, Tom, or did you just decide to do it on your own initiative?"

"We're close to forming a coherent theory as to the origins of this planet. The water, the big thaw, *everything*. It's a masterpiece!"

David tore back the sheets and pulled off his shirt, exposing his lean and hungry torso. If Tom saw this as crass, he was mistaken. David was trying to sleep.

The older man resumed.

"And don't give me any of that shit about not giving a damn! Don't give me any of that shit about coming here under orders! I know who you are?" The man in the bed stiffened. "Do you think we never even heard your name before? Before you even got here?" David's eyes opened. "Smith told us!"

Quietly: "Tom! Get outta here."

"Look, David," this regression to first-name terms was painful. "I'm down. Rachael's not up to this. And we both know there'll be another window in the spring. I mean what about the Chinese? Have you thought about them? If we get back there at warp speed, what do you think the navy are going give you? Your own game show? You'll be out there in the Pacific, waiting to get hit in some newfangled boat."

Very, very quietly: "That's where I belong."

Tom's arms were in the air.

"Nuts! Have you done all this to die like that? Don't you understand? If we hold out here 'til the New Year, this thing with China will blow over. There'll be a settlement and the fighting will stop. Has anybody ever told you that?"

"The Chinese are taking low-Earth orbit," said David, revealing a secret that might have been better held in reserve. "If we stick with Marshall's schedule, there's still a chance we can survive."

"And if we wait another six months, we can finish our work here and this crisis will have blown over. Like it always does."

"Tom! The Lexington has been sunk! My crew are dead! Your son –"

"Not if he got off."

"He was in the engine room!"

"What if it wasn't his shift? Look, *you're* in charge of this outfit, not them. They can't make you do anything!"

But Eliot was beginning to repeat himself. His appeal had fallen on deaf ears. He was ordered to leave and left without a fight. Shielding his eyes with the heels of his own palms, David prayed for some sort of break from the conflict and got it for the best part of an hour.

CHAPTER FIFTY

The door opened quietly and David returned to the present. Sarah Connolly was back in his bedroom. She pressed her butt against the latch and he heard her undress. Her first few seconds beneath his sheets seemed to be more about body heat than affection. This was no big deal. Life on Mars had a lot to do with coping. Another breath, another sip of richly flavoured fluid. Another step on the blood-red sands before the frost and the cold could make it through your boots. Just one more.

Her legs were unshaven. Her breasts fuller than he remembered. Ample. In many ways reborn. But this was not the body of his red-hot flight attendant from the jet copter. This was the body of a woman whose life was half spent and carried all the wounds that come with time. On her belly, he felt ripples and he stroked them softly in the darkness. Some of them, he knew, were down to childbirth. Others were the hallmarks of starvation and had persisted in part because her natural body fat had yet to recover. Connolly hadn't come to his room for data or a seat on a ship she was bound to be given. She might well be the angry Greek goddess of Daniel's prophesy but as David saw it, there was nothing left to fight for.

Several minutes passed by. He felt the need to speak.

"You were sleeping with Marnix."

"Yes," she agreed.

"Is that his son? In Charlotte?"

Post-coital and exhilarated, she sighed in the half-light.

"Can't you let go?"

He followed the line that led down from her neck and then her shoulder and across her breasts and on to the mature and womanly body that had been salvaged by the supplies on the Ajax. He thought of her ancestors, just off the boat in New York and the lands and the homes they had left behind. Not for them the luxury of inherited wealth or soil. Only the clothes they stood in and the luggage they could carry. And yet, somehow, this distant descendent was a fine woman, strong and tall, and able to hold her own in the cloistered, freezing world of Mars. The essence of life here was much more abrasive than he had been led to believe. It broke his heart and smelt of diesel oil. For most of the crew, it meant weeks underground with just the occasional forage on the dunes to break the boredom. Besides data and the next ticket home, it was hard to see what anyone could really fight for on Mars.

He faded out and slept soundly until Rachael Callaghan arrived and clambered over the pair of them to lie against his right flank. He turned to face her, feeling the first woman's legs rub up against his own. She kissed him – very slowly – and he revelled silently in the wake of her mouth. They progressed to sex and the protracted exhaustion that followed until she was rested and ready to speak to him again. In a sense he had waited for this moment – though he had not known he was waiting – since he had first set eyes on her in a mad house. Now that it had come, physical weakness and his mild dehydration made it all the more raw.

"Lighten up," she whispered. "You're on a different planet."

And he did and he saw that within the confines of this strange New World, she was right.

They made love again, unrestrained and ignoring Connolly in any case who was standing to leave, devoid of any kind of rivalry or rejection. When Rachael had finished and when he was breathless again, he found himself distracted by his mentors in Houston.

"For Christ's sake!" groaned the woman, suddenly alone in his cot. "Can't it wait?"

Over by his desk, David glanced at his latest message. It was too large to be verbal. A message of this size had to involve images. In his mind, that could only mean one thing and he wasn't glad about it. "Shit!" he whispered. "Hutchings!"

But he was wrong.

It was Christine.

CHAPTER FIFTY-ONE

At first sight, the lobbyist from Washington seemed much the same and this constancy would later trouble him, because in time, he would begin to question the credibility of the film.

"David, David, I didn't contact the NASA people, earlier on, earlier on in the pregnancy, because ..."

It was Christine alright but she was speaking in a new rhythm. She had been changed, significantly both by childbirth, and by the arrival of her son.

Killing the sound, David Hewish watched her colourful gestures beside a dozing infant.

"This is our child ..." she went on. "I didn't tell you about him earlier because ..."

Had they persuaded the girl to stand in front of a camera with some other likely-looking offspring? No. There were subtle changes in the texture of her face and skin that seemed to be speaking the truth. Locked, organically into the competitive Washington social scene, it was hard to imagine how Christine could have gained weight in any other way.

"You see that!" Rachael raised her voice. "You see that!" she snarled. "That's bullshit!" He turned back to the screen, infuriated, more than anything, that he should find himself harassed at this juncture. "Bullshit from another world!"

Quite apart from anything else, there was the issue of privacy. All too often on this mission, he had been awakened by the sound of sobbing, barnyard sex, or some other form of early-morning angst. It went without saying, the last few hours would not have gone unnoticed.

His mind sharpened by this latest bombshell, David started to grasp just how much mayhem he might have caused tonight. In the meantime, Rachael's scowl was starting to bite him and he grabbed her. Seconds later, the two of them fell heavily, David's right hand firm across her lips.

Her nostrils were flaring, her breathing fast and laboured. "Why …" He was asking for her help. "Why do you think it's a lie?"

He let her speak.

"They're trying to control you! That's what they do. They know you loved that woman. You called out her name."

"When?"

"Under the ice." David's grip began to weaken but she didn't try to run. "Kazu told me."

"Did I – did he talk about –?"

"No. Kazu only talked about his wife."

David's mind seized up. Nothing came. Then, "What – what wife?"

"On the Lexington. Kazu was married to his commanding officer on the Lexington."

He let her go, rising and turning around awkwardly, possessed by a desire to drive back to a heap of ice in the sand and ask for confirmation.

"They offered him command on the bridge. He asked them why. Then they said the thing like he kept saying, they told him not to ask. He took it. That was Kazu's problem. He did everything that was asked of him." And Rachael returned to the present, adding, "They know you're gonna break –"

"Do I look like I'm giving up? Rachel Callaghan, Ph-frigging-D? *I don't break.*"

He stepped away.

"But you will. You will, Colonel David Hewish M-fucking-B. Believe me, I will watch you break!"

"No!" he stated. "A man can hold it together. If he wants to. Kazu held it together. Right to the end. I was with him!"

"Like your boys on the Lexington? None of them screaming! None of them –"

He punched her in the stomach with an explosive burst of emotion and with all the strength he could muster. Flying backwards, she bounced off the wall and rolled over to the floor, a mass of red hair hiding her face. The impetus to follow through with his feet was overwhelming but he managed to suppress it. Feeling no guilt, he watched her crawl for a corner and turn to jeer at him some more.

"What bothers," said David, standing over her, catching his breath, "what bothers me most, is how you had two spacecraft on the ground and sat here on your asses while the tanks bled dry."

"What bothers me," said the woman, "what bothers me is that you guys were so smart, but you missed the fucking obvious."

"Such as?"

"Major Smith."

It wasn't just the words. It was the delivery.

"Smith died," he said.

And with no discernable change in the speed or rhythm of her speech, Callaghan corrected him. "Major Smith was murdered." They sprang apart. "Ha – you didn't see that coming!"

"Did you kill him?" Ditching the smile and pulling a sheet across her breasts, she shook her head.

"Are you sure?"

"We saw the body."

"Did you –" His thoughts switched from the surveillance cameras to her face. Houston was blind but it was likely that their words were being recorded.

"They had to send up a Gossamer wing to find his body. Tan said it was a waste of good money but Kelly said we had to get to him. Like she thought he might be still breathing, six weeks after we lost contact!" David Hewish grabbed his clothes. "Smith went out before a storm. Then he didn't come back. The storm got going, then we were cooped up in the base. By the time they got to him, the footprints were blown away!"

Seconds later, the colonel was gone, gone to a horseshoe-shaped table, aching to stare at a jet-black sky.

"God Almighty!"

"Are you going outside?" He spun around. She had followed him.

It was too obvious. What excuse could he muster for an EVA at this hour? Back by the door to the office he scanned the corridor. The village was silent. His crew were still sleeping.

In the office again, he spoke with more purpose.

"How do you know he was murdered?"

"He was shot in the head."

"Suicide?"

"Twice."

"It could have been an exit wound."

"No, there were two exit wounds. Two bullets."

"What about the fuel leak? Sabotage?"

"The taps were turned by hand. We found them open. Kelly thought it was Tan."

"Why?"

"Because he doesn't want to go back."

This idea had more credence than he would like to pretend.

"What about the radio beacons?" he said. "There's a beacon in every helmet."

"Foguet disabled the beacons."

"Why?"

"Tan told him to."

"So they could hold back all their findings from Marshall? Write the definitive history of Mars from their own survey? Get to be famous before anybody else could see their data?"

"Yes."

"Did you try to figure out who it *couldn't* be?" he asked, knowing full well that they must have done. "On the day that Smith died, was there anybody still in the settlement, someone who never left the base?"

"Bose."

"Shit!"

"Everyone else was out there. That's why he did it. That's why he did it on that day. Even Tan and Eliot were outside. They were going out lots then, 'til Smith got murdered and they nearly starved to death. There was no duty roster. It was chaos."

"Where did they find him?"

"Five klicks north of the Von Braun."

"What was he doing there?"

"He was outside," he said. "Smith had taken to going outside. On his own. On foot." Rachael shook her head with genuine contempt. "Never go outside on your own, Colonel. Not on this planet."

Suddenly, they heard a knock at the door.

"Can you keep it down!" The voice was muffled and angry. Maybe Eliot. "We're trying to sleep out here!"

"Er, yeah – sorry!"

"I liked it better when you were humping!"

The footsteps receded. Had they heard something?

"So, you've got a problem, *Commander* Hewish," said Rachael. "No medic ever craved the helm of a ship." This was too precise. He must have told her. "But you've got it. What-a-ya gonna do? How are you gonna get us home? If you know for a fact that one of us has gotta be psycho? Because you're not the sort of guy who could dump a crew on Mars, are you, David Hewish?"

He was not.

"This stays in this room," he grated. "You speak to no one but me on this one. Remember, I'm the commander of this base."

"Third one I had."

"Did you hear me?"

Rachael had. She was laughing.

CHAPTER FIFTY-TWO

Over in the Ajax buggy, David Hewish set up a secure link to Houston. Cross-legged on the floor, arching his neck to a distant Sun, he called out to a hidden mike.

"Speed of light in this universe was 300 million metres per second, last time I checked. That means you should be getting this message in just over 20 minutes. I want –"

But the Earth was cutting in. They must have prepared this one as he slept – or struggled to sleep – with Callaghan.

"Hutchings!"

Indeed it was. The emeritus good guy Hutchings had been wheeled back from retirement for yet another keynote address.

"David, we're still reviewing your discussion with Doctor Callaghan last night. Obviously some interesting material there …"

Conscious of the lag in transmission, Hewish snapped a couple of senseless questions.

"Did you know that Smith was murdered?" he demanded. "Smith was on the Serpentine with me! You must have known that!"

Deaf for the next 20 minutes, Hutchings rambled on.

"Smith's fate remains a mystery. Callaghan's come out with this new claim, but that's all we've got to go on. Internal surveillance was disabled long before Smith took a walk and as a group, we'd been losing them for weeks. The homeostatic data was still coming through as was some of the B Division raw data but the bulk of the down-link was heavily constrained. We knew what they were doing but we couldn't stop them. As you've discovered, Mars has a lot to do with isolation. People start to think they're beyond reprimand."

"How am I'm going to get home with a killer on my ship?" asked Hewish.

"We aren't convinced that Smith was murdered at all. I'd ask you to give some thought to this woman, Callaghan. She's interesting. She's not just the gardener. I'm sure you know that. She's gifted. And in some respects she's been lucky. Total shutdown of the farming system followed by reactivation with all this water and then the thing with the mirror too – it just fell into her lap. Her achievements on the farm are on a par with anything that happened in the forbidden zone, completely overlooked by one or two of the other self-obsessed oddballs you've been forced to shack up with these last few months.

We know that Callaghan has sought physical attention, firstly from Smith, then Kazu and now – seamlessly – from yourself. No outward sign of grief associated with either of the previous two deaths." David's soul hardened. "She has not sought intellectual recognition from her colleagues. The data stream on the greenhouse has never gone off-line. Not even once. She never sought media attention as Marnix sought it and she never asked for medication as Weissman did. In short, Callaghan has sought and has consistently sought physical but not intellectual attention from her peers.

That episode last night in your room, this deliberate act of revelation. That wasn't random." Suddenly Hutchings – of all people – was speaking with a clenched fist. "Don't forget that Daniel Tan tried to *warn* you. Daniel must have overheard some kind of exchange between the two women.

Now, son, I know – I wanna tell ya –" This wasn't the kind of man to stumble on his words and yet he had stumbled and this was not a good sign. "I want to tell you, not just on behalf of the agency but on behalf of all Americans of my generation, that this isn't the world we wanted you to live in. These aren't the problems we wanted you to face. It just happened. We couldn't stop it – or we could stop it and we didn't – and like a lot of guys my age, I can't bear to think about our legacy."

Hutchings was almost tearful. He was building up to something worse.

"I know who Smith was. Of course I know that. But, son, the fact is, we just don't have a lot of choices left. We have to know how this man met his demise. If he was shot …"

In the back of the buggy, the colonel went down in a prayer of his own.

"Oh God no!"

"... then there ought to be gunshot wounds on his body. As I'm sure you know, this is a matter of the greatest importance. Justice here has a priority second only to survival and there's simply no one else we can ask."

"There'll be nothing left of him!"

"Smith's body was given up to the elements more than a year ago. In these conditions, that same body will be well preserved. You can't trust anybody else. You're just going to have to go out there alone. We figure that if you tell the others you're doing a supply run back to the Ajax, they'll buy it."

"No!"

"You're going to need the excavation kit you used by the ice lake. It's still bolted to the buggy and it ought to be kosher ..."

David wasn't listening. His mind had already fled through the fractious air of Mars. The next launch window was less than two weeks away. He knew from experience that this time would pass very quickly. An immediate visit to the graveyard might attract attention and it was vital that he kept this matter secret from his colleagues. For the next few days, he made a big deal about shovelling ice in person. A degree of frank swelling marred Rachael Callaghan's face but the community as a whole seemed oddly blind to it. Rachael made mention of her own bombshell and David played dumb too.

Then, some 72 hours after his conversation with Hutchings, he spoke to his crew over supper.

"In the morning," he told them, "in the morning, they want me to go out to the Ajax."

To begin with, his audience decided to spare him by expressing disinterest. Then, after about a minute, Tom Eliot started to list reasons why he wouldn't be able to help. Flaked out to his left, Daniel Tan was nodding in non-specific agreement. A few seconds later, Foguet came up with an idea of his own. He suggested unbolting the excavator arm and detaching it from the buggy.

"There'll be more room for the cargo if we take the thing off," he added.

"No," said David. "NASA wants it in place."

NASA wanted all kinds of things and they seemed to accept this.

Shortly after sunrise Colonel Hewish boarded the vehicle and returned to the Ajax. Close by the spacecraft, he unloaded the remaining supplies alone and on foot. It took five hours. Then, about halfway through the afternoon, he turned off the radio beacon on his buggy and drove out towards the hills.

By the standards of his previous escapades on Mars, this journey was a brief one. The final ascent was severe although the buggy seemed to take it in its stride. In contrast, the driver approached the graveyard with undisguised concern, his heart rate soaring on his own instruments. Soon, he could actually see the brightly coloured flowers laid out beside a wooden cross. Turning to his computers, David Hewish played with the imaging systems and tried to home in on the grave itself.

The burial service had not been recorded and he had no idea how deep the body would be. There was only one way to find out. The mechanical arm on the back of the buggy swung purposefully towards the dust. Seconds later the wooden cross keeled over and the flowers and the smaller boulders were rolling down the hill. Major Smith, the strong-willed schoolboy from Australia, was about to be disinterred.

Right on cue, a pristine visor appeared in the sand. Taking over on manual, David trailed his metal teeth along a torso. Smith – it seemed – had been buried in a full pressure suit. Either that or the body was elsewhere and the suit would turn out to be empty.

Toying with one of the legs, David Hewish reluctantly acknowledged that the outfit was too rigid to be hollow. There was something stiff in there and he was going to have to take a look. He dug a gentle ramp towards the corpse and began the laborious task of donning his own, identical pressure suit.

Out on the surface, he grabbed a shovel and a rope and checked his gas. Five hours on his current cylinder, more than enough for the job in hand.

He remembered his conversation with Erkhart in the seismometer lab and her passing reference to the Viking death rites. Weissman, she argued, would only need a stringed instrument but Smith needed more than that and he was all set up for that big adventure in the sky. His tool kit – indeed, his entire backpack – was fully prepared.

David tied a rope to the man's legs and began to slide him, unceremoniously, up to the surface. By the time he got the body into the cargo canister, the light was beginning to fade. Sealing the door behind him, he cranked up the air pressure in the canister and shut down the life support in his own suit.

It was time to remove two helmets.

There was no smell. The body was a block of ice.

"You're getting all this?" he asked.

There was no reply. He'd been here for over an hour. Mission Control should have reacted to his initial discovery. He might have paid more attention to this issue but something else was flashing through his mind: his first encounter with Greaves.

"Did you know Major Smith?"

"I – we met at NASA, sir."

"And before that?"

Weissman had once told Hewish that he thought there was a place, a place that came after this life, where a man would get to meet those friends he had already lost. And Hewish had told him that no, there was no such place. Well, Hewish was wrong. That place did exist and it was here on a slab in the back of an over-worked cargo canister on Mars. Major Smith was with them alright, and though he lacked the power of speech, the snarl on his retracted lips was more than enough to make his presence felt.

Smith and Hewish had first met in an evacuation centre in Sydney. There had been grown-ups all over the place, trying to tell them it would be alright but David

295

didn't believe them. Having just come down from Alice, the 12-year-old was under no illusions as to the savagery of their foe. Some people were choosing to stay in Oz, making speeches about the humanity of their opponent and remaining calm. Others were shitting themselves. For his part, Smith was already restless. He had been trapped in this institution for six long weeks and was all for getting out. The American Senate had approved the evacuation of Queensland and they were flying people out in batches of 1500.

On the face of it, Smith and Hewish were only kids but they were ageing rapidly and they knew that if they wanted to live they would have to run. It wasn't realistic to get to Queensland and by this stage, the airfield in Sydney had come within artillery range of the Chinese army. America – as they would later say – was about to be "strengthened" by the arrival of some six million Aussies and this particular pair of stranded adolescents were hell-bent on being in on it.

There were still a few cargo ships in the harbour and one of them was the Serpentine. News came through that the US embassy had agreed to evacuate children by sea with the threshold for getting a ticket being placed at 13. Hewish counted four or five uniformed personnel on the Serpentine although official accounts would later describe 50. In any case, they were never on deck and fresh water was in short supply. Staying south of New Zealand, the captain kept them cold for the first few days, heading north beyond the date line. There were Chinese submarines in the area and the bulk of the crew were distracted by their duties to the ship. Kids teemed over in the hold like maggots in a rotting steak and there were torsos going overboard every few hours.

Unsupervised by the water supply, a bunch of nine-year-olds made short work of the stuff, dousing themselves down in the stuff they should have been saving for the second half of the journey. Six days out from Sydney and there was nothing left. Water loss in relation to body mass increases rapidly in the young. Especially the very young. A 12-year-old is relatively protected and as the crew sealed themselves off from the hold and the storm warnings arrived, Smith and Hewish scaled the walls and tied themselves to the deck with a plastic bucket between their legs. The rain came down heavily and they drank from the skies. A few of the older boys came up to share their rainwater and in time, when their limbs began to weaken, and sunburn kicked in, the 12-year-olds managed to fight them off.

Splayed out in an equatorial Sun, waiting for the next downpour, some of them finished up in the drink but Smith and Hewish were not amongst them. Years later, the Serpentine remained famous – not for the kids since most had expired, but for the tales of the men who had been asked to explore the decaying mess in the hold.

At Harvard, Smith would introduce him to friends as "another survivor" and in a way, Hewish realised, that's all he was. In the whole of their adult lives, Smith and Hewish would continue to rise above the throng. No mater how bad it got – no matter how brutal their remote military boarding school became – they would come through, meeting again in medical school and then in the Astronaut Corps.

By the dockside in LA they had counted a thousand dead bodies in the hold of the Serpentine and less than 200 still breathing on deck. *"America gets the survivors!"* Smith would tell them. And he was right. The boys had survived because they had the physical and mental strength to kill for rainwater and there were countless others who had died because they lacked it. In another age, he might have been wracked by guilt but this was no other age – the values of his time had been skewed towards the living. Even now, even with a hundred boffins back on Earth to help them, he'd already lost Bose and Kazu. As far as Smith went, if this was murder and the killer was still on the planet, he'd probably have to kill him too because he would never fly back in the Ajax with a murderer in his crew and he would never leave a man behind.

Could he kill Callaghan? If he had to? Could he kill Kazu's lover or the other woman who had come to his bed and offered to screw him this week? *Yes.* In the end, he could kill all of them, just as he'd been able to sling one screaming nine-year-old after the other into the Pacific because they had asked to sup from his mug or hide in his own patch of shade. Smith had been right about one thing: the people who survived the Serpentine were tough guys and they had no intention of laying down. That ship was still a part of him and when the time came he would call on it again.

Sliding his hands into a pair of rubber gloves, David began to examine the head. Smith had suffered from acne in his late teens and his cheeks were heavily puckered.

"The gardener's right," he said. "There are two bullet holes on the skull. He couldn't have pulled the trigger twice. Two independently fatal wounds excludes suicide."

Awkward and apprehensive, Hewish undressed the body in stages, searching in vain for additional injuries.

Who had shot Smith and why? Could it be some kind of professional rivalry? Sexual envy? Smith was screwing Callaghan and she wasn't screwing anybody else.

And if this was murder, where was the killer right now? In between worlds on the Von Braun?

No.

He doesn't want to go back.

"Do you want me to do an autopsy?" David asked out loud. "He's going to be solid for another day or so. I'm not driving to the settlement with this bloke in the back. They'll go berserk …"

Houston had failed to comment for some time. Maybe it was the down-link to the canister. He could try them again from the cockpit in the buggy in a few minutes. Eager to get out of here, he retrieved some tissue samples from the skin and also some clumps of subcutaneous fat, though he had to use a hammer and screwdriver to get it. Then he sealed the fragments in separate pots. He could keep them hidden in the Ajax and then – if they ever made it back to Earth – someone could do toxicology.

"I'm sorry pal," he muttered and began to redress the corpse. "And I'm sorry, Houston. That's your lot."

It was time to scrub the post mortem. This was Mars, where a man could do whatever he wanted and feel no guilt. Confirmation of the double gunshot wounds was enough. Returning the body to the grave, he kicked a little dust across the face and felt the urge to leave.

He couldn't.

Kazu had gotten his own ice. Smith deserved his sand. Reaching for the shovel, David began to move soil back over the body. Another few minutes and the body was fully covered. "Rachael, you bitch!" he breathed. She'd seemed pretty crazy from the day he'd first set eyes on her in the village.

"Hewish!" There was a voice on the com.

An astronaut works with transducers in both ears and it can be hard to know which way to turn. Somehow, right now, David Hewish looked back to the buggy.

"Who is it?"

"What are you doing?"

"Who sent you here? Did you follow me out?"

"No, no, no, my friend. What are *you* doing?"

It was Foguet. He had recovered a firearm from the buggy and was aiming it loosely towards the grave.

"Orders from NASA," said David, looking down the barrel of a gun.

"What do they care?"

"Maybe the major was murdered."

"'You seen his body?"

"Didn't you?" Foguet offered no response. "How did you get out here? It's too far to walk."

"The outrider."

"Did they tell you –"

"There's no voice link."

"How's that? Did you shut it down?"

The colonel took his silence to mean yes.

"Did you come here to be a hero?" asked Foguet.

"I came here under orders."

"To preserve *the American way*?"

"That's what I meant."

"To make some great discovery? What about life, Colonel? Did you find much of that on Mars?"

"Just about all of it," said Hewish, low on oxygen, stuck in a trench with a rock-solid corpse by his feet. "Why? Pablo? How the hell are you going to get away with this? Where is there to go? When you get back to the States–"

"Why should I want to go back to the States?"

"You asked to live in the States."

"Would you have me live in Spain?"

"Spain doesn't exist."

The response took the form of a scream.

"America exists!"

One bullet from the pistol and his suit would instantly depressurise. David realised he was going to have to try and talk his way out.

"It's not right that Europe should die and that America live!"

"And Mars is a shithole!" David reminded him. "We've got to get home before our supplies run out, Pablo. Man! We've gotta get back."

The Spaniard was stepping forwards, his body a dark silhouette against a dying Sun. The gun itself was still visible, moving in close now.

If he wanted to kill me, he'd have taken his shot. Keep talking.

"Look, Pablo, what about your wife –"

Pablo raised the weapon as if to fire. David Hewish was reluctant to turn his head away from the barrel. Besides, he was still debating with himself whether a pressure suit would cope with a small arms hit on Mars.

He needn't have worried. On standby to play dead with the first shot, Hewish received a left-handed crow-bar blow to the neck and went down beside Smith in the process.

CHAPTER FIFTY-THREE

Coming to with his visor in the sand, Hewish rolled over and took stock of his position.

The outrider buggy was stationary and a good 20 metres from his feet. Some time ago, Foguet had pulled up in this silent airless world and waited patiently at the rear of the nuclear-powered buggy. That vehicle had left and Hewish caught sight of it making steady progress down an incline, heading back towards the plateau and – presumably – the only settlement on Mars.

Trotting towards the outrider, David confirmed that the smaller vehicle had been sabotaged.

Gaseous hydrogen had leaked from the fuel cell in much the same way as liquid oxygen had once seeped from the Von Braun. The motor wouldn't move.

Foguet, you bastard!

Checking the vehicle quickly, Hewish located the radio: smashed with a mallet. Foguet might not have told the village where he was going. What were the chances they would have guessed?

Unless they were in on it too.

There was less than 30 minutes of oxygen in his cylinder. In broad daylight, he figured that it would have taken four or five hours to walk back to the village.

After sunset, without a light source …

"It's Foguet," he said out loud. "Foguet's nuts! Liberal intellectual from a dead country …"

He was calm. There was nothing to be gained by panic. He remembered a bedroom in DC.

The sea's as good a grave as any.

The voice link was down. He was on his own. It was going to be pitch-black in under an hour and he'd been pencilled in to asphyxiate shortly after that.

But the link was stronger than he knew. Unknown to David, a whole bunch of people were watching the drama in Mission Control. The transmission lag was well understood here. Whatever they were looking at, it happened some time ago and there was widespread speculation that their man was already dead. All voice links with the village had failed. Pretty much the only signal they were getting came from the camera on David's helmet and for the last ten minutes this had featured only sand.

Alarm bells were ringing. Senior personnel were dragging themselves out of their meetings and over to the control room where five or so guys on the night shift were suddenly crowded out.

On their monitors, the images had changed. They could see sand being thrown in the air. Their fallen astronaut was alive and upright, back in the grave and digging it deep.

"What's he doing?"

"D'ya think he wants to lay down with Smith," asked a youthful engineer.

"No!" said his supervisor, more slowly. "This guy doesn't give up!"

Over on another planet, David's shovel had struck glass. Ignoring a dead friend, he started work on the tool box.

There was no one of consistent faith amongst the villagers, but perhaps in respect for their Nordic namesakes, they had surrendered to tradition and prepared their dead colleague for a mythical afterlife. Trudging through his first sand storm in the sky, the first thing a man was going to need was a good supply of oxygen. With this in mind, they had thoughtfully filled the cylinders in his backpack. Unclamping them in the half-light, Hewish blew on the nozzle and watched as a patch of water vapour appeared on the inner aspect of his visor.

"You're losing it, Colonel!"

In the tool box he helped himself to a torch. The battery had been less keen on internment than the gas cylinders and the beam was hardly there. Scavenging on the high ground, he found Foguet's crow bar in the sand. A little further on, he even found a gun. Was this a thoughtless error? Or a conscious invitation for suicide?

Walking back to the body, David held the weapon through gloved hands and let off one shot. A tiny squeal reached his ears through the tight Martian air and a hole appeared in the major's visor. "Yep!" muttered David, hooking the firearm to his belt. "This thing goes through plexi-glass."

There was no time to lose. Clinging to the outrider, he released the brakes and began to push. With the engine disengaged, the wheels turned well, hurtling down the hill at what felt like 20 kph. By the time his momentum ran dry, the sky was jet-black and he had gained a thousand metres.

Abandoning the outrider, David resumed his journey on foot.

The oxygen cylinder on his suit had been reading zero for some time but he had decided to wait until his helmet was really foul. That moment had arrived and he switched over to the first of Smith's oxygen cylinders.

Twenty minutes later, the flash lamp decided to give up the ghost. He dumped the thing in the desert and kept walking. Seconds later, his feet went from under him and he landed heavily amidst the magnemite. Rolling over, he found the wherewithal to get upright and resumed his march at a slower pace.

There are no street lights on Mars and it was impossible to orientate by ordinary means. Peering up at the heavens, he looked for a familiar constellation and saw something else.

There was a new star in the sky.

Tens of thousands of kilometres away, the solar sail had rotated on its gyros. Responding to an order from Houston, an immense mirror would soon be facing David. At this altitude, the Sun was still visible and would remain so for another hour. No mirror could banish night forever, but an extended twilight might just see him home.

From the colonel's perspective, the movement of the sail was too accurate to be random. The NASA people had to be conscious of his predicament. How? Helmet cameras? Probably. Voice communication was down but the image link was on a separate frequency. What's more, if they'd bothered to move the sail, they must be giving him a reasonable chance of survival.

And so he soldiered on, until even the sail went black and true darkness returned. But it wouldn't stop him. Having already made it as a gravedigger, Colonel David Hewish had fast acquired a miner's sense of footing.

He remembered Weissman's natal cleft and his bizarre fantasy about the desert. *Like Smith.* Was David going to lie down in this desert? No. Not like this.

He remembered his last days in Taiwan. These days were distant from him but they were familiar too since he replayed them in his head on a regular basis. The only good thing about getting hit in Taiwan was getting out.

Because he always got out. And he'd get out now, if not by the reflected light of the Sun then by the moons of Mars or failing that by the residual electronic glow that seeped out from his helmet and down to the sand. And as he cleared the horizon and paused for breath, he caught sight of the green pilot light on top of the dome and knew he would make it. He would inhale on the frigging vacuum if he had to. He would find Pablo Foguet and blow his fucking brains out.

CHAPTER FIFTY-FOUR

Fifty feet short of the village, David paused by the green pilot light to check his oxygen reserve and ready his gun. One bullet had been wasted on a dead man's skull. There were 11 more rounds in the magazine.

Shaking and on the edge of breakdown, Colonel David Hewish slipped through the southern airlock unnoticed. Establishing some kind of new record for pressure suit egression, he entered the settlement on tiptoe with his pistol cocked and ready. Close to the dome, he heard voices. Suddenly, the woman Rachael appeared in front of him.

Without reference to the rules of polite society, David crushed her up against the wall and held one hand across her mouth.

"Where is he?" he hissed. "Foguet? *Where is he?*"

The gardener made no sound. He slid his hand from her lips.

"I *don't* know," she whispered, all but screeching the second word. "I don't know! He was under the dome."

"Did you know? Did you know he was coming to kill me?"

Her head made an effort to shake but she was too constrained.

"He found the buggy in the sand," she told him. "We thought you'd gone AWOL."

He sealed her mouth again, swinging her round and dragging her struggling body along the corridor and towards the dome, where four desperate people were clustered around the dinner table.

"Wanna see a ghost, Foguet?"

David's entrance was ill conceived. Foguet stood upright with the startled look of the guilty. Seconds later, he was ready to respond.

"What are you doing, David?"

The girl went down on the floor.

"He was shot!" shouted David, his own eyes wild, with both hands holding the weapon. "He was shot!"

This wasn't some kind of mad idea that had sprung up in his head. Though David Hewish was missing it, this statement had caused a major change in mood.

"Who was shot?" asked Foguet, with real calm.

"Major Smith! He was shot! Two fucking bullet holes in his brain!"

"How do you know?" demanded Eliot, unthreatening with his hand in a plastic cast.

"I dug him up!"

Gasps all round.

"You *dug up* the body of a dead man? Are you mad?"

"Orders!" He gestured to Foguet. "He wants us to fucking die out here!"

Everyone who has ever lived in a Kevlar bubbles lives in fear of a hole in the wall and wielding a handgun in public was never going to go down well. For her part, Connolly was disbelieving. She jumped at Hewish and brought him down, the handgun letting off a round in the process.

Hewish let off a round at the ceiling but managed to miss the plexi-glass roof. Thus far, there was no audible gas leak and Foguet broke into a sprint. Hewish got a grip on his own weapon, just as a second bullet brushed softly by his cheek.

Foguet was armed.

People were heading for the deck. There was screaming. Hewish heard distant footsteps and shut down the main lights.

"You're gonna die on this rock, Hewish!"

In the vacuum, on the radio, it was impossible to track a man by the sound of his voice. Here in the base, it was easy and the colonel declined to respond.

"She was a good woman!" shouted the Spaniard, his voice noticeably breaking at the mention of his wife's name. This was a mistake, Foguet took a round in the shoulder and almost went down. To Hewish, the retaliatory shot that followed was little more than a flash but within a few seconds, their ears were popping.

"Seal the holes!" shouted Hewish. "Seal the frigging holes! Now!" Their reaction was slow. "You knew he'd murdered Smith! You bastards!"

He ran down the corridor, increasingly conscious of his lack of cover. In the dome there were pictures on the walls.

"He's in the greenhouse," shouted Rachael.

Was she lying? David Hewish ran further and found himself on the edge of the greenhouse airlock. This was the only entrance to this area and it might have been more rational to stake him out from here. Yet he couldn't. The distant voice of Kazu was goading him on. It couldn't hold a prisoner for 17 weeks in the Ajax. It was time to finish the job.

David ran into the garden and gagged briefly on the noxious gas he found there. Going down on all fours he crawled between the hydroponics. He saw a flash and heard another round above his head. If Foguet had a plan then he was doing his best to hide it. Upright with his torso stark against what little lighting there was here, he was an easy target. Hewish ran into him and the guy came down with his face in the algae. And although

Hewish was tired, his victim was older and wounded and bleeding. The Spaniard struggled for a difficult minute then expired slowly and without resistance in a full six inches of soup.

Over by the airlock entrance, more lights came on and a couple of villagers came through to help.

"It's the CO_2," said Rachael, her own face covered, her right hand offering him a mask.

"It's a lot more than that, honey!" he replied, retrieving a weapon from the floor. "It's the Great Galactic Ghoul."

David took aim at the body and let off three rounds in rapid succession. Behind him, a voice screamed, *"He's already dead!"*

The next voice was more pragmatic.

"There goes our supply problem."

The killing was over. Rachael helped him drag Pablo's body onto the Kevlar and draped something over it. All around them, a strange silence had descended on the village. It wasn't shock. It was fear.

David went to the kitchen and filled a glucose bottle from the tap and poured in the soft coloured powder and then drank it quickly. And then he turned to the elder statesman figure of Tan and kicked him, rather thuggishly, in the lower part of the abdomen, lashing out a second and third time as he hit the floor.

Over to his left, Eliot tried backing off a little. It was no good. The colonel punched him hard, hard enough to bring him down and hard enough to expose him to a second explosion of violence that no one replied to. He moved onto the women. They didn't scream much. And when it was over, he thought of Jones and D'Alonzono. He thought of Smith. Bose. Kazu. All of them lost in a deadly sequence of events that had started in this base.

Finally, he asked them this question: "Why didn't you tell me that Major Smith was murdered?"

They offered no response, nor would he ask for one again.

There were things to do, images to be uploaded and another body to be disposed of. Barefoot in Smith's quarters, Hewish received a formal message of congratulations from Hutchings and news that he had been officially promoted to mission commander. No medic ever craved the helm of a ship but the helm was his and he was free to use it as he wished.

In the first instance, he rounded up his colleagues and briefed them on their journey into deep space. This was the order they had been waiting for and they were quick to heed it.

The latest batch of fuel was transferred to the Ajax. The Russian novelists would not be coming with them. Having watched him deal with Foguet, Connolly closed her eyes and made no attempt to stop him. "We launch in five days," he said.

News came through that the Von Braun had arrived in low-Earth Orbit. All five crewmembers were alive and well as was their very own store, still holding out in a pool of his own. Later that day, they also received an update on the strategic situation. A massive force of Chinese marines had landed in the horn of Africa, desperate to dislodge an Indian army that had controlled the peninsula for the last two decades. US intelligence was reporting a full-scale commitment and the Pentagon was beside itself with joy. Although eager to dispose of the United States, the allure of African mineral resources had proved too much for Beijing and the Americans had been given a breathing space.

Limping down to a half-empty pool, David took off his clothes and slipped beneath the waves. Even in

Martian gravity, it hurt to weight-bear and he hoped that this water might ease his pain.

It did.

Hitting the surface at the far side, he realised he was not alone. Tom Eliot was squatting by the wall, ready to give this explanation for what had gone on.

"Who are ya gonna kill? I mean after Smith? Anybody but Bose? Maybe it was just a guy with a one-off grudge. There are grudges all over the place out here. Maybe we'd all get home and no one back on Earth would ever know what transpired. And if he never did anything like it again, how would it matter that he was free? Surely *you* can understand that? Yeah he might turn out to be a psychopath. He might come and find you in the night and try to slit your throat, but on this planet, so could the wind."

"It doesn't matter," David told him. "You had a duty to report your status."

And Eliot walked away.

CHAPTER FIFTY-FIVE

It was almost midnight. Rachael Callaghan trod softly on a Kevlar floor, a yellow wicker basket slung loosely across her arm. Anything that she left in this greenhouse would soon be wasted and anything that was ripe was soon to be eaten.

Of all the research efforts on Mars, hers had been the most successful and when they returned to Earth, Tan and Eliot would find themselves humbled by the plaudits she received. To those who were familiar with her, as yet brief life story, such prominence would come as no surprise.

At 19 she had won awards in the state figure skating championships. At 22, she had triumphed nationally and might have gone further had there still been an international community to skate against. By the age of 25, she had handed in her PhD thesis to a bunch of white-haired supervisors in Stamford who would have rather ravished her naked than check the text. At 27 she had been accepted for astronaut training and at 28 – in part due to a mental breakdown in her rival – she had been slated for the next outbound flight to Mars. Though she never got to see it, someone on the selection panel had pencilled a single hurried line in the margin of her file: *"Gets what she wants."* That had been a good day. On that day she had been euphoric. She had celebrated, totally blind to the pain and the horror and the screaming that awaited her on this world.

Twenty-four months and a few hundred million miles down the road, Rachael Callaghan looked up at the clock. It was 23:28 hours. She was not yet 30 years old.

Pausing by the exit she took a last look at the fields that had been her own: the bags of algae, the human waste, the exotic fruits that were a nightmare to culture and a joy to eat. All of this would soon be taken from her and as she strolled out from the greenhouse and into the commander's office, she shed a rare tear for her loss.

Slumped against a wall in a pair of boxer shorts, David had blacked out with a single e-book across one thigh. Conscious of his change in status, a thoughtful sensor had dimmed the lights.

She knelt beside him and thought of Tan and Eliot and the grating encounter with NASA aristocracy those men would surely face. In comparison, her own behaviour on this planet had been exemplary but Rachael was only human and she guessed, correctly, that her collusion on the issue of Smith would bar her from future missions.

At ease on a cold stone floor, she reached out with one hand and touched his face. Alone amongst the men in the village, he had never asked her for sex and alone amongst the men she had slept with, he had remained unchanged by the act. Nothing that she had done to please him had shaken his will. Even now, even in sleep, the scars of his life were still there to be seen. And this troubled her deeply because by the standards of this settlement, David Hewish should have felt no pain, should have had no self-doubt. For it was David who had escaped from the horrors of Chinese expansionism, David who had arrived penniless in a distant country and battled his way through the increasingly brutal ranks of the US Navy. He had explored an empty desert and returned with fresh water. He had encountered Foguet in his own graveyard and clambered home alive.

And there was something else. Something that Major Smith had hinted at, each and every time they said his name. Something that more than one of the marines in David's apartment had spotted from his sofa, that had muted the recruitment committee in Texas and drawn down that smart ass on the space station, pretending to talk about the ghoul.

He was beautiful.

Rachael glimpsed the dense white scar on a mangled thigh and ran her fingers from firm to healthy tissue, trying to imagine the pain and suffering he must have felt. Soon, they would return to the world that had given him these wounds and for many in the village, debriefing was going to be painful. In Houston, she knew, David would be feted in a different way. He would be marched before the same committee that had once dispatched him to Mars and be told that he would be given any post, or any mission he asked for.

His eyelids fluttered and he pulled her closer in, until the vertex of her skull lay soft beneath his chin. Reaching out with his other hand he got a grip on his fluids and sucked eagerly from a narrow tube.

"Do you need some?"

"No," she murmured, touching his face against her own. There was a clock on the wall. It read 00:12 and the naval officer must have seen it too because she heard him whisper, "Happy birthday."

CHAPTER FIFTY-SIX

David Hewish skipped over to the horseshoe to feast on his obligatory pre-launch breakfast of steak and scrambled eggs and fresh orange juice.

Making small talk whilst he ate, the villagers were polite, even reverent. Five minutes into the proceedings Doctor Tom Eliot made an unexpected appearance with no beard and with a sharply trimmed head of hair. No one knew what to say. Finally, the scientist looked up from his food and said something about the length of the journey and difficulty of getting a really good stylist in zero g. Controlling his surprise, Mission Commander Hewish turned to Daniel Tan.

"Are you predicting a safe launch?"

"Hard to say," said Tan. "You're talking about the future there."

"What about the schedule? Our flight plan? I thought that was part of your job."

Tan shook his head. "Commander Hewish," he said, "I thought you'd have guessed this one by now."

"And what's that?"

"The one thing you can't predict is the future."

Breakfast was done. They could have left the dirty dishes on the table but he made them to clean up, not just because a delay to the launch might see them back in the village by nightfall, but because this act of courtesy to their successors would be seen as a sign of his confidence in the future of this settlement. The American presence on Mars would be renewed. And then David gave the order to go on ahead of him and suit up in the southern airlock that he might perform one last task alone. He had prepared a small package and he left it on the dining table with a sealed and hand-written note beside it. Someone asked for permission to read it. He refused.

Suiting up by the airlock, there were no formal speeches. Preparing to close his visor, Tom Eliot asked about the Lexington and the fate of his son. Did he get out? Had Josh made it to his raft?

"Yes," David Hewish reassured him. "I'm sure he did."

"And you know what?" said Eliot, "I think that kid on TV might just be your own."

The saga that had begun for David in the southern airlock had nearly run its course and he was ready to leave. Two guys entered the chamber and then another two followed. Daniel Tan was discernible by his residual limp, Eliot by a minor hunch.

As is the tradition in such matters, the commanding officer was the last man to leave, climbing out onto the blood-red sands of Mars with a mothballed base behind him and his crew up ahead. His friend and erstwhile lover, Rachael Callaghan was waiting by the exit hatch, the rest of them having already boarded the vehicle.

Would they share the storm shelter all the way back to Earth? He couldn't say.

Bounding around the vehicle, *Commander* Hewish made one last check of the axle and tyres and the condition of the sole surviving trailer. David was running the show now and it mattered to him that things should go well. He recalled his speech on Thanksgiving, citing the heavy mortality rate that had beset the Pilgrim Fathers. And he accepted, without cynicism, that the nation that had itself saved him from the sea had been founded on sacrifice.

Then, just as he was on the verge of saying "C'mon, let's go" David Hewish stalled in his suit.

The gardener had seen it too and they shuffled towards the wide transverse window together. In less than 20 minutes, images from their helmet cameras would be arriving in Houston. They would drive the agency wild.

On the corner of a single pane of glass, David and Rachael had seen something new. Something that that had been here for many weeks but that neither they nor anybody else had noticed. Something so fantastic that even Nobohito Kazu might have taken time to stand and stare.

Something *green* was growing, on the *outer aspect* of the window. Ahead of him already, the gardener leant forward and wiped a little off with one finger.

It looked like the stuff that they had to scrape off the inner aspect of the glass. Most probably, David reasoned, it represented stray spores from the greenhouse.

"Rachael?" asked David. "What's the temperature? Right now? Right here?"

"Are you breaking off for science, Commander? OK. -3, maybe zero."

"No. It must be higher than that. Heat bleeds out of the settlement, even with insulation. If this is green, then it must be alive. If it's alive then there has to be liquid water in these cells. I think the temperature here has crept above zero. Must've been the rain from the exhaust plume on the Von Braun. Melted on the outer surface of the glass, then the soil got moist, picked up some spores from our boots …"

Observing the delay, but unable to appreciate its significance, Daniel Tan called out on the com.

"Colonel Hewish! Or should I be using your more recent title, *Commander* Hewish. I would like to remind you that we are on a clock, that the hour of our departure is fast approaching and that at this point in time, you are the only man on this planet capable of flying the Ajax!"

And if I don't want to go?

Overturning a stone with one foot, Hewish realised that the evidence was overwhelming. Shaded from the fierce ultraviolet light from the Sun, life from Earth had established itself in the sand beneath the stone and a tiny patch of Mars was turning green. It might not be the miracle year, but he had found it and the villagers were about to give Albert a run for his money.

"It'll die soon," said the woman. "When we cut off the heat and all, it'll go solid. You don't have to worry about touching the planet or anything."

His reply was in the form of a whisper and failed to make it on the com. *"He wanted to be with me when we found it."* Then, more audibly, "Besides, we've already touched it." Facing the buggy, Hewish spoke to his crew. "Tan! Open the hatch from the inside. Callaghan, don't clean that finger. We'll culture the stuff in the ship."

And when they reached the vehicle and as he gestured to the ladder, something very unusual happened. The gardener caught sight of a man's face through a silvered visor. "Commander Hewish!" she said, taking the first rung, "I do believe you're smiling."

Lost within the confines of his helmet, Commander Hewish declined to reply.

There was life on Mars.

THE END

319